No one thought of the foolishness of the moment. Here was a rescuers' camp by a flooded river, on a barely moonlit night. A young girl was almost on the brink of taking a wrong turn at a twoway junction into the shadows. Into the bush?

Mark or Dean? Dean or Mark?

"Look, you lie down and go to sleep, Nairee," Woolarooka was saying.

But a new Nairee had that minute been born.

"Not on your life," she said clearly. Then being in a certain cloud-happy way, she overlooked the meaning of her words as she added—"Which will I sleep with, Woolie? Mark or Dean?"

NOBODY READS JUST ONE
LUCY WALKER!

SO
MUCH
LOVE

Lucy Walker

BALLANTINE BOOKS • NEW YORK

I

❦❦❦❦❦❦❦❦❦

THE PLANE CAME DOWN AT ALICE SPRINGS. RIGHT on time.

The voice of authority was heard from the flight deck.

"This is your captain speaking. Will all passengers remain seated until the security officers and their party leave the aircraft."

So now I know what that bevy of men is all about, Nairee thought. There must be someone important on board.

She had been perplexed when all bags had been searched before they left the Adelaide terminal. Never before, over the years, had they had to pass through an X-ray unit. Nairee thought perhaps these precautions had become the *in thing* against hijackers. But why Adelaide Airport and not at other cities?

She gazed curiously at the group of solemn-faced men as they went down the gangway. They were all dressed alike in monotonous gray suits. Hatless, the men descended, each with one hand in his right pocket.

Then she saw the small boy. And the penny dropped. The papers had been full of a young Asian prince's visit to Australia. This boy surely was the Prince.

He is just like *all* twelve-year-old boys, she thought. Only the cloud of security officers makes him different. I've never made this trip without seeing something marvelous. The Prince had come to Alice to see Ayers Rock, of course. It was said to be the biggest monolith in the world.

Then—of all people—she saw Mark Allen, the Bush Ranger. He was walking out of the terminal building toward the plane.

Something stirred in her heart. That quiet, deliberate tread! So purposeful! His tallness! Watching him, she felt little knives stabbing at her heart.

She had rarely seen Mark in his official uniform. Her heart lifted now, almost as if Mark really *belonged* to her. This was ridiculous, of course. Nobody belonged to her—except Gamma. She had no home except the place known as *The Patch*—Gamma's place. She supposed she had no near relatives—although in an adoptive way there was Mark's father, Sergeant Jack Allen of the Mounted Police. And—also adoptive—*Woolarooka*. It was Woolarooka who had found her—a lost child, not even at the talking stage. She had taken her to Sergeant Jack who happened to be in the Outback that week. Sergeant Jack, in the fullness of time, became *Uncle* Jack. Gamma became *her* Gamma for ever after.

How time had passed! Nairee only remembered her childhood in little flashes.

Funny how people get names bestowed on them in places like the Northern Territory. And in the Kimberley too—just across the West Australian border. The names stayed with Nairee for keeps. The little white-haired lady of The Patch had become Gamma because that was how Sergeant Jack had told the little girl to call her new relative. She couldn't say "Grandmother"—she was so small when Woolarooka had given her to Uncle Jack. She could say "Gamma" and had been saying that ever since. She was eighteen now.

Being eighteen was the reason for her taking the Alice Springs route home from the College of Advanced Education—"C.A.E.," for short.

About being eighteen? A mythical figure! A few weeks either way didn't matter. They'd made a guess at her age when they found her along the creek bed —all those years ago. She had had to be registered somewhere somehow. Since Sergeant Jack had—as far as officialdom was concerned—been responsible for "bringing her in," he had fixed a birth date for her by guesswork. And that date, late in the year, had been Nairee's official birth date ever since.

The very sight now of his son, Ranger Mark Allen, across the tarmac had brought first a lift, then a lump to Nairee's throat. It was simple enough always to say she was "Gamma's Girl" and settle for that. Everyone in the north knew her as that. Yet sometimes in the dark of night, or on an occasion such as this, there came a little whimpering voice inside her that asked: "Who am I? Where had I been before being found by Woolarooka in those grasses down in the old creek bed back of Gamma's Place?" There was nobody in all the world who would answer that question for her. So she never uttered it aloud. After all, she . . .

The stewardess was standing there at the gangway. She was saying good-bye to each passenger as he or he reached the top stair and then began the descent down to Mother Earth, the hard red-brown soil of Alice Springs—the center of Australia.

At last she was at the gangway and it was her turn to be farewelled by the stewardess. She made the first downward step.

Again she looked across the tarmac for Mark. He wasn't there now. Her heart dropped. He hadn't come to meet her after all! Then she caught sight of him once more. He was way off to the right of the posse of security men walking in fan formation across the tarmac. They were walking almost shoulder to shoulder in an inverted arch to shelter their precious protégé, the little Prince.

Nairee's spirits lifted again. It was all so commonplace. Yet so safe! Mark, the only man in uniform—a Ranger's khaki uniform—walked ten yards behind them. Just behind the little Prince.

Knowing now that Mark was on duty Nairee was disappointed as she descended the steps. It was only because it would have been wonderful for somebody —*anybody*—to have come to meet her. As if she *belonged*—or something. Funny how if you were an adopted child—or just a stray child—you always wanted to *belong*. Did ordinary girls with ordinary fathers and mothers ever feel like this?

She stopped thinking about herself because she had now reached Mother Earth, and there was another uniformed stewardess holding out an envelope to her.

"Miss Peech?" she asked with a pleasant smile, handing Nairee a note. "And would you please wait in the reception hall for Ranger Mark Allen? He may be delayed. But only for a short time."

Nairee's spirits rose again. It was her "seesaw day"! "Thank you," she said, taking the note. Oh yes, she would wait in the reception hall for the Ranger. For ever and a day, if necessary. She no longer felt that familiar sensation being on the outside of places and events. Someone—anyone—to meet her was a particular glimpse of Heaven for her.

There had been two other girls from southern schools on the plane. Not from the Tertiary Technical kind of school she herself had attended, they wore the uniforms of a well-known private school. They were younger than she was, of course. Their chief claim to fame, as far as Nairee was concerned, was their frantic waving from the top of the gangway to a group of people—*relatives,* no doubt, each of whom had waved back. The younger members of the group were waving with joy, and jumping about drawing the attention of adult members of the party to the girls now crossing the tarmac.

Nairee was no longer envious. She felt now a certain kind of pride. Those girls had families to meet them. She, Nairee, had a handsome Bush Ranger. One who walked, drove, and flew all over the Kimberley Territory to see that all was well with birds, animals, and even humans. His duties took him all over the vast tropical domain of mesas, plains, valleys, forests, and creeks. The district's Bush Ranger—who would presently greet her!

She hoped with some excitement the people about would take notice when Mark arrived in the reception hall. She wanted in a half-shy way for *everyone* to see her with him. With Mark! Heaven!

The stewardess at the foot of the steps had bestowed an extra-radiant smile on her as Nairee had said, "Thank you. It was a lovely trip!" She could not explain, of course, that in the country of her heart there suddenly was at least one little bird singing. Like everyone else, she would have—openly and in public —someone to whom she would belong. Someone important too. An Outback Ranger of the Kimberley and the Territory. A young god—caretaking the people's bushland heritage.

Nairee watched through the window in the hall as the phalanx of gray-suited security men ushered the small Prince into a blue station wagon. Several of the men got in with the Prince. The others stood and waited as the car U-turned and, throwing up an enormous cloud of red dust, wheeled onto the outroad and made off into the distance toward an outback town called *Alice*.

Would the little Prince feel homesick—being so far away from home? Perhaps he was used to it. All the security men were Australians. Nairee knew that by their sun-browned faces, their slouch hats, and their khaki clothes. He was among strangers, wasn't he? Yet he hadn't seemed nervous or lonely. Perhaps princes never felt lonely? They always belonged, didn't they?

Nairee turned away from the window and as she did, she caught sight of Mark again. He strode in through the side door of the airport waiting room. There were still quite a number of people about as the passengers had not been able to leave until the Prince had gone.

Nairee waved. "Mark! Mark!"

He turned and saw her. One hand went up in a kind of salute. Then he came toward her in his quiet purposeful stride. His fugitive smile and his clear blue eyes. Oh! Mark! Partly for Mark but mostly for the people still around, Nairee held out her arms and ran to meet him. Everyone would see that some-one—especially *this* someone who was tall, handsome, sun-browned, and distinguished looking in his uniform, with the badge on his sundowner's hat—had come to meet her.

"Hullo, Nairee!" Mark said, unaware of his new hero status. "You have my note? Good. I'll be only a minute. I have to ring headquarters and sign off. I won't be long."

Nairee had had her arms wide open to receive him, but they were still three feet away from one another when he gave her an official salute then turned toward the airline's office.

"Hullo Mark!" She was saying it to his retreating back. He'd never know that the tiny bird that had for one little moment in time lifted its head and sung in her heart had now fallen silent. Just like that.

Why did she always expect, and hope too much? It used to be like that at the first school she had at-tended. It was a small private school and the other girls there would ask about her way of life in the far tropical north. When she told them of the day her Dandy won the local cup, "How many horses run-ning?" one girl had asked.

"Oh, six that day," she had said. "There'd been a flood, you see, so lots of the station men who would

have come could not get across the river." Somehow
the girls had not seemed amused, much less impressed
that Dandy had won the Bush Cup from Outback
Cabarita. One girl had actually said she had never
heard of Cabarita. "It's an aboriginal word for a place
by the river," Nairee explained, trying to retrieve
something for herself. But the girls were still not impressed. Some of them came from big station properties along the Murrumbidgee. Which was an aboriginal
word for "that river." But *it* was on the maps and
was famous all over Australia. It was important.

Nairee had learned the hard way that there was
nothing original about Outback station races. What
was home and a kind of heaven to her was no more
than just another place to the southern-bred girls. And,
of course, the snapshot of Gamma feeding her birds
—with half of them on her shoulders and some on top
of her gray hair, and the three kelpie dogs at her feet,
a drove of goats to one side, and the funny old mud-
brick and iron shack—were, to them, only *astonish-
ing*. Not praiseworthy.

Nairee rather painfully discovered she was something of a quaint person herself. That was till Mrs.
Lacey from the big station, Beelagur, ten miles northeast of Gamma's Patch had come to the school to see
her. She had taken Nairee to the most comfortable
hotel—the Grovernor, in Adelaide—and the next day
taken her shopping for beautiful clothes, a haircut,
shampoo and set. She had bought Nairee a silver-
backed brush-and-comb set, some shiny leather cases,
and new shoes. Finally she had taken her to another,
quite different tertiary college. One for teaching young
women how to work, and speak properly, and finally
discover some of the pleasures of tending gardens—
flower plants, vegetables, and tropical fruits—and
the solutions to the riddle of how to keep station
books, without the pains of not understanding why she
was different from other girls.

This college was large and pleasant, and everyone
had taken an interest in her in a helpful way. Nairee

by this time was a little older and a little wiser. She had discovered the wisdom of listening and learning rather than telling and explaining. Except when she was asked she did not talk about the Outback, nor about Gamma and the birds and the goats and about Uncle Jack who was of the Mounted Police. He had come to see Gamma once every six weeks just to make sure Gamma loved and looked after Nairee as well as she loved and looked after her goats, her birds, and her kelpie dogs. *And* two donkeys—once wild, but now tamed.

Oh yes! Nairee had grown up now. And knew it. The only sad thing was that though she knew she owed so much to Mrs. Lacey from Beelagur Station, she could not always understand her ways. She was a little nervous around Mrs. Lacey, but did not know why. There was something about the way Mrs. Lacey stared at her while she talked or gave advice, something searching in Mrs. Lacey's eyes as she spoke to Nairee, as if she were always looking for something that she might be able to read in Nairee's face.

Strange, but each of them was a mystery to the other. Or so Nairee thought. Why was the rich Mrs. Lacey so good to her? Was it that Mrs. Lacey was wondering—like Nairee herself—who she, Nairee, was? How could it possibly matter that much to Mrs. Lacey?

Once Mrs. Lacey had flown into town on some station business, collected Nairee from the college and brought her to the hotel in Adelaide for the weekend.

Mrs. Lacey had invited a Mr. Byrne to dinner with them at the hotel. She had explained that Mr. Byrne was her solicitor. After dinner they were to talk over business affairs. Mr. Byrne had been very kind and very gentle with Nairee. He'd taken a lot of notice of her, and had asked her lots of questions about herself and about what she remembered as a very small girl. All she could think to tell him about was Gamma and the goats and the birds, and about Uncle Jack—

the Outback mounted policeman. Oh . . . and there'd been some talk about the aboriginal woman Woolarooka, whom Nairee had greatly loved as a small child. Still loved her.

It was Mrs. Lacey who had answered Mr. Byrne's polite questions about Woolarooka. She told him about Woolarooka's tribe and how she herself had known them all very well indeed. Some of them had actually worked from time to time at Beelagur, the Laceys' cattle station.

"I know them all. Every one of them," Mrs. Lacey had said brusquely. "From the eldest to the youngest of the children. They're nomadic. In and out of the area. Sometimes there is trouble with other tribes. But they did not know Nairee."

Mr. Byrne had looked at Nairee, and though she tried to hide it she knew that he saw she was troubled. She couldn't contradict Mrs. Lacey, could she? Better to say nothing. She realized she herself knew more about the tribe than did Mrs. Lacey. This was because of Woolarooka, of course.

That was the first and most important time that Nairee learned to keep silent, to keep her own counsel except where Gamma and Uncle Jack were concerned. Oh, and the social welfare lady—Mrs. Gray —who sometimes came out to The Patch with the Flying Doctor. Always unexpectedly too.

Nairee liked Mrs. Gray very much indeed. But she had noticed how Mrs. Gray would look her over. And look Gamma over too. She would look all over The Patch. Very curious. Curious about Mrs. Lacey too. She would ask was Nairee happy? And did she love Gamma? Or just *like* her, which was something quite different apparently.

All that had been when Nairee was very young. Mrs. Gray, Uncle Jack, and the Flying Doctor were "government." They had a right to look at tonsils and her teeth, feel how much fat—if any—she had on her arms. Also look at her clothes and shoes to see if they were weatherproof.

Of all the people in and around the shack when the Flying Doctor came in, he and Mrs. Gray were most interested in Woolarooka. They would talk to her for a long time, as if trying to make Woolarooka remember something. Or tell them something. Always Woolarooka sat cross-legged by the old leaning log and just smiled. She would shake her head, and say nothing. Always this happened and always the doctor and Mrs. Gray would, in the end, stand up, shake their heads, give hopeless lifts of their shoulders, then give up on talking to Woolarooka. The same pattern every time.

Nairee didn't really know exactly what it was all about. Woolarooka would smile at her, even giggle aloud. It was as if they had something between them that they shared. As a little girl, Nairee had thought that it was because Woolarooka loved her, and she loved Woolarooka. It was a nice warm thought for the small child to carry in her heart. And they weren't going to share this love with anyone else.

One day Nairee had collected some very beautiful rain-washed colored stones. She drew a circle on the ground and put three of the stones in it. It was her "secret place."

Then on another day when Woolarooka came to The Patch by herself, Nairee showed her the circle, now fenced by small sticks and eucalyptus nuts. Woolarooka had said, "What name you give this fella?"

Nairee said, without thinking, "The circle's me. This stone is Gamma, and the next one is Uncle Jack, and this pretty one is Woolarooka."

"That circle all around bin your heart, eh?"

Nairee nodded.

"That's good fella, awright," Woolarooka said. "You keep them alla-same, one day a big fine fella come an' you put the big stone in there for him."

This mysterious advice had buried itself in the small girl's mind.

Then Uncle Jack had brought his son Mark out to see The Patch and its strange occupants of goats, dogs, birds, Gamma and Nairee.

Nairee did not realize she was enthralled by the tall sunburned youth that Mark was then. All she knew was that now she would put another stone in her circle. This stone was called Mark, and when Nairee saw it sitting there beside Gamma, Uncle Jack, and Woolarooka's stones she suddenly, with a wonderful awakening, knew a kind of special *different* love.

This was her world and these were her people.

When she first went to school down south she forgot about the circle. She did not think of it for years. But it was still there.

When she was sixteen and home from college for the holidays, Nairee—quite accidentally—came upon the circle with its group of stones. A ground shoot from the beauhinia bush had grown over it.

Discovering the circle again had an extraordinary effect on her. She remembered instantly what it meant, and yet she was physically incapable of touching it. She just knew it had a message and she must cover it up from anyone else's sight. It was a painful exposure of herself as she had been when she was very young. Yet she could not destroy it. She covered it with the tree shoot again and walked away. She did not look back even once. Instinctively she knew this was something akin to the aboriginals' tribal secret place. Where had she got that knowledge? Why was a circle important? And why was each stone a different color from the others? She felt as if the pattern was speaking to her.

She did not know who she really was. She had a sort-of knowledge that once she had been with the tribe, and that Woolarooka had mothered her. Even though she was a white child. From where had she, Nairee, got this knowledge? She had no idea. It was just there. Definitely *there*. A lost child, found by the tribe and mothered by Woolarooka. The circle "sang" to her and told her this. Why? How?

2

NOW, TODAY, NAIREE WATCHED MARK CROSS THE area back to the airline's office. How tall he was! How broadly set those shoulders! He was a special kind of tall man now. Not just Uncle Jack's son. He was himself and belonged to nobody else.

Watching Mark cross the floor with his firm stride, Nairee noticed that others watched him too. This was because he was so striking. He had a sort of innate air of command in the way he held his head, in that ease about him! Yet a certain reticence too. Nairee was aware of a certain "something" in her own heart as she watched him. It wasn't just belongingness. Nor that she was glad he'd come especially to meet her. It was as if he were someone else now. Someone who in some strange way—just by walking like that—had caused a chord in her heart to sing. Not in the ring of stones now: but in her heart!

In the midst of this newly discovered feeling, other familiar persons arrived in the airport's entrance. Here came Uncle Jack and Mrs. Gray. Behind Mrs. Gray was a tall, slim, distinguished-looking man who, as he walked, seemed as if he might own the place! Dean Lacey of Beelagur Station!

Good Heavens. Everybody! Nairee thought with a leap of joy in her heart.

Dean was the owner-manager of Beelagur Station, and was Mrs. Lacey's son. Only Gamma was missing to create a near-family party. But of course Gamma never ever left The Patch.

Here in the dead heart of Australia was a group of those Nairee loved or liked most.

She was all smiles now. As there was no mirror in evidence anywhere, she had no idea how lovely she looked. Her white teeth flashed and her gray-green eyes shone. Glad-tears put that shine in her eyes.

She ran forward, her hands held out as if to encompass them all.

"Hullo, hullo!" she cried as they met near the entrance. "What a lovely homecoming! I know I'm only halfway there, but . . . well, I've finished school now —forever. I didn't think you would all be here . . ."

Mrs. Gray kissed her gently on the cheek.

"I think you've grown another inch," she said. She held Nairee at arm's length. "My, you *are* smart. What a lovely dress!"

"Yes, isn't it?" Nairee agreed, shyly. "Mrs. Lacey helped me choose it when she last came to Adelaide." Then, turning to Dean, she held out her hand. She was very shy now. "Hullo Dean! How do you come to be in Alice Springs?"

He barely smiled, but then, as Nairee well knew, he was not the smiling kind of man. His eyes looked at her as if he thought highly of what he saw. Yet he was aloof from them all—even though he stood there in the group. He was a station owner. King of twenty thousand acres! And he looked it. He had that air of ownership.

"Hullo Nairee," he said, quietly. "A good trip?"

"Perfect," she said. "Now it's perfectly perfect. Hullo, darling Uncle Jack. I suppose you know Mark is here? Somewhere over there in the office. Using the telephone, I think . . ."

Even as she spoke Mark appeared and strode toward them across the rapidly emptying reception hall.

Father and son each lifted a hand in salute to the other.

"Quite a posse to meet your favorite client. Hullo Nairee!" Mark smiled at her then gave his father the benefit of a grin. Then: "Hullo Dean! How goes it?"

"Well, thank you. The cattle sale at Wyndam was fair to good." Dean Lacey shook hands with Mark. His glance came back to Nairee.

"A special welcome to you, Nairee. We're not exactly on home territory, but welcome back this far."

Nairee had hugged Uncle Jack, shaken hands with Mrs. Gray, and now gave her hand shyly to Dean Lacey. He held it for just a fraction of a second.

"Welcome home, Nairee," he said again. "Home for good, this time I think?" His gray eyes stared into hers and she blinked.

"I can't believe it." She looked around at the group. "So many nice people here in Alice, I was afraid there would be no one at all. Not in Alice, anyway—I'm still hundreds of miles from home."

She broke off and looked at the group once more. This time a little curiously.

"Why . . . why was I to come only as far as Alice, Uncle Jack? Is there something special on?" Then with sudden anxiety, "Is Gamma all right?"

"Absolutely. Just as she's always been. Waiting for Gamma's Girl to come home."

"Oh, thank goodness for that! About being well, I mean. I know she'd never leave The Patch."

"The fact that you have come of adult age, Nairee," Mrs. Gray said gently, "doesn't mean a thing to Gamma. You'll always be her girl."

"I know," Nairee said soberly. "But of adult age . . . ?"

"Of course," Mrs. Gray agreed. "Eighteen. All eighteen-year-old people have a vote now. And, our department no longer has a looking-after role any more. At eighteen you're out in the world . . ."

Nairee looked puzzled for a moment. Then she smiled—at first gladly, then a little sadly.

"I like to be grown up and have a vote," she said. "But does it mean you won't come out to see me every three or four months? It was generally in the school holidays."

"I'll always come as a friend, if you and Gamma invite me," Mrs. Gray said, smiling. "But as far as the government in the territory—and the Commonwealth Government of Australia—are concerned you are on your own. Think you can take it, Nairee?"

Nairee nodded, then looked from one face to the other. They were all smiles. Even Dean Lacey smiled, just a little. Suddenly he looked marvelously handsome. He so rarely smiled. Nairee noticed several people who had not yet left the airport looked at Dean with interest. And at Mark too. Everyone, even strangers, always looked at the Ranger, and at the badge on his broad-brimmed hat.

Yes he is very striking, she thought. And caught her breath. Then she realized she was not keeping her thoughts in rein. She glanced at Mark again and gave him a wistful smile, unconsciously excusing herself for suddenly being so drawn to Dean.

Mark Allen and Dean Lacey were several worlds apart. One was a rich station owner, a man who, from wherever he stood, could never see more than one boundary of his great acres. The other, Mark, was a man who worked in the service of the great mysterious land around. He would never be rich like Dean Lacey. But he would be there to watch the well-being of *all* the people. The Outback Ranger was a soldier in service of a cause. Help and contact were what he gave to the people in isolated places of the Outback. He would not be as Dean Lacey was—an *owner*. He was mostly a *giver*.

Nairee slipped her hand in the crook of Mark's arm, then as quickly withdrew it. Dean Lacey's look had clearly disapproved, as if she, Nairee, had taken an unwarranted privilege. She straightened herself. She felt at peace again as she saw Mark's smile.

She glanced now at Mrs. Gray.

"What do I do now that I'm eighteen and the government is throwing me out on my own?" she asked, wanting to forget Dean for the moment.

"Come and have some tea," Mrs. Gray answered, "Mr. Lacey has an air booking to make. Perhaps he'll join us later. Meantime I'm thirsty. What about you, Sergeant?" she asked Uncle Jack.

"I'm thirsty," he said. "Mark? You on duty?"

"Yes sir!" Mark said, saluting a senior officer—even though he was his own father.

Mark turned to Lacey and asked about his station.

"At the moment all is well," Dean said. "Not a bush-fire this season so far. The brolgas are back in the lagoon north of the homestead. Always a good sign . . ."

"Always," Mark agreed.

"That last cyclone we had settled the one and only bushfire since Christmas," Dean added.

"Any damage?"

"You ought to know. You're the area Ranger," Dean replied, with an edge to his words.

"Then 'no damage' is the answer," Mark said easily.

"None that would interest you," Dean replied, turning away as if he had other and more important matters on his mind.

Tea in a large room at the side of the lounge was of the Outback kind. Mrs. Gray held up her basket. It contained a thermos flask in its nest of cups, and a plastic jar of biscuits. A tea party had been thought of in advance.

"Sorry, Nairee. Sorry, Mrs. Gray," Mark said abruptly. "You were all so busy talking you didn't hear what I heard—"

They fell silent as they half turned to where an airport officer was speaking over the radio. The sky outside had lost its burning shield of light.

"First repeat: Wind clouds mounting southeast are increasing. Visibility is decreasing. All light aircraft grounded until further notice. However the Ansett 727 for Darwin—flying north—will proceed as scheduled."

There had been such a sound of greetings in the party that none of them, except Mark, had paid the least attention to what was going on elsewhere in the airport. Now there were cries of disappointment, even annoyance from several groups. People had been patiently waiting to board one or another of the private planes standing out on the tarmac. The planes had the desolate look of small birds grounded. No life in them at all.

"That lot will have to find someplace here, in Alice, to bed down," Sergeant Allen said. "By the look of the sky out there they won't be leaving today."

Mark, ever vigilant, had noticed that a small, privately owned Cessna had just taken off from the far end of the tarmac.

"Could be trouble there," he said, concerned.

"Can't stop it now, can they?" Mrs. Gray said. "I think it's the manager's plane from Boodarra Station. I did see Owen Prentis in town this morning. He said he was flying back this afternoon. The Boodarra plane *is* a Cessna, isn't it, Mark?"

"I'll soon find out," he said. "Excuse me, please. Sorry, Nairee, but it looks as if I might have a job of work to do."

"Oh dear!" Nairee said regretfully. She had so wanted Mark to stay.

The small plane had taken off into a coming windstorm. Its direction had to be the Simpson Desert, since Boodarra Station was hard by the last waterhole, only twenty miles southwest of the Simpson. It was flying now. Into the crosspath of the coming storm.

Mrs. Gray caught Sergeant Allen's eye. "Owen Prentis must have heard some kind of weather report before he took off, surely?" she said.

"He should have done so. That's for sure. But those

Prentises have wills of their own. No ordinary rules for them."

Mrs. Gray shook her head. "They had to have that kind of will in the early days or they would never have pioneered out there on the verge of desert land."

"Will he be all right?" Nairee asked Sergeant Jack.

"Well, he knows how to come down in any wind. Let's hope his radio is working. If not it'll be a long trek for Mark—and one or two of his men. Mark is the only Ranger hereabouts on duty today."

"Oh *no!*" Nairee protested.

The excitement of seeing Mark when her own plane had landed at Alice Springs was all gone. He had come but to go. She could have cried. Then she was a little ashamed of herself. After all, somebody's life might be at stake. It would be dangerous for Mark traveling in a Land Rover too. Planes that came down in a windstorm did not necessarily choose dry claypan, nor a made road. The Cessna might come down anywhere amidst the Simpson Desert's notorious dunes.

"Nairee, dear. Let's get down to *our* business," Mrs. Gray said, taking her arm. "You are to come along to the government office . . . Sergeant Jack is coming too. After all, he has been your guardian. He has to do a little bit of paper-signing too."

"Yes, of course." Nairee gathered her wits and got her feelings under control. Funny, she thought, how everyone just takes it for granted Mark will go out into that desert! All because it is assumed that Owen Prentis, Nabob of Boodarra Station, a big cattleman, and self-willed into the bargain, will have to come down or be blown to bits in that storm. That is, if a storm really does blow up.

She tossed her hair back and pulled herself together. Neither Mrs. Gray nor Sergeant Jack would ever guess how glad she had been that tall, blue-eyed, khaki-clad Mark had come to meet her.

Nairee's luggage was retrieved from the pile now off-loaded from the plane. They all three went out to the stationwagon which Mrs. Gray was allotted for her work as a district welfare officer.

She insisted now that Nairee sit up front with her. "It's your day, Nairee," she said. "You must have the front seat."

"It's such a big car." Nairee edged nearer Mrs. Gray, who was already behind the wheel. "Come on, Uncle Jack. Please, *please* ride with me. There's lots of room, and this way we're all together."

"Right you are!" he said with a grin. "We're all three in on this affair. What does it feel like to be out in the world and on your own now, Nairee? Scared?"

"Of course not. I'll still have you and Mrs. Gray as friends. But most of all, I'll have Gamma, won't I? For always. Why doesn't Gamma have to sign something too?"

There was the smallest silence. Nairee wondered if she imagined it.

"You don't sign off there—*ever,*" Uncle Jack said, very serious now. Yet with a sort of heartening note in his voice. "You're Gamma's Girl, aren't you? Mrs. Gray's department, and I, had to act . . . well, let me think—Mrs. Gray, why did I have to act? I've forgotten."

Nairee knew very well he had not forgotten.

"You probably had to act because Gamma wouldn't sign something she couldn't understand," she said. "Those legal documents would have bothered her. Uncle Jack, you had to sign for her. You explained that to me years ago!"

"Excuse me," the sergeant said with mock haughtiness. "I signed because I *wanted* to sign. I wanted a stake in the nicest little girl I'd ever seen."

"You signed because you guaranteed that Gamma *could* look after me," Nairee said sternly, not to be taken in. "If ever anybody turned up to claim me you were to see that right was right, and that Gamma wouldn't be pushed aside because she is a quaint little birdwoman who lives on her own Patch. And looks after the birds and the animals round and about. What you really did, Uncle Jack, was guarantee *Gamma*. Not me. And Mrs. Gray's department guaranteed that her department would look after *me*. Right?"

"Right," Sergeant Jack said. "You been doing your homework, Nairee?"

"Of course. Wouldn't you—if you didn't know who you were, and where you came from? Nearly everybody is here today except Woolarooka. Why wasn't Woolarooka told it was my coming-home day?"

"My guess is she wouldn't need to be told," Mrs. Gray said. "The tribe would have known all about it before we did."

"Oh, smoke signals!" Nairee laughed, but not unkindly.

"Maybe just the elements talking," Sergeant Jack said casually. "Nobody ever knows how the tribes really get their messages across. The smoke-signal theory doesn't always hold water. You seen any smoke talking in the sky today, Mrs. Gray?"

They had had only one corner to turn and now they were slowing down outside the government building.

"No," Mrs. Gray said with a laugh. "But ask Woolarooka. There she is by that old pepper tree!"

The car came to a standstill under the shade of the tree. Sergeant Jack eased out in order to let Nairee scramble after him as fast as she could.

"Woola, Woola, Woola?" she called, holding out her arms. "I just knew you had to be here!"

The bush woman, neat in a new print dress, flashed her white teeth in a broad smile. Their arms went around each other, both of them half laughing, half crying. Then they stood back and looked at one another.

"My, you bin come home a fine big girl, Nairee. You bin eighteen your own boss now. How you like tha', eh?"

"I like it fine, Woola. But I'm just the same—I'm *me*."

"No you not. You bin fine lady now—" Woolarooka

fingered the material of Nairee's dress. "My, that cos' you plenty. Mrs. Lacey, eh?"

"She chose it for me, Woola. But Gamma paid for it. *My* Gamma."

"Now you bin go to work help your Gamma, eh?"

"Of course. That's why I came back. Down there at Adelaide they wanted me to stay and take up nursing or teaching, or something. Mrs. Lacey wanted me to do that too. But I said, 'No. I'm going back to look after Gamma. She's getting old.'" Nairee's smile was threatened by tears as she looked at the little old woman. "And look after Woolarooka too. They're my family. Gamma and Woolarooka . . ."

"An' the goats, an' the birds, 'an the donkeys. You know Gamma got two them cattle fellas now? One day there be calf, eh?"

Nairee threw back her head and laughed. "Not *Gamma's Patch* anymore? Gamma's 'cattle station,' and Gamma's 'homestead'!"

They all laughed. It all seemed just that little bit ridiculous. And quite impossible. The *Patch* to become a station? Gamma to be a station owner? Gamma who couldn't or wouldn't *write,* and couldn't drive a motorcar let alone fly a plane. Though she could play Patience, and loved to cheat herself a little. It could be ridiculous, but only Nairee knew it was not. As yet they didn't know the ideas Nairee had in her head. They had no idea themselves the things Nairee had taught herself—in addition to what the schools had taught her—these last five years. There was time another day for Nairee to explain it all to them.

3

LATER, THE RITUAL OF THE TERRITORY'S WELFARE department writing Nairee off their books as their ward was full of fun-making and laughter. The formalities over, they all went off to the post office to watch Nairee fill in her electoral cards. There was more laughter as she signed her address as "Gamma's Station" instead of "Gamma's Patch."

Then came tea and cakes, this time in a tea shop. Only Woolarooka was missing, now. Woolarooka had other things to do, she had said. Notably, visit her relations camped out under the gum trees along the edge of the dry river bed.

They had all meant it to be a wonderful celebration for Nairee. So it was. That is, except for the moments when Nairee's thoughts kept playing lost out along the sandy wastes on the other side of the ranges where Mark's Land Rover would be ploughing through the dunes . . . in a dry storm. He was looking for a plane that just had to come down in that turbulent wind, and for its pilot perhaps. Well, maybe not too!

Then came time to be going. It was at that moment

that Nairee saw Dean Lacey again, striding along the footpath.

How tall! she thought. And handsome. But then he had always been tall and handsome, hadn't he? Those times long ago when he used to come down from the Lacey station to see Gamma and the child Nairee. Then over the years to see the young girl that Nairee had become. He had always seemed tall as a youth. He had taught Nairee to ride his horse. Later he had given her a horse from the Lacey stable. They had gone riding together. Those days.

When they were very young he had been bossy. But then, one hot day Nairee had walked away from him through miles of bush and heat back to The Patch, and he had learned his lesson and stopped trying to rule her. Yet, strangely, Nairee was always aware of that capacity in him. That touch of the master. Because he was stronger than she was, of course. There was always a hint in the long run he could best her— if ever he wanted to do that.

Yet she was not ever afraid of him. Just wary. And somehow, somewhere in her heart there came a wish, a dream. Of what, she did not know.

Strange, that this day he should be in Alice Springs, just as she was. She had not told Mrs. Lacey when she last saw her in Adelaide that she was dropping off at Alice Springs on her way home. Nor that her eighteenth birthday—her *alleged* eighteenth birthday—and adulthood were being celebrated today.

Funny, but as she saw Dean Lacey, better-looking than any other man in or around Alice, striding along the footpath, she had that old feeling of something unspoken and unknown between them. There was always this tiny whisper of *anxiety* clouding that old old feeling. . . .

Nairee had a vague hope that Dean Lacey would come across to them. Speak to her. Welcome her home *truly*.

But Sergeant Jack had other ideas. He, like Nairee, had noticed a sudden slowing in Dean's stride.

Then a quite extraordinary thing happened. Sergeant Jack and Mrs. Gray suddenly were standing side by side, almost shoulder to shoulder, as if screening Nairee from someone. Dean himself had faltered and turned his head. Nairee knew for the second time since the plane landed that Dean *had* seen her. There was a split second of silence, as if all of them were waiting for something—something memorable but yet quite unknown that could possibly happen.

Nothing happened. Dean Lacey looked front again and strode on.

Yet Nairee knew he had seen her. Why did he walk away? Why were Sergeant Jack and Mrs. Gray standing like that, jaws firm and something almost baleful in their eyes?

Nairee felt as if a shadow had walked across her path. It was cold, and just a little bit frightening.

Then it was all over. Sergeant Jack and Mrs. Gray turned back to Nairee.

"Since Mark has had to go about his Ranger duty I'll drive you up country to The Patch," Sergeant Jack said, taking Nairee's arm gently.

"But . . . it's hundreds of miles," Nairee protested. "Couldn't I stay in Alice for the night and catch the overlander tomorrow?"

"Oh no! That wouldn't do!" Mrs. Gray was looking anxiously at Sergeant Jack as she spoke. He caught her eye, and nodded his head.

"Keep Gamma waiting?" he said with a smile to Nairee. Intuitively she knew this was a cover-up. It had something to do with Dean being in Alice. The Patch was on the track to Dean's station, Beelagur.

"Gamma never knows the day. Or the month," Nairee said quietly. "Am I being a nuisance? It's an awful long way, and the track is pot-holed—"

"I've done it on normal duty, and I know every inch of it better than you do, young lady," Sergeant Jack said. "Besides, I want to see Gamma, myself."

"Yes, of course," Nairee said. "I didn't mean—"

"You didn't mean anything Nairee," Sergeant Jack

took her arm, "except that you feared you might be a responsibility to me. No chance. In addition I've a job to look at round at Gotby's Rock Pool, so I'll set off today instead of tomorrow."

Sergeant Jack caught Mrs. Gray's eye again, and something passed between them again. In spite of Sergeant Jack's kindness and his words, Nairee still did not want to be a bother. What was wrong with going up bush in the through-coach anyway? Or better still, with Dean—if he would only ask her.

It was good to know that Mark had offered to take her home. The last lap, as it were. He *had* thought about her . . .

"Bother that Cessna taking off into a windstorm!" she said aloud. Then bit her lip. They all understood what she meant, though words wouldn't wring such knowledge from them.

The day was just past middle-aged, so Sergeant Jack and Nairee set off almost at once.

Someone in police headquarters rustled up a carton filled with fruit, sandwiches, a double-sized thermos, the routine ration of tea bags and dried milk and —just in case—an extra can of water. At the rate at which Sergeant Jack drove they would reach The Patch by sundown. A police car—even if a four-wheel drive, or station wagon—was always stocked with the equipment to deal with blown tires or a stake in the gas tank.

The road, once they left the overland, was no road at all. It merely went by that name. It was only a track. Once across the border and onto the Northwest Highway they would travel in comparative luxury. Sergeant Jack was Territory Police, but across the border he would be accepted by the West Australian Police as "one of them" for whatever jag he was on.

"We are all of a kind!" he remarked with a grin to Nairee. She knew what he meant, of course. Now and again when a transgressor was sought, the two police forces joined company or—at the least—changed territory to lend a hand in an "incident." Or a search for a lost party, usually someone who, in ignorance of this "hell's own country" of the Outback, was ill-prepared for its difficulties. Borders didn't mean anything in the Outback when the Mounted Police were on the *Search and Find* leg of their work.

As the vehicle, a Land Rover on this occasion, raced out of Alice Springs Nairee brushed aside her hair and leaned against the seat-back. She drew in a great gulp of air, then said:

"Oh, Uncle Jack I do love coming home this time! It's for good, isn't it?"

He did not reply because he still couldn't see that it was right and proper for this city-college-trained girl to live permanently in that isolated stretch of the bush in which The Patch was located. He didn't know how in Heaven—let alone on The Patch—she would make any use of what she had learned down south in Adelaide. "College of Advanced Education" indeed! Well, better than that fancy dame school Mrs. Lacey had put her in in the first years. A place where they changed for dinner every night! Ye gods! At The Patch she'd be lucky if she changed out of soiled shirt and jeans into clean shirt and jeans before she and Gamma sat down to bush turkey or a stuffed lizard.

In his mind Sergeant Jack was annoyed with Mrs. Lacey for her interference, and for wringing permission from the welfare department to allow her to have that girl sent to *her,* Mrs. Lacey's, choice of school. That girl was now *this* girl. It had cost him plenty of time and talk interfering himself and—along with Mrs. Gray—insisting that poor lonely little Nairee would do better in a boardinghouse—carefully appraised beforehand, of course—and going to the technical side of the C.A.E. Where was her future to be? Back with that crazy but loving old female hermit, Gamma? Along with beasts, birds, and that growing pack of goats!

He had a kind of hunch that Dean, since his father's death majority owner and station manager of

Beelagur, had had his say too. The girl had been lost in, found in that northwest spur of the great Outback. Sergeant Jack, realist all the time, hoped that Dean Lacey was lofty enough to marry—when he did marry—some *other station owner's* daughter.

Sergeant Jack Allen was shrewd enough to know a man like Dean Lacey was too high and mighty for a quiet soul like Nairee. Well, surely?

He had another thought. He turned his head sideways to look at her. After all those years down there, was she still the gentle trusting bush girl she was once?

He ran over an ironstone rock. He and his passenger lifted off their seats and dropped back again. Sergeant Jack swore, but under his breath.

Nairee looked at him, and smiled. "You mad at something, Uncle Jack?"

"Yep. That flaming rock."

"It was waiting for you," Nairee laughed. "I thought *you* never, but never hit rocks, reptiles, or kangaroos in the Outback."

"Goes to show you sometimes think wrong," he said. "How you going to like being back in the wild bush, Nairee? The heat? The emptiness—which also means the loneliness? There's little society up here."

"Wrong. There's lots of society. Apart from you and Mrs. Gray, and Gamma . . . and Mark—there's two ponies . . ." She paused, then said, "Oh, my darling ponies! How I long to see them and ride them!" She looked quickly at him and then back again to the outside world of bush, a long snake of dirt road, and bush again. "Oh, I love it. I love it all. It's wonderful. My land! That great red lump of monolith—Ayers Rock back there near Alice! And the huddle of the Olgas further on. And the gray gray miles of bush, grass spinifex, and every single snake tree. The sun out there westering, shining on the side of your face, Uncle Jack. I love it all. Every single thing. I never, never want to leave it again—"

"Not even for a holiday?"

"Well . . . sometime, maybe a holiday to Darwin. Or

maybe further west to Wyndham. I would like to sail across the Timor Sea a bit, and watch the pearling luggers or fishing dhows coming in. Sails against a tropical sunset! Red fire on the sea! What could be more wonderful?"

Ten yards ahead of them a kangaroo crossed the road. Sergeant Jack swerved to miss it.

"I'd have jumped out and walked home if you'd hit it," Nairee said.

"I'd have jumped out and walked all the way with you if I'd hit it," Sergeant Jack said. A dead 'roo on the road always hit him in the heart.

"Watch for lizards too," Nairee said. "With your kind of eyesight, Uncle Jack, you would see a two-footer twenty yards away."

"A bit late in the drive for that. I need to see it forty yards away to be sure."

"Well, darling Uncle Jack, do slow down a *little*. It won't matter if we don't get there till after sundown. I do love the moon over the bush. I'm longing to see it. I'm longing to see *all my Outback*. Never to leave it again."

"You love it that much?" Sergeant Jack asked quietly. "There's practically no *real* social life out there at The Patch. You must have had some gay times down there at Adelaide. Won't you miss all that?"

Nairee shook her head. "I did have some lovely times. But not always. I was sometimes that little bit homesick for Gamma. And for the birds and beasties. Even the goats. And the bush. And my ponies. I never want to live away from the bush."

"No sweethearts yet?"

"Oh, there were young men. Boys, really—I did dance a little. But nothing, and no one to take my heart like the bush does. Besides, up here, they do have races at Beelagur Station. I'm sure the Laceys will go on asking me to them. They ask everybody, don't they? Their parties are sort of district parties, aren't they? Even the aborigines come to them. They come there walkabout from all over when a Beelagur show is on."

"Yes," Sergeant Jack said slowly, reluctantly.

Nairee caught the hint of questioning in his voice. There was quite a silence.

"You couldn't possibly mind my riding over to the Laceys'," Nairee said, puzzled. "Mrs. Lacey has been wonderful to me. All my clothes for my schooling. And the extra studies like music and domestic science—if one could possibly bracket those two together! I know Gamma doesn't have very much money—only when she sells something like Ratter's litter. Ratter is the best kelpie in the district. And sometimes Gamma sold some goats, though she always hates to do that. She is afraid they might be passed on as 'bush mutton.'"

"Uh huh!" Sergeant Jack said. "Gamma's goats are for living, not for the swagman's dinner."

There was another long silence, during which Nairee glanced at him and could see there was a troubled frown on his forehead. She had always sensed he did not like the Laceys to do so much for her. Mrs. Gray felt that way too. Mrs. Gray had twice come down from the territory to see Nairee at school, and both times had seemed concerned about the nice things she, Nairee, had. The silver-backed brush-and-comb set. The little trinkets that other girls had as a matter of course. Even some of the clothes. Nairee sensed all this but she did not ask questions. And Mrs. Gray did not say anything much. She had just *looked* it. Only once had she said, *"This won't do!"* But when she had seen Nairee's puzzled face she had broken off. Then added: "Ah well, we can't do anything about it, can we? But you must remember, Nairee, that when schooling is over and you return to The Patch—what you will be is an Outbacker. Gamma's Girl. No finery. It would be useless."

As if Nairee ever wanted to be anything else but an Outbacker! She had been sensible enough to know that Mrs. Lacey only provided her with these things so she, Nairee, would not be too much at a disadvantage with the other girls. At least Mrs. Lacey had said this. Nairee had seen the point, as well as been very grateful. She only wished she really liked Mrs. Lacey better. She could not understand the strange undercurrent that made her think, in spite of all Mrs. Lacey's generosity, that the woman was wary of her. Nairee too was wary. Mrs. Lacey had only been doing her duty. She was like that. *Duty* was written large all over her somewhat handsome face. Tall, austere, black-haired, pale-gray-eyed—Mrs. Lacey was quite a personage. But for some reason, at least when Nairee was around, she *never* smiled.

"Then why did she put up with me?" she asked aloud.

"Who?" Sergeant Jack demanded, glancing sideways at Nairee. His face was expressionless, but Nairee knew him well enough to see an undercurrent of concern in it.

"Mrs. Lacey."

His expression did not change.

"Possibly because she needed a daughter of her own," he said quietly. "You are very modest, Nairee. Could it be that she was also very fond of you? *I'm* fond of you—"

"Oh, I know, Uncle Jack." Nairee touched his arm. "I know—but I never know quite how to say it. You . . . and Mrs. Lacey. Perhaps . . . perhaps Dean? I never know about Dean! Sometimes he looks and looks at me as if he likes me. Other times he is cold and distant."

"Just his manner, child," Uncle Jack said gently. But he frowned, and seeing it, Nairee wondered. Oh, she wished she knew all the riddles of her life! That old question plagued her once again: *Who am I?*" But she didn't say that aloud. Years and years ago, Mrs. Gray had explained to her that she was an orphan. And since she did not have parents, and as there was no near-relative, the department had officially made her their ward in the personal charge of Mrs. Gray. Mrs. Gray was to take the place of a mother.

Gamma was to be her grandmother. That was the beginning and the end of it.

Meantime it was a lovely day. She was going home
to her beloved Outback and to dear funny Gamma.
To all the goats and birds and animals too! No more
ever saying good-bye. College days were over now.
She was her own self . . . without any strings . . . forever more.

Gamma was getting old. And one day—well, one
day, she, Nairee, would be the only one to look after
Gamma. Just as one day years and years ago, Gamma
had taken her in—a lost child—and looked after *her*.

4

THEY HAD LONG SINCE SWUNG WEST AND CROSSED THE
West Australian border. Now they were on a dirt-and-
gravel road so straight it might have been ruled by
some giant's extended ruler.

As far as the eye could see there were the low
humps of spinifex. On both sides of the road was the
dull gray-yellow of spiky grass. Now and again in the
hazy distance to the east and north were glimpses of
the Breakaway country. Great walls of red stones of
every shape and size, some vast, some rounded like
footballs could be seen flaming in the westering sun.
Red mesas broke the skyline. They stood their ages-
long sentinel stance over the plain looking westward
to the distant coastland.

To Nairee, motionless things like Breakaways,
mesas, old ghost gums, and the occasional twisted
snake trees all had a life. They "spoke" to her, as
they spoke to the aborigines. She believed this as the
tribe believed it because nothing else in this strange,
beautiful, sometimes terrible country could so touch
her heart. The land was so old. So incredibly old.

Everything seemed to say it had always been here, like this, for millions and millions of years. And they would be here for millions more years—if only man did not come with giant drills, in his search for water, or oil, or gas, or uranium, or some such—and destroy it all!

Never! Nairee had arrived at her favorite solution of her who-ness by giving her heart back to her own country—the wild loneliness of the vast Australian Outback. Her country where trees and stones and monoliths spoke straight to the heart. "Keep it, my country!"

Sergeant Jack stopped once for billy-tea at the king of all black stumps by which every lone traveler gauged his distance to or from his goal. It was a big grotesque black stump, this one, the last remnant of a majestic tree burnt out by bushfire long ago.

Then the gray-brown spinifex gave room to greener bushland. Larger eucalyptus trees, and here and there a runnel of water! They were nearing the harnessed spread of the Ord River and its many tributaries.

Sundown would come soon. The scorching red of the sunset already flamed across the sky, wounding the eyes with its light and color and spreading fan-like up to Heaven. A salute to departing day.

It was then, at sundown, in a crimson cloud of glory, that Gamma's Girl came home to The Patch.

It was then too that Sergeant Jack's radio told him Mark had found the fallen Cessna from Alice Springs. And that there was no sign of the pilot. His tracks led away from the plane so that at least he was—as yet—whole and mobile. Mark would follow the tracks and find him. If the aborigines found him first they would lead him to a waterhole; and care for him.

"Meantime," the radio said. *"Give Nairee my love. When this job is finished I'll be up to Gamma's to see her. Gamma and Nairee both. Tell them to keep the billy boiling and a bush turkey hot in the pot. Mark will be there sooner if not later."*

If only he'd said that—"Give Nairee my love"—
back at Alice!

The little white-haired old lady was down by the
waterhole. Trailing homeward through the trees and
bush were the goats—splashes of gray-white against
the darkling undergrowth. The magpie geese were
pecking round the rubble of bush. The minor birds
were at the food scraps Gamma nightly spread for
them.

As Sergeant Jack drove in through the trees a gray
arch of galahs flew, whirring and wheeling here and
there, into the red sunset glow. They were coming
home to roost in the tall trees all around. And oh!
what a screaming, tumble-turning clatter they made.
A song of joy.

The plains of spinifex and the spread of the pindan
bush were behind them. Nairee was home again in the
heavy tall growth of the water country now—tropical,
hot, and beautiful. And very still. When the galahs
finished their nightly scream session, a gum nut was
heard as it dropped. Dead dry leaves cracked, breaking the air like gunshots muted in a new quiet place.

There were no arms out and no kissings where
Gamma was concerned. She was poling the first of the
trailing goats into their enclosure, looking over her
shoulder, shyly smiling so that her lined and sunburnt
face told its own story. Her girl had come home to her.

Sergeant Jack sat in his vehicle, his hands resting
on the wheel, his eyes thoughtful and watchful, as
Nairee jumped from the passenger seat and ran toward Gamma. He had seen this reunion so many
times, each time he had brought Nairee home to The
Patch. The humanist in him savored with some amuse-
ment the ritual with which this old woman and Nairee
would be at home together once again.

"Hullo Gamma! Hullo Gamma!" Nairee cried as
she ran across the short distance. Gamma said not a
word. Nairee took the pole from her and said, "How's

the billy, Gamma? Can Uncle Jack have a cup of tea?"

Gamma's faded blue eyes watched Nairee pole in a couple of the goats, then she turned to the Land Rover.

"Sergeant Jack? Cup of tea, hey?"

He nodded and let himself down from the driver's seat, and slammed the door behind him.

That was all!

Sergeant Jack had often wondered if Nairee's long absences were no more than long nights to Gamma. Whenever Nairee came home, it was a nod, a shy smile, and on with the job. Nairee might have gone for no more than a stroll in the bush and come home again at sundown.

Once inside the quaint little shack with its tree-trunk, wattle and daub walls, and iron-roof things were different. A low fire gleamed in the old iron stove. The old handmade colonial furniture shone, the timbered floor shone. This from recent scrubbing and polishing and from much use of oil. The curtains, though old, had been recently washed. The china, the billy cans, such little glass as there was—all shone.

There had been no outstretched arms. No kiss.

But the cottage shone.

This, Sergeant Jack knew, was the "welcome home" for Gamma's Girl.

Nairee took it all in with a glow of pride. This was her home. Not the fine mansions of Adelaide, nor, for that matter, the notable colonial homestead of Beelagur Station—the home of Dean Lacey and his mother. Home to Nairee was just a little cottage on the outflanks of the water glades.

Nairee did not wait for Sergeant Jack. The last goat was in and she had run to the door, then was lost in the shadows of indoors. A bare minute later she had emerged, and ran toward Gamma. This time she kissed her on the cheek.

"Oh Gamma darling! It looks gorgeous. Who? Just

who did that polishing? And where did you get that oil?"

Gamma smiled again.

"Dean Lacey came down from the big station, last week," she said, her voice soft and just a little bit cracked—from sheer want of use. Whenever Nairee went away Gamma spoke only to her birds, and the animals.

This time Nairee's own voice carried into the trees at the back. Before she really had time to turn round, there was a fluttering and crackling in the trees behind the cottage. Then a wild flurry of a racing scamper through dust and grass. The flight of pink and gray galahs that had come home at sundown, like Nairee, and made their presence heard again. The brown short-haired kelpie dogs that had been indifferent to the sound of the Land Rover driving up now heard the sound of Nairee's *voice*. They lifted their heads, sprung to their feet, and raced round from the paddock at the back. In their excitement, they all but knocked Nairee over. She only had two arms but she took the three animals in one embrace of joy.

"Hey! Down, Banjo. Down down, Rogue! Piker, darling—not such big licks. Please, please you'll knock me over!"

Sergeant Jack, his hands in his pockets, rocked back on his heels.

"I'd call that a welcome and a half," he said. He thought to himself that the birds, the bush, and the dogs seemed to sense that *this time* Nairee had come home for good. They were more noisy than usual.

Nairee ran back into the house to escape. Any minute the dogs would have rocked her right off her feet, so great was their excitement.

Gamma was smiling now. Really smiling.

"I guess she likes to come home," she said. "You think she'll stay?" she asked Sergeant Jack, a little tremble in her voice.

"Stay?" he said. "You couldn't keep her away, Gamma." He paused then, his face deadpan, asked:

"What's Dean Lacey been doing down here . . . besides bringing you a bottle of oil?"

"Other things!" she said anxiously, suddenly worried, as if she needed to keep Sergeant Jack's good will. She knew well that Sergeant Jack did not care for Dean Lacey—nor for his High-and-Mightiness from the Big House calling at The Patch too often.

"Other things? Like what?" Sergeant Jack asked, almost sharply.

Gamma shook her head. She would not tell him of the wool-woven mat Dean had brought for Nairee's room. Nor the aboriginal wood carvings for the little sitting room. Gamma knew Sergeant Jack had the power to put her in a "home for the aged" if ever she did anything to—or was neglectful of—his ward. She did not yet quite understand that Nairee was now fully adult, and was her own mistress. When these sort of situations had arisen before, or when that Mrs. Gray from Alice Springs had visited The Patch and asked questions, and said "This must not be done," and "That must not be done," Gamma had always been a little afraid that one day they might take her away and put her in a home. She was uncertain as to what authority they might have for the present. Her wits told her that now Nairee was home there was someone to be with her. Sergeant Jack would not have to visit so often. Just maybe call in when he was passing through.

Yes, Gamma knew well why Sergeant Jack did not like Dean Lacey coming this way too often and bringing presents, and Nairee being asked to go to Beelagur Station. She knew everything, but she did not tell anyone her thoughts. There were a lot of things the little old lady kept in her head—except that sometimes she talked to the goats or to the kelpies. She knew she did this, and was on occasion afraid that Sergeant Jack might come silently through the glades—as once or twice he had done when he was on a search—and catch her talking when there was no one but the animals and the birds to listen to her.

So she smiled that tiny quivering smile of hers, pretending she did not understand, and said nothing.

Nairee had come to the door again.

"Come on, Uncle Jack! Come on, Gamma," came her young voice. "The kettle's boiling. *Tea-o!*"

It was a call of joy.

5

THE THREE OF THEM SAT ROUND THE TIMBER TABLE
and had their tea. Sergeant Jack could not help smiling every now and again because he could see that
though Gamma had her girl home, they were a little
shy of one another. Gamma did not ask Nairee about
her life down south. Nairee said nothing of it. Sergeant Jack guessed—rightly, he knew—that it would
take days with little-by-little talk before the two of
them broke down the wall of their divergent experiences of the past year.

"Well, I must up and off," he said at last. "That
track home to my own pad is not too good at any
time. Worse than the worst if I let the night overtake
me."

Nairee went to the door with him. He bent down
and kissed her cheek.

"So long, girl!" he said. "Take care of Gamma. Call
the dogs off, will you? I'd rather get to the track whole
and not in rags." He lifted a hand to Gamma, then
slammed his wide-awake hat on his head. "So long,
old girl!"

He often called Gamma "old girl," and for reasons that he didn't even try to understand, she liked it. She *never* said good-bye to him. Sergeant Jack and Nairee had a theory that Gamma was afraid that if she said good-bye he might not come back ever again. She was dependent entirely on Sergeant Jack to bring out her monthly allowance from the money her husband had left when he had died more than twenty years before. Nairee had never known Gamma's man, and Gamma had only once or twice spoken of him in all the years Nairee had lived with her.

Way off by Beelagur's southern boundary fence was a little graveyard with a small fence around it, and it was known all around. Gamma's husband was buried there. She never spoke of him now, but there were many other matters of which Gamma never spoke. By the time Nairee was twelve or thirteen she knew there was much locked up inside Gamma of which she could not—or would not—ever speak. Nairee, like Gamma, also had the gift of silence. She loved the little old lady with everything she had in her, and she knew Gamma loved her that way too. Their silences spoke.

So Nairee could never stay for keeps down south, and live and work in the glamour of cities or even small towns. They belonged to each other, she and Gamma. And that was that!

Nairee waved Sergeant Jack off as his Land Rover ploughed its way through the rough bush track to the west. In one way she was sad to see him go, but in another way she was glad. Now she could talk to Gamma and tell her some things about the way of life in the south, and show her the exciting things she had brought home.

First opened was the carryall in which she had brought her little gifts. She unfolded a blue denim blouse with a double-strength matching blue denim skirt and presented them to Gamma. Gamma loved the buttons with their bright pearl-like polish. There were two soft-cloth shade hats: one for hot summer sun and one waterproofed against rain and the monsoon. There were leather boots and a chain belt from which hung clips to hold pocket knife, a grass knife, a whistle, and any other gadget Gamma might use in the bush. Her old sunburned, lined, and bush-scratched hands stroked their shining surfaces. There was a new aluminum kettle with a whistle stop on the spout. This last was magic to Gamma. Nairee had never known a time when Gamma had gone into a town, or even to the small bush store twelve miles away at the nearest crossroad. It was south of the Everglades, nearby yet another enormous black stump burned to a likeness of a dark "statue" of a camel. So the corner store was naturally named the *Black Camel*.

Gamma was delighted with the things Nairee had brought. There was even a hint of tears in her eyes. Nairee knew her choices had been right. Her Gamma was bewitched by Nairee's own bright and pretty things. She was delighted while Nairee folded and packed up the delicate underclothes, the one or two dresses she had brought home with her against that race day or homestead party to which she knew Mrs. Lacey would invite her, and to which she would have to go in the guise of a well-educated, well-dressed *young lady*. Oh! That "schooling" down there in Adelaide!

Much of that and most of her thoughts about those things Nairee kept to herself. She knew Gamma did not like her to go often to Beelagur station, and nothing in the world would make Nairee do anything that would upset Gamma too much.

It was at least an hour after Sergeant Jack had gone before Gamma really came out of her shell and talked.

"You didn't want to stay down there in the big city, Nairee?" she asked.

Nairee laughed.

"No. I'm here. Right here. You didn't think I'd ever leave you, Gamma? You know jolly well I wouldn't. This is my home."

Gamma shook her head and the tiny little crooked smile touched her face with a soft light.

"No, I didn't think—but someday, Nairee, you might . . . Well, Sergeant Jack and Mrs. Gray . . . they thought someday you would have to—"

"Have to what? Go south to a big town? How would I be able to take *my* goats. Some of them are mine, Gamma. You gave them to me when they were born. And I couldn't take *my* share of the birds. I'd have to put them in cages. Never. Absolutely *never*."

She *knew* how terrified Gamma was that one day they—"they" being the government authorities—would take her away and put her in a home.

"Never," Nairee had said repeatedly. "Never, never, never!"

Yet someday—she knew in her heart—Gamma would no longer be self-sufficient. She also knew in her heart that she herself would never leave Gamma alone. However, she would let time take care of itself. There was nothing else she could do about it, was there? Sometimes she had the awkward thought that one day she might have to get a little cottage on the outskirts of one of the nearer Outback towns. Just in case—

She had always banished this thought with that leaning post of a saying: "Sufficient unto the day is the evil thereof."

This day of her homecoming Nairee ran outside to call sundown remarks to the galahs who were still making a mighty racket on the tree boughs. She patted and laughed as she played with the kelpie dogs. Lastly she took a goodnight peek at the goats in the yard. Again she had that sundown thought. "Sufficient unto the day . . ." But not *this* day. It was not such a convincing backstop to time as it used to be. *Time was passing!*

Gamma limped a little, just a very very little, as she walked. She had never done this before. How old was Gamma? No one seemed to know, and those concerned had given up asking long ago.

As much as could be traced by records, Gamma, not much more than a girl, had come with her young husband in a horse-drawn dray, their meager bags of personal belongings strapped under canvas. No one of the few oldies who had seen them on their way through the bush had any idea what were, in fact, their worldly possessions. Nor from whence they came, or where they were going.

They had taken a liking to what became The Patch. Her husband had felled trees and built their first wattle-and-daub cabin. There was nothing unusual about this in that place in that era. There had always been, since the very early days, bagmen and swaggies who "squatted" in the no-man's-land of the vast uninhabited Outback. The more wealthy people had arrived, and established cattle stations. They took little notice of this "lot" on the far side of the creek.

Ben and his wife lived there in peace, quiet, and industry, until years later Ben was thrown by his horse —a wild bush brumby—against a tree trunk. He never recovered from his injuries.

The authorities were called in by the station people on the uplands across the creek. The Outback policemen came to check events. They buried Ben Peech by the boundary fence neighboring the Laceys' station. His was not the only sad grave lying beside a boundary fence in the Outback.

Gamma, known at that time as Miz Peech, refused to move to a town. There was no law that said she could not live alone. She could not forcibly be moved out. So, in the early days of live-and-let-live she was allowed to stay on. People were good people in those neocolonial Outback days. The station people said they would keep an eye on her. A transceiver set was provided and set up by the Flying Doctor Service. The Outback policeman and the then Ranger who traveled that track called in regularly to share billy-tea with Miz Peech. Really it was to see how things were going with this strangely uncommunicative lady. Legend said she had become silent after her husband's death. The nearby aborigines had more than befriended her. This was because she herself became something of a hermit, and did not want to mingle with the station people. She was a true loner.

Already several of the wild goats round and about —mostly regarded as nuisance-next-to-vermin by the other inhabitants of those latitudes—were kept at The Patch. These bore kids that were brought up as pets. It was these last, together with *their* offspring, that Gamma nurtured and made her own.

This is how things were by the time Nairee was a small girl.

Sergeant Jack, a rookie policeman sent out on an early patrol, was the first to discover the little girl living at The Patch.

No one could part Gamma from this child. Nor part this child from Gamma. Sergeant Jack reported that the child was healthy, well-clothed, and happy. The benign authorities, because they could not trace the child's parents, decided to leave her there with Gamma —whose hair was now going prematurely gray. They would leave other welfare matters to a later day. The bush mailman called from time to time, but this was mostly to deliver parcels of clothes, towels, and books for the small girl.

Nairee lived her early childhood with the little graying lady, loved and loving.

The welfare people kept a watchful eye open behind their blinkers. In the fullness of time Rookie Allen became Policeman Allen, and finally Sergeant Allen. In the years that had slipped past he had very soon become "Uncle Jack," always loved and welcomed by the growing girl. From Miz Peech the now-white-haired elderly lady had become "Gamma" to all. Later comers to the area had never known any other name for her. Station properties had changed hands— except for the Laceys' at Beelagur—so most assumed Nairee really was Gamma's grandchild.

The Patch had grown to become a bird sanctuary, and an animal hideaway.

Percy the swagman had come by to leave a bitch—
the part-wire-haired-terrier offspring of a border collie
who spent many nights cohabiting with a "wild dingo"
out on the range. Hence came the so-called kelpie-
type dogs that lived and loved in their own particular way at The Patch.

Gamma and Nairee, on this night of Nairee's return, sat by the darkening coals of their outside *cooking* fire. Little was said, for each knew the other, and
each understood silence. But Nairee had a full
heart. She wondered how, in these last four years, she
had ever been able to leave The Patch. Yet when
each holiday had ended, she had gone down south
readily enough.

For one thing she knew she had to go. Mrs. Lacey
at Beelagur had rarely been to see Gamma, but she
had used her powerful station-owning prestige to see
that the authorities insisted that Nairee have a complete education. First there had been the "School of
the Air" over the radio. Then there had been the
boarding school in a city down south. She had been
so homesick there that once again Mrs. Lacey had
used her influence to have Nairee—older now—trans-
ferred to a College of Advanced Education where she
could learn more useful things. No one could teach
Nairee bushcraft. She had known the bush all her remembered life. But the manual and technical subjects
could and would be of use. She could now do simple
accounting, and understand the covenants of law. She
acquired an understanding of the mechanics of motor-
cars, especially of those equipped with four-wheel-
drive. She herself had concluded that one day it might
be necessary to acquire some form of motor transport.
She and Gamma could not be forever beholden to
other homesteads to come to their rescue if either of
them—particularly Gamma—needed hospital treat-
ment.

"Gamma," Nairee said this golden evening of her
return. She was looking into the shadows and occa-

sional lights of the dying fire. "The Patch is getting big now, isn't it? I'd like my own back-paddock to be bigger. We could grow sorghum. Perhaps some other things to make a little money—"

"We have enough money," Gamma said, stubborn now. "I've the pension. And the rattler brings it out in stores."

"Yes, Gamma. But we should have our own rattler. A utility. Better still, a four-wheel-drive vehicle. It's better, stronger. But it does cost more. A lot of money—"

"We don't need money, Nairee. We grow our own food. And get our beef from the store at the camel stump."

Nairee stared at the coals. How could she tell Gamma that one day she, Gamma, might need more than make-do? Might need a rush trip to the coast?

She couldn't tell her. Gamma would say she could manage for herself. She had always managed for herself. In Gamma's book *it would go on forever*.

Nairee knew that things as they were would *not* go on forever. Gamma, like herself, and all living beings, grew older year by year. They were mortal.

They could not always think that "over the mesa breakaway" was a store. To the northeast were Geko and Beelagur stations. If trouble came those station owners, Hank Brown and the Laceys, would be on hand.

Nairee fell silent now, for once again she had the troubled feeling she always had when she thought of the Laceys.

Was it because of Dean?

Funny how she always, somewhere inside her, felt his presence. Yet his distance.

Dean!

Once, when younger—not much more than a very young girl—she had a kind of hero worship for Dean. She recognized this fact now, but not without a blush. What had he thought of her? A silly girl, she supposed. Fearing that, she felt uncomfortable now because she kept thinking of him. He was the heir of Beelagur station, one of the biggest cattle empires in their vast state. A bush king in his own right. She herself was a stray. A no one's child from nowhere—found in the bush by dear, kind Woolarooka. Then brought to Gamma to be cared for. And loved.

Who am I? Oh! If only that recurring question did not haunt her so!

6

NEXT DAY, NAIREE TOOK THE HOE OUT TO THE SMALL
paddock that had always been her own estate. Together, she and Gamma had made the paddock. They
had searched the bush for short-length broken boughs
to set uprights in the tough, hard ground.

How they had chopped and dug to get those fence
posts deep into the hard red ground! "A man's job,"
the Ranger, Mark Allen, had said with some indigna-
tion when he had come upon them at work. He had
thrown off his hat and pulled off his shirt, and set to.
He dug the holes and then fixed in, and sanded down,
the posts. He had stayed a whole week, and come
back another time to finish off the job. He had brought
with him not only rolls of fencing wire, but also two
of his own offsiders, and another man from a small
station that dominated the western plains and the timber country near Great River. They had brought other
tools and these they left behind—on purpose—when
the job was finished.

How Nairee had loved that time! How they had all
laughed, teased one another, and worked!

In those days Mark used to call Nairee "sweet-heart." Then the other men did too. She was every-body's sweetheart, they said. And she loved it. So did they. So did Gamma the teamaker. That was four years ago. She was fourteen years old then.

Now this day, her first full day home for keeps, Nairee thought about it as she tilled and dug out the grosser of the grasses. And about Mark too.

Two men in her life! Mark the Ranger, and Dean the station owner. Which, in her teenage mind, had she dreamed—secretly—of loving for keeps?

Both of them, of course! First one and then the other. At least first one dream. Then later another dream.

Nairee rested the hoe against the fence and sat down on a red gravel mound, her back to the iron-stone spear of rock, her arms wrapped round her knees. She had on her thinking cap now. She was older. It wasn't as easy as all that. It wasn't the girl's choice, was it? It was the man's choice.

There was a sound in the bush. It came from the northwest corner of the paddock. She could see the flight of disturbed birds, then the movement of the half-grown trees, their low branches in a wind-made curtsey as someone passed by.

He came, a shadow first because of the thick, trop-ical growth of the young saplings. The shadow was tall—Mark? In her heart Nairee was troubled—or was it "excitement muted"?

Because of the down-trailing creepers from the big trees she could not quite see his face. But she saw his shape and knew it was not Mark. It was Dean. She did not know whether she was glad, or *very glad.* How long had he been up there on the tumbled rocks from the mesa? Watching her as usual. Always from a distance—*watching her.* Rarely ever coming close.

Now that he *had* come through the veiling creepers, he stood quite still. Nairee did not stir. If anything, her arms were locked more tightly around her knees.

He came on, not looking where he was going. Not smiling either. Just coming.

Then suddenly he stopped still in his tracks. He turned his head a little, as if listening. Nairee was listening too. Her bush-trained ear had caught the sound, and instantly recognized it. Mrs. Lacey's Holden station wagon.

Dean was bush-trained too, of course. He knew how to go on looking like a grass tree instead of a young man. It was a trick they all learned from the aborigines. "Stand small"—according to the height of the low-growing grass tree. Have its black body-sized trunk between you and the person from whom you are hiding. As that person moved outside the straight line and came round in a semicircle so you moved around in the same arc as that semicircle.

Anyone who had lived and worked long enough in the Outback could camouflage himself. Most grass trees were the height of a man and their mop of foliage hid the head and shoulders.

The Holden's door had been opened, and it shut now with a slam. Nobody ever drove that car but Mrs. Lacey. Nairee knew who it had to be coming through the undergrowth. She stood up herself and leaned against one of her fence posts. For want of knowing what to do with them, she folded her arms. The hoe lay abandoned on the ground.

Mrs. Lacey, in a dark blue cotton dress, came through the last veil of trees. She saw Nairee leaning against the fence, her hoe lying slantwise on the ground. She lifted a hand in greeting. Then she came on.

"Hullo Nairee!" she called. Her voice had a flat, anxious quality. Nairee had heard that note before. Always it had been something to do with Dean.

Mrs. Lacey came on as far as the side fence and looked across at the girl.

"You came home safely!" she said without a smile. Nairee had seen her like this before. The only factor common to each of those times had been that Dean was out of Beelagur territory, and somewhere around *this* way.

She wanted to say, "Looking for Dean?" Intuitively she knew that that could be worse than impertinent. Mrs. Lacey stood quite still in her cold arm's-length way for half a minute. She was looking across the diminutive, partly hoed paddock. Then, as if collecting herself, she relaxed.

"Hullo Nairee! Glad to be home, and at work already?"

"Oh yes!" Nairee relaxed too, as she answered over the short distance. Perhaps Mrs. Lacey had come to see her, after all! It was only her imagination that said whenever Dean was southwest of his own boundary in this area, Mrs. Lacey sooner or later happened by.

Nairee dropped her arms, and now almost ran across the ground to the far fence.

"Will you come in and see Gamma?" she asked.

"You know I rarely come and see Gamma," Mrs. Lacey said, not unkindly but firmly. "And Gamma does not want me to come and see her. But when she wishes she too can come and stay a day or two at Beelagur. She has in the past—as well you know, my dear."

"Yes, but—" Nairee was leaning her arms along the top wires of the fence, her right foot resting on the lowest one. "I always ask you. You've given me ever so many lessons in being polite. I have to show I haven't forgotten—" She paused, then added wistfully, "I would so like you to come."

"Yes, of course. I'm glad in some ways you are home, Nairee. But I would have much preferred you to take up some pleasant work in one of the southern cities. There's nothing for you hereabout. I had that in mind all along."

Funny how her gray eyes never seem to have any expression in them, Nairee thought. Sometimes I think she doesn't really like me at all. Other times I think she likes me too much. Too possessive—

"Well, I just came to see that you were all right,"

Mrs. Lacey said. "You know, Nairee—and I have suggested it before—you should put gardening gloves on your hands when you do that kind of work. It is not a girl's work."

"But who up here in the Never-Never is going to look at my hands?" Nairee asked with a laugh. Even as she said it she thought of Dean. She didn't know why. Would *he* ever look at her hands? Or be *allowed* to look at them? A silly thought, that last. Dean was strong-minded and king of all he possessed over there at Beelagur. He owned all the cattle and the general livestock, anyway.

Her eyes strayed up to the distant mesa. She lowered them slowly, and came back to the scrub bush below. She glanced at the grass trees behind one of which she was sure Dean, aloof as ever, had been standing.

Which one? She could not tell now. Her interest had been deflected and there were so many of those trees. Small, slim, big, double-headed, long and wiry-haired at the top. And the surrounding scrub, all so dark grayish-green, and impenetrable.

Why did he not show himself when he knew Mrs. Lacey was here? It wasn't as if his mother was bossy with *him!* The opposite, in fact. It was Dean who was the autocrat on the other side of the mesa. King of his acres. And yet . . .

It was a mystery to Nairee. But then she had never lived in a cultivated, affluent, streamlined homestead like Beelagur. She had been there often as a little girl and as a growing adolescent, but mostly when Dean was away. Not so much the last year or two. Only to the races on Dandy at the Beelagur race track that was a mile away from the homestead.

"You must come over and see me when you have settled down," Mrs. Lacey said. She looked around, as if searching for something. Someone? Dean? Following him? "Dean will be out drafting cattle next week," she added. "We'll be able to have a good talk without interruptions."

"I would love that," Nairee said. "I could come anytime. Only—"

"Yes?"

"Well, you used to say—when I was younger—that it was polite to wait until I was asked."

She glanced away into the bush. Dean was no longer there. Yet he hadn't made a sound.

Mrs. Lacey was looking at Nairee steadily, those gray eyes veiled as if she had some sadness in her. Which was *impossible*, Nairee thought. Mrs. Lacey's life was surely without troubles. She was in a special sort of way above all the other station owners. Some called her "Queen Bee," but never to her face!

Nairee had noticed this expression in the woman's eyes before. She had always been grateful because Mrs. Lacey had taken such a kind interest in her, and had taught her quite a lot of the customs of her own way of living. Nairee realized—and Mrs. Lacey had told her—it was in order that she would not feel out of place when she went south and mixed with other girls at school. And later at college.

"You must be like the other girls," Mrs. Lacey had repeatedly said. "You are one of them now. They come from good homes, and their manners will be polished."

Nairee had been particularly grateful for these kindly teachings when she was invited to a couple of the girls' homes for weekends. She had, on those occasions, watched carefully what the others in the household did and often thought of Mrs. Lacey's pronouncements. But why was it so often *different* when she came home to The Patch? Mrs. Lacey was kind—when occasion demanded—to Gamma, but became distant in her manner. She was like someone from another world. She kept herself enclosed in some private place of her own.

It just didn't make any sense to Nairee. Now that she was grown up and home for good, maybe things would be different. But here, today, this was not so.

Had Mrs. Lacey come down in her car because she had seen Dean coming this way? Why?

The old mystery deepened. Why had Dean walked away? He *had* walked away, silently. Nairee knew he had gone because she could see the sunlight shining through the leafery of the scrub bushes. So he wasn't there anymore. No one was there.

"I must be going, Nairee," Mrs. Lacey said, her voice cheerful now. "I just wanted to catch a glimpse of you, and know you were well. I will take the north track back to the homestead. Have the Rangers had the far track cut through to the lake yet?"

"Oh yes!" Nairee said eagerly. "Mark Allen wrote to me, and told me about it. On account of Gamma. The stores can come right through to her now instead of being left by that old black stump at the bend. The camel stump—"

Mrs. Lacey had been on the point of turning away. She half turned back to stare at Nairee. Her smile was gone and her face quite blank.

"Wrote to you?" she asked. "Have you and the Ranger been writing to one another? It's not very wise, Nairee. You are still quite young—"

Nairee took defense behind a little fib. "Only to give me news of Gamma," she said. "He always called on Gamma when he went through this way and brought her extra treats—stores. You see, it kind of saved Uncle Jack making a special trip out to see if Gamma was all right." Actually "the Ranger," as Mrs. Lacey called Mark, had written to her, at least twice a term. And she to him.

"Well yes, I can understand that," Mrs. Lacey said thoughtfully. "You are grown up now, Nairee, and you don't have to call Sergeant Allen 'Uncle Jack' anymore." She broke off and bit her lip. Then Nairee said something which she had never said aloud before:

"I know he is not my real uncle," she said firmly, but not quite indignant. "And I know Mark couldn't be my cousin. But I wish they both were . . . I mean,

Uncle Jack at least. I would like to have a real uncle."

Mrs. Lacey was obviously taken aback. Even worried. But *why?*

"Well, so long as both men know they had a duty to do," she said briskly. "They won't be so necessary anymore. To Gamma, that is. The Beelagur stockmen can attend to your stores now that lake track is going through."

Nairee said, "Yes—of course. At least I suppose so . . ." She did not know what else to say. For some quite inexplicable reason she did not want to tell Mrs. Lacey that she had hoped—with all her heart—that Uncle Jack and Mark would keep on calling in at The Patch whenever they went through to distant places beyond the mesas. For ever and ever. She intuited that Mrs. Lacey's objection was because salaried people did not have the same wealth as people who owned stations. Big stations at that!

She listened to the crackle of the undergrowth as Mrs. Lacey found her way back to the track and her car.

Why does it have to be like this? Nairee wondered. Tears welled in her eyes.

First Dean, and now Mrs. Lacey herself! Yet Mrs. Lacey had helped her so kindly over the years. And Dean . . . yes, tall handsome *Dean!* He too had been a friend. Well, most of the time . . .

Where was he now? Why had he gone? Was it that old sense of social distance? Yet, all those years back when she had been only nine he had given her her first pony and taught her to ride. The Laceys together had given her *Dandy*—her prize-winner. She had loved Dean then—just a little bit anyway.

She brushed her arm across her eyes, and started once again to hoe out a small square in the paddock corner. This was to be her new "all-sorts" garden this season. Some brush flowers; some vegetables. Nairee always, since she was old enough to wield a hoe, had kept her garden in small squares. The red hardness of the ground had been too much for her to till in larger sections.

She was cross with herself now. She had been so happy to come home. Everything about the bush, the creek, and the little old homestead had seemed so wonderful. To be home for good! The sun had been shining bright. The bush smelled so wonderful.

And now—

"Oh blow!" she said, literally shaking herself. "I'm just not going to let other people bother me!"

She turned, and as she did she saw Gamma, her funny little narrow-brimmed cotton hat pulled down over her eyes. She was walking in her quaint sturdy manner, toward the goat track that led through the bush. She was going to bring the goats home herself today. Only when Gamma felt happy, well, and energetic did she go herself to shepherd the goats home. Other times they came home themselves—in a flock.

Nairee dropped the hoe beside the pick and ran to the fence. Her momentary unhappiness had been only momentary indeed. The familiar and loved sight of the little mud brick wattle-and-daub homestead in the slanting rays of the westering sun, and Gamma, shoulders back, trudging toward the goat track, was enough.

She was home indeed!

"I'm coming, Gamma!" she called. "I'm coming too." She stooped to climb between the horizontal wires of the fence, then ran after the little gray-haired lady—both of them heading for what most people far off in the Outback, called "vermin." Beloved goats! For the dwellers on The Patch, the goats were never vermin, only loved ones, "part of the family."

≈≈≈≈≈≈≈≈≈≈

7

HOME AGAIN LATER. WHILE GAMMA POLED THE LAST
truant goat into the yard, Nairee lit the fire in the iron
stove in the lean-to kitchen. Gamma came in and
stirred yesterday's stew in its massive iron pot. Neither
spoke a word, for each were busy at her own chores.

Then suddenly Nairee lifted her head. She had
heard a sound. It was far off but becoming louder—
second by second.

Gamma took no notice.

Was it a truck? No. Not a plane either. They had sel-
dom heard that strange foreign sound before. It was a
helicopter, and belonged to the Ranger staff. Could it
be? Could it really be . . . Mark Allen?

Through the window Nairee saw the helicopter sink
gently to rest out on the dried grass plain, and Mark
Allen step from the cockpit.

Nairee puffed and blew on the fire till it was a glow-
ing blaze. Gamma went to the shower house and
washed her face and hands, then came back and added
the contents of a jar of ready-to-serve stew to the one
already cooking in the iron pot.

The fire was now going full blast. Nairee set the table against the wall—for *three*. . . . .

The only person who could ever come to The Patch in a helicopter was Mark, surely? Sometimes, Gamma said, he'd come with another Ranger. Sometimes alone.

As Nairee ran out to greet Mark, he pushed his broad-brimmed Ranger's slouch hat to the back of his head. His fine teeth flashed shining white in his browned face. He moved easily and with purpose, with that innate air of command. An air of mastery. And security in himself.

"Oh Mark!"

The declining sun made gold shafts of light through the trees. The sky was a red glory. One's eyes were dazzled when looking west at this hour of the day.

Nairee ran straight into his arms. Was *that* accidental?

"Oh Mark! I'm so glad you came." Could it have been only a few hours ago that she had seen him in Alice Springs. No . . . it had to be all of two days ago!

"Steady! Steady!" he said, holding her at arm's length. "Why all the hurry?"

She blinked her eyes as she drew back and stood upright.

"Surprise!" she said. "I . . . that is, I thought—I mean, I didn't know for sure it was you, did I? Then it *was*—"

He had taken off his hat now. That brown broad-brimmed Stetson with the Ranger's badge in front. His sun-bronzed face was almost the same color.

"Someone else?" he asked skeptically. "This stretch of the Outback is as empty of man-power as a . . . desert. Unless—" He stopped smiling. He dug his hands into his pockets and rocked back on his heels. "Unless the high-and-mighty Dean Lacey had been around this stretch of the river beds?"

"Well, he *was* . . . I mean, I think he was somewhere up there," she said, with a wave of her hand in the air. "Past these grass trees. But I could have been . . . I mean, I might have been mistaken."

"But if he had really been there you would have come running to him—right into his arms—like this?" He put out his arms. Jokingly, of course.

Nairee took a step backward. She avoided looking into Mark's eyes.

"I might have. I don't know. Since he didn't come I don't know what I would have done. One doesn't think—"

"Then my welcome was because you didn't know it was 'just me'!" The teasing in his manner was marked by that clever smile.

Nairee half turned away.

"Don't be so muddly, Mark. It's only my second day home. I'm glad to see *everyone* living round and about. And you especially. Just because you are *not* living round about."

"I've received the message," he said, miming a rueful droop of the mouth.

They both stood and looked at one another. Straight in the eyes. Then laughed.

Mark took her hand, turned her around, and said: "Come on. Let's go see how Gamma is doing now she has her bodyguard home for keeps."

"*Me?* A bodyguard?" Nairee looked surprised. They were walking along the foot track now, swinging gently held hands as they went toward the house. A boy-and-girl affair. Their feet swished in the long dry wiregrass that almost hid the earth track. They didn't notice it because they knew their way, and could have walked it in dark night—straight on without a thought.

"Was the flyer inside the Cessna when you found him down in the desert?" Nairee asked.

"He was all right. Mostly because Lady Luck looks after some people, whether they deserve it or not," Mark said a little grimly. "He brought his plane down on the desert rim himself. Emergency landing was what he called it. But nowhere near water. Not there anywhere."

"Was he injured? How did he manage?"

"Desert aborigines were on walkabout, thereabouts.

They found him. They abandoned their walkabout—which is quite something—and led him to water. He'd never have found that pool himself. It was cached away in a rock pile. One of the aborigines' last secrets on the edge of the Simpson Desert."

"But Mark, how did you know where it was? To find him, I mean?"

"Tracks in the mud, for one thing," he said. "He'd had that once-in-a-lifetime luck of a shower of rain. Bang over the desert too. The dunes will be sprouting green on their ridges. Probably for once in a lifetime too."

"Oh Mark," Nairee said ruefully. "You are making fun of something that could have been a tragedy."

"But it wasn't a tragedy, was it? That fella is an experienced pilot, and he should not have taken off when he did. One needs luck as well as skill to fly in tropical storm weather if it comes up. Right? Now let's not talk about him. Let's talk about you. What everyone wants to know is what are you going to do now that you are home."

"Maybe build a proper station homestead," Nairee said. "I could, you know."

"No, I don't know," he said, smiling again, setting up little vibrations in her heart. His big smile was so rare. But it was beautiful when it came.

"I didn't just learn sewing and dancing at the college," she said, very seriously now. "Those Colleges of Advanced Education—C.A.E. to you, Mark—have a technical side to them. You'd be surprised to know what subjects I took in my last year. I was afraid they wouldn't let me take some of them. They were mostly for males. But they did, you know. Because I was an Outback girl and needed to know how to use tools."

"Fire away and tell me."

"Well, Motor mechanics to begin with. A three-month course. Did you know that when you buy a Land Rover you are given a course in the mechanics of the rover, and road management, along with the purchase?'"

"And did you buy a Land Rover?" Mark asked, smiling.

"No. But I'd know how to look after one if ever I did buy one. And one day I will."

"Good for you." When he saw the look of purpose in Nairee's face, he became serious. "And what else?" he asked.

"Woodwork and carpentry. And how to mix and fix cement. Lay tiles and also—for fun—to lay bricks."

He was laughing now. "What did you build, Nairee? A doll's house?"

"You're poking fun, Mark. Actually it *was* something like that. Obviously there isn't room for everyone in a course to build a house. So we built a small one between us. Not a waste, either. It will later be used for storage at the C.A.E.

"How did you get on with all those young men, basking in the sun and building, while you were learning?"

Nairee stood looking at him.

"It wasn't a game, Mark. You might not have noticed it, but there has been an *International Women's Year*. The C.A.E. recognized it by allowing some women—girls, if you prefer it—into the all-purpose course as an experiment. I was one of them."

"So from now on, I can call you 'an experiment' instead of a 'female'?"

Nairee was standing on her dignity again. "You may call me what you please, Mark, so long as you don't call me too early in the morning."

Mark laughed out loud this time. "I've never been near you early enough—at that time—*yet*. But . . . ?"

Nairee nearly asked what that "yet" and that "but" meant. Then thought perhaps he hadn't meant anything by it at all—except it was *something* to say.

"You'll be glad to know I studied English, some economics, and history as well."

He put his arm along her shoulders as they walked. "Just as long as you learned to stay the way you've always been, Nairee. Quite a few people hearabouts were dead scared you might have changed after that dose of town life. Then what would become of Gamma? Worse still, what would have become of the rest of us? I can't imagine the Outback, let alone The Patch, with Nairee all different."

"Thank you very much," she said. Her heart struck a glad chord. She could almost hear the twang herself. "You are now Ranger No. 1 Mark. Have *you* changed any?"

"Not a whit."

"Same with me, then."

"Good for you!"

They had stopped to clamber over a fallen tree log. Nairee found herself staring into his eyes. Her heart began to beat fast and she was afraid he might notice it. "*Dear Mark, dear* Mark," she was saying inside herself. Unexpectedly, and unannounced, she would have liked to shed a tear, but had no idea why. For being past play years? She had to be a grown-up now.

Gamma's postmanlike whistle, a silver-sounding lifebuoy, came from the homestead and interrupted her thoughts.

"That's Gamma!" Nairee said. Actually she knew the whistle was mostly calling in the animals and birds for the evening meal, but it had always included her too. Not that Gamma meant to whistle her in. She just came, as from habit, when the animals came in.

"Let's go," Mark said, taking her hand. They were laughing now, back to the safety of youth. Nairee was happy again. The misty window that glimpsed into the realm of the worldly was shuttered down. They were friends. "Cobbers" as the bushmen would have said. She had been silly to think—to hope—*what*?

Yet that evening, after dinner, and after Mark had gone, Nairee thought about it all again. Why had there been something different about Mark? It had to be that now he was No. 1 Ranger for the area, he might just have *seemed* older. More serious, though friendly of course. And teasing, as he had always been. A man of authority. All the vast bush, and the creatures in it, were his to care about. And the trees, and the mountains, the swamplands, the desert lands. All *his*!

What a strange day! She had been in love with being at home. The bush, the red ironstone line of mesas in the distance. The great red spear of rock that pointed skyward on the horizon half a mile away. The blazing sundown sky. Gamma just exactly as she had always been. The animals, especially the kelpie dogs; the birds, especially the galahs and rainbow colored parrots. Gamma's beloved goats. They were all here as if not altered one whit, waiting for her, Nairee, to come home again. This time to stay.

She could still hear the strange sound of the Ranger's helicopter departing. For some reason the buzz, and the fading whirligig sound, made her feel just that little bit sad now. Almost as if a bird were flying away, and might be lost once it was over and beyond the mesa.

8

Nairee's spirits lightened as she remembered the "good news" part of Mark's visit. There was to be a party at Geko Creek, the station northwest of The Patch. She would see Mark again, there. Actually she would see everybody, for when one station or another gave a party everyone came from all over. She would see her beloved horse Dandy. He had been put to grass at Geko Creek. He was getting old now. The best news was that Dandy had had a son. Dandy Two. He had only been a foal when she had come home for the long Christmas holidays last year. He was breaking two years now and Hank Brown, the Geko manager had broken him in and been training him for Nairee.

Nairee stopped being what she called a "misery miss" when she thought of Hank Brown and Dandy Two. But mostly because there were so many marvelous people in this part of the Outback. They had each in their own way given her a welcome home. Mrs. Lacey had come—only as far as the rise above the creek, of course. But then she never came much nearer than that at any time. She liked to keep her distance.

Dean Lacey had come. She was sure of that. He had come to see her at her own house because she had come home now for good! She was sure that was what he meant by being there—very still, just beyond the trees.

He hadn't come any further because of his pride. She was sure of that too. The proud, aloof station owner—Dean Lacey! So stiff, sometimes, with that pride! Yet sometimes not quite so much.

Even as she thought of him Nairee felt a strangeness. A wishful thought that she and he could be more natural when they met. Really interested in one another.

Last but not least, there had been Mark. Mark! If she'd had someone of the other sex really to love, she was sure he would be someone like Mark.

She had felt something really *great* for him when she had arrived at Alice. She had thought, or hoped, he had come to meet her. She'd had that "belonging" feeling. Had he perhaps *really* come to Alice to meet her?

He'd had other things to do. Oh well!

Now she must think only of the party at Geko Creek, and of Hank Brown and Dandy One and Dandy Two.

Gamma had cooked her own favorite dinner while Nairee had been tilling the paddock, then tilting at misunderstandings with Mark.

"He should have come in to eat," Gamma said. She spoke so rarely that this was the best way she had of saying Mark was welcome.

"He has a job to do, Gamma. Something over the range. Maybe strangers are going through there. They have to be warned away from the river glades. Uncle Jack said once . . . that people who go in there don't always come out again. They lose their way."

"One day some people came out of the glades," Gamma said. "The other Ranger, the old one, heard about them. They'd left crossed sticks for tracks."

"Must have been boy scouts once," Nairee said. "Boy scouts leave arrows or crossed sticks when they're going into strange 'no path' places.

"You learn that at school?" Gamma looked at

Nairee as if she herself had discovered something new, even alarming about her girl.

"Actually I read it in a book first. Then they had girl guides at school. They had the same rules as boy scouts." This last was a simplification and she knew it. One always had to simplify for Gamma. Gamma had long since lost her interest in books, but not her knowledge of birds, reptiles, and animals of the bushland. Sometimes, even very learned people came to interview Gamma about the animal inhabitants of the region.

Behind her quiet no-talk, Gamma was really quite shrewd. Nairee knew that. If Gamma surmised that these enquirers were sometimes from zoos or other places where caged animals were kept, she pretended she had forgotten all she knew. She also pretended she was deaf. Most of the few residents round and about on the scattered stations thought Gamma really was a little deaf. Nairee never gave her away. When Gamma played deaf, it was really because she didn't want to talk. It was easier to pretend. That way she could hear more being said than others knew she was hearing.

Sergeant Jack called her "the wily trickster" and she loved it. Coming from Sergeant Jack, it gave her a certain importance.

Sometime after Mark had gone, and when together Gamma and Nairee were washing the few dishes, Gamma broke the silence to say: "I like that one—Mark."

"Oh you do, do you!" said Nairee, surprised. "Why that one?"

"Guess you'd better marry him one day. Not the other one. Nairee, you keep away from Dean Lacey."

"I don't go to Beelagur much, only when I'm asked, sometimes for a day or two—also for the rodeo, of course. Everyone goes to the rodeo," Nairee said regretfully. To go to Beelagur was to enter the fascinating world of wealth.

"He was here today," Gamma said. "Dean Lacey was out there over the creek."

Nairee nearly dropped a plate.

"You mean *here*? At The *Patch*?"

"No. Up by the trees on the far side. Over the creek."

"Goodness me. What was he doing up there?" Nairee went on rubbing hard in an attempt to deal with both the plate and the subject.

"Looking at you," Gamma said bluntly.

Nairee peeked at her around the plate. The little old lady was wiping the top edge of a bowl.

"You couldn't see that far, Gamma. You're making it all up." Strange how they sometimes changed roles and Nairee became the adult, Gamma the child. Nairee finished with the plate and lifted another from the tray. Her own voice had just that much of a tell tale creak in it.

"I can see that far when I want," Gamma said.

Yes, Nairee thought. I guess you can. Well nearly, anyway.

Sometimes Gamma was like the aborigines. They too could hear and see and identify from great distances. Was it because, like them, Gamma had lived all her life in the Outback, and had "long sight"? She didn't know anything about the sounds in a town, or even in a village. Was this also why the aborigines could hear and identify things in the bush of which ordinary white people were unaware? An extra sensitivity? The eyeballs shaped for long sight?

"Woolarooka!" Nairee said suddenly.

"What you talking about? What about Woolarooka?" Gamma seemed just that little bit anxious.

"Woolarooka was in Alice Springs when my plane came in," Nairee said. "She came to the welfare department. She couldn't walk that fast, and that far, and be roundabout *here* today. Someone gave her a lift. So she's been up to something!"

Gamma had finished with the bowl and now put it away on a shelf. Nairee still had a few things to dry. She finished them quickly, then sat down on the lid of the firewood box and wrapped her arms round her knees.

"How did Woolarooka get here?" she asked.

"Maybe someone give her a lift in the store truck," Gamma wiped her hands on a hessian towel behind the door, not quite realizing that, in effect, she was giving away the fact that someone *had* told her about the near-visit of a certain person from Beelagur. Nairee was quite silent for some minutes. She was putting two and two together.

Woolarooka had arrived. Her tribe was probably somewhere near the Laceys' homestead. They knew all about who was going, who was coming, and where. Smoke signals, maybe. More likely the disturbance of birds—especially the big eagles above the rock piles along the breakaway on the west side of the mesa range. The tribe had known where Dean was, where Mrs. Lacey was, even where she herself had been, and when. And why. Woolarooka knew what they knew by the heightened perception of the aborigines.

Woolarooka would have known where she, Nairee, was. And have known about Mark coming too! Yet she had come here to talk to Gamma and not to Nairee herself!

Gamma looked sideways out of her old faded blue eyes at the girl sitting hunched up on the wood box. She knew instinctively that Nairee was troubled.

"It was Mark brought her from Alice, Nairee," she said slowly. "I guess he left it to Woolarooka to tell you," she added. "Woolarooka came to see you, all right. She went out along the creek. Don't be sad, Nairee. She'll go off walkabout a little. Then come back again and see you."

"She'd just better!" Nairee said, jumping up and smoothing down her blue jeans with a quick flick of first one hand, then the other. "I'll find her, Gamma. And I'll give her what-for pretty quick, all right!"

She didn't realize she was speaking something near pidgin English herself.

Gamma looked at the girl with tired eyes.

"You come home with a temper, Nairee?"

"No. I love Woolarooka and she loves me. Why is she telling you tales and worrying *you*?"

It was Gamma's turn to look doubtful.

"Maybe you'd better ask Woolarooka yourself," she said. "Maybe she knows. It's all strange to me. Nairee, you have come home for good now! Things have to be right for you. When it comes time for you to go back in eight weeks' time, you *don't go back anymore,* do you? So you have to see pretty quickly how things are up and round The Patch."

Nairee put her arm along Gamma's shoulder, and gave her a hug. Her mood changed back to near calm.

"Don't you worry, Gamma dear. I'm your girl come home, and I'm going to stay now. For ever and ever."

"Don't you go making a promise you can't keep, Nairee. Just wait and see." A slow smile stole over the little old lady's face. "I guess Woolarooka will watch out for you, so no harm comes . . ."

"I guess so. I just wish I knew what harm is likely to come. Everything seems mystifying all of a sudden. Yet The Patch hasn't changed. The birds are here, and the goats come in at sundown. Even Woolarooka is playing 'I spy' in the bushes round and about. I guess that it's because I'm older. I'm all of eighteen years, now. That's why I sense something *different.* Sort of unusual. It's like *eyes* are looking at me all the time. From all around—"

"You have a pink-and-white skin instead of a brown one. That's living down south. Makes you look different. Some people think maybe you've changed, Nairee."

"Some people?"

"Well, Mrs. Lacey from out at Beelagur."

Oh ho! Nairee thought. So Gamma knows *for sure* that Mrs. Lacey was up there on the far side of the creek this afternoon. And that Dean was there—further round the creek bend, by the pandanus trees.

And Woolarooka having a walkabout! Well, she'd go herself and find Woolarooka. *Now.*

Too late.

Woolarooka had disappeared behind tall grass bush and trees beyond the creek. Nairee knew she could never beat Woolarooka at that game.

So she went to attend to the white Mitchell cockatoo that had a damaged leg. Whenever Gamma went far enough down the tract it was sound to forecast she would come back with some bird or animal that had met with disaster. Mark was like that too.

Mark in his short stay had named the not-yet-adult cockatoo *Beaut*. As an official Conservation Ranger he had the right to view and pronounce upon any of the native birds, reptiles, animals, and even trees that mere mortals had taken from the bushland for whatever purpose.

"You little beaut," he had said as he bent over the box Gamma had made ready for the invalid. With a slim sapling stick Mark had half lifted the bird's wings to take its weight from its leg. "You'll do all right if Nairee and the old lady can keep your feathered ma, pa, and a myriad cousins, uncles and aunts, from trying to prize you loose," he had said.

Nairee had tilted her chin. "I don't forget *anything*," she had said firmly to Mark. "I am to put in a report on any or every bird, animal, reptile, and even any noteworthy tree that I have seen and to which I have given my undivided attention, plus skill. . . . So you didn't come to see me or Gamma? You are just out this way on duty?"

"Sure!" But he had glanced sideways at her, and wore a Mark Allen grin. A wicked yet somehow heartwarming grin.

He had taken Nairee's arm, as he walked.

"I'm not being chivalrous," he'd said, still smiling. "Your being so much down south, the muscles of your legs and the tendons of your feet wouldn't be in good condition for walking, let alone running through scrub bush . . . Mind now!" He had guided her past a halfburied old tree branch near the little house's doorway.

"Why should I 'mind now'?" Nairee had played his

game his way. "You are looking after me, aren't you?"

"Always," he'd said, then fell unexpectedly silent. For a fleeting moment his expression had been serious, full of subtle depths, and anything but detached.

Nairee had fallen silent too. Something had wafted into the air between them. Yet a minute later had come that relenting smile—so inexplicable, yet one that touched her heart.

Oh Mark!

9

THE DAYS PASSED AND NAIREE BECAME IMMERSED
once again in the way of life she had known during the
long annual holidays from her school in Adelaide.
Dandy Two arrived, brought to The Patch by one of
the stockmen, Bash, from Geko Creek. And Bash also
carried a note from Hank Brown, the manager of
Geko.

Welcome home. For good this time? Dandy
Two has been broken in the long way. Roped and
poled to the center tree in our yard. You know
how it goes with us. Six weeks and no let-up unless necessary for feed and sleep. He won't know
you, and might need the half-hour "break and
make" method. If you want help—don't do it
yourself. Old Gamma mightn't be strong enough
to pick you up. Woolarooka is always prowling
round The Patch. Give her a call and she'll bring
a message. I'll send Bash or our Tom over. Somehow I guess you'll manage yourself. But take care.

Dandy handles easy if you sit tight and don't get thrown.

Shindigs up here at Geko on thirtieth! Whole district is coming. We know you won't prize old Gamma out but you'd better come yourself as the big idea is to give you a welcome home for keeps. Love, Hank.

Nairee was delighted not only with Dandy Two but with Hank Brown's letter. Not a word or a sentiment wasted. He was a dour Outbacker, but with a heart of gold.

Bash was given tea and stove scones and thanked warmly before he set out on his way again.

"Give Hank my love!" Nairee called after him.

"Just as well," Bash answered over his shoulder. "No one else 'ud send it."

Holding Dandy Two by the mane, Nairee laughed and gave an extra wave of her hand.

She *really* was home. Word from Hank Brown in a manner meant to disguise his neighborly kindness, and a rejoinder from Bash, were typical.

Dandy Two had come home to Nairee, saddled and bridle knotted to stirrup. Hank Brown knew her, all right. He knew the first thing she would do after talking Dandy Two down to earth, would be to spring up and try him out. In the Outback the silences between man and man, and even between man and girl, said more than spoken words, or even written notes for that matter.

The moment Bash was out of sight between the trees in the bushland, Nairee patted Dandy Two's cheek. Then stroking the mane, she waited till the sound of hoofs thrashing through the bush had faded out of hearing. One foot in the stirrup, the other springing from the ground, and she was up in the saddle.

Dandy Two stood rock still, sizing up the situation. Nairee knew exactly what he was doing. She sat perfectly still, the reins firm but not tight in her hand. She gave Dandy Two roughly two minutes to register this new creature on his back—the firmness of her knee pressure and the light "speaking-hold" on the reins.

Two minutes later, she urged him forward just those few paces necessary to let him know what she was doing. Two minutes after that, she eased the reins, nudged him with one firm gesture from her right foot and called . . . loud and clear.

"Get on, Dandy Two. *Get on!*"

He took one tentative step, then another more meaningful one. Nairee firmed her leg grip under his belly, then leaned forward onto his neck while she tightened the bridle strap. She whispered right into his ear: "Get along, Dandy. Get along. You heard me!"

With a smart kick-up of his hind legs he made a try at throwing this new two-legged creature off his back. Nairee stayed firm, pressing down and inward with her knees. She was not in the least nervous. She knew Bash would never have gone off if Dandy Two were unreliable. She knew the horse would know what she knew, and was only having a tryout.

"You do that again," she said, lying forward with her cheek near his ear, "and I'll wop you into the creek, saddle, me, and all."

Dandy did not do it again. Instead he shook his head, rattled his bridle, and took a step forward. Then another. And another. The girl in the saddle on his back was very kind now.

"That's the boy!" she whispered, and holding the bridle in her left hand, patted his cheek with the right.

Out of the corner of her eye she had seen Gamma half hiding herself just behind the creeper.

" 'Bye, Gamma," she called. "See you in ten minutes."

She rode off. First at a slow walk, then at a moderate trot round the wire fence of the vegetable paddock, out onto the single track that led north to the creek.

It was just heaven as she and Dandy Two learned the feel of one another. Nairee straightened her back, threw up her head and called:

"Whoa, Dandy Two . . . we're at it!" Over the creek

and into the wider vehicle track they broke from a trot into a canter, then as they got onto the grassland, from a canter to a gallop.

Half an hour later they came home, friends forever!

Nairee walked Dandy Two into the side yard that once had been his sire's home. As she slid down, Nairee explained it all to him in gentle words. She slipped the straps, then threw the saddle over the fence rail. It was a beautiful hand-stitched saddle, and she told Dandy Two about it as she worked.

"Now for your sire's brush, and a good sweep down. There you are! Don't shiver. I'll do it more firmly as I go along. That way you'll get to know my hand by its feel, won't you? Dandy One did, and now Dandy Two will." She paused, then went on: "Goodness me, I'm talking too much! Depends on what's in the heart of it, doesn't it? Your heart and mine. Together, aren't we? Forever and ever!"

Out of the corner of her eye Nairee saw a movement in the bush just over to the left.

"Come out of there, Woolarooka!" she called. "I didn't get thrown, so you can stop worrying, right now." Then to Dandy Two: "You knew Woolarooka was there, didn't you? And you didn't bridle or shake your head. So that means you and she know one another already. But I won't mention to her the fact that you know and I know that all the time old Hank Brown from Geko was tuning you in and getting you ready— you see I didn't mention the word 'breaking' at all. . . . Woolarooka was peeking and spying. Just all of you tuning in for Nairee. For *me*."

Suddenly and quite unexpectedly, there were tears in her eyes. She leaned her forehead against Dandy Two and spoke with a lump in her throat.

"Everybody. Hank, and Bash, and Gamma, and Woolarooka, and you, Dandy Two. Everyone cares. Why? Who am *I*? *Who am I?*"

Woolarooka had come up. She put her arm up around Nairee.

"Aye now! What you telling that horse already? Eh?

Why you want to know '*Who am I?*' You Dandy Two's girl, and Woolarooka's girl. You, most of all Gamma's Girl. What more you want. Eh?"

Nairee brushed her arm across her eyes, then looked at the plump dark-haired, dark-eyed bush woman. She tried a smile.

"All right, Woolarooka! I'm Gamma's Girl." She looked up suddenly to where there had been a movement behind the creepers. She saw the shadow of the small white-haired elderly lady move toward the homestead.

"Yes, Woolarooka," Nairee said loudly. Very loudly for Gamma's benefit. "I'm Gamma's Girl. I get tired of telling you that. Now, once and for all—*I'm Gamma's Girl.*"

She turned round again still pretending she did not know Gamma was there. And that Gamma had heard these words. She was meant to hear them, of course.

"I'm going to put this hoss of mine in the stall," Nairee went on. "And I'll put a bucket of chaff in the trough. Then I'll come right out here and ask you, Woolie, just why you have been skirting around—first in the bush, now by the creek, then by the far fence, out amongst the trees—all day? What's worrying you, Woolarooka? Think up something to say by the time Dandy Two and I settle for each other with one bucket of chaff, one bucket of water, and two buckets of straw on some ole sacks."

"Tha's Nairee," Woolarooka said approvingly. She laughed and laughed, showing magnificent white teeth in her ebony face. "Tha's better! You sound just like yourself. That school and all those people down south done nothing to spoil you. Not one bit."

The party at Geko was meant to be a "goer." Everyone in the far-flung district—some of them living hundreds of miles apart—agreed to that. There were usually only two or three big parties in a year, and so each was an event. From Gamma's Patch to the Beelagur it was fifty miles, then twenty miles of tougher going northwest to Geko first along an old cattle track that followed the creek—some of it through a corner of the everglades. Only a Ranger like Mark, and the aborigines who squatted nearby the Boobera water-hole, ever took other tracks. Except for the natives, in a way it was all but no-man's-land out there.

In times past, the squatters and cattlemen had sometimes been isolated beyond Boobera. There they had stayed till the Wet and all its muddy devastations were over, leaving only the remnants of dried bushland behind. But then, almost overnight the young bush plants came shooting up. It was then the bush animals and reptiles and birds came back. The Wet brought the widgies out of their holes. The temperature brought out the buds on the bush, and the wildflowers in the undergrowth. The whole mammoth wild land stirred and lived again. The great wedge-tailed eagles kept watch on the mesa heights, the honey-eaters swarmed in the trees, the finches went mad, and the galahs came and went in noisy waves.

The Wet did not keep strictly to any timetable. Sometimes it came before Christmas. This was mainly from some rogue cyclone. Such a cyclone would rip the trees out of the ground and sometimes even the cracked mesa tops would have their outlines changed. Most years, the real drowning of the land would come about after December, often accompanied by a wild-fella cyclone bent on ripping off roofs and sending sheets of galvanized iron whizzing through the air like vast troubled metal leaves.

So the "welcome home for keeps" for Nairee had to go ahead now. Before there came the time of weeks with no access to Geko station.

Gamma sat on the one chair in Nairee's room and watched her dress. This was a sort of ritual for her. She had never seen anything like some of the clothes Nairee had brought home with her. It was a moving-picture show for Gamma. She smiled, even laughed, and nodded as Nairee put on first this, and later 'that'. She watched as Nairee folded and put away her change of clothes in a suitcase.

Gamma knew that Mrs. Lacey—who went south to the big cities every few months—had chosen Nairee's wardrobe. She never said whether she minded or not. Nairee had told her that Mrs. Gray from the social welfare department had given her approval a long time back, when Nairee had first been taken "down there" to school. But Gamma had not said one word about what went on. She was a little old hermit lady and she understood that Nairee had to go to school, but had kept her opinion of Mrs. Lacey's doings to herself.

Nairee knew intuitively that Gamma did not want her to go too often to Beelagur—the Laceys' home. Strangely, Nairee had come to realize that her Uncle Jack also wasn't very keen for her to go to Beelagur *too often*. Now and again, *yes*. But not too often. Hers was a nomad way of life compared with that of the Laceys. And so it had to stay that way.

As she grew older Nairee had come to believe that the big settled station people were thought by Uncle Jack and Mrs. Gray to be too wealthy and too important for Nairee to become used to their way of life. This made sense, so Nairee settled for it easily.

The Geko people were different. They owned vast acres too, but their parents and grandparents before them had settled and grazed a fine livelihood out of this cruel yet marvelous country by their own labors, with the help of the friendly aborigines. At school Nairee learned all about what "social differences" meant.

She thought she understood why Beelagur, in spite of Mrs. Lacey's goodness, and watchfulness on her behalf, was just that little bit out of bounds for her and therefore must not be visited too often. She only wished that other people would stop making an issue of it. They—other people—said little. But they watched warily. Was it because of Dean?

However, this day, today of the party and the fun, was an open go for all who cared to come—invited or just as passersby and drop-ins.

Nairee always felt just that little bit sad that Gamma did not come to parties. But Gamma rarely went anywhere beyond the boundaries of her own Patch. Nairee was old enough now to know that it was Gamma herself who was "different."

She had no wish to leave The Patch since her husband had died. She would not leave her birds, her bush animals, and her goats for a king's ransom. Nairee sometimes wondered if in the funny dear world of her mind, Gamma was waiting for her long-lost husband to come home again. But she never asked. And Gamma never said. They, Nairee and Gamma, loved one another and that, till time and destiny told them something different, was enough. One thing was certain: in her own silent world Gamma was happy. And Nairee was happy. They both knew that. If the rest of the district sometimes pondered over them, even worried about them, it did not have the slightest effect on either of the residents of The Patch.

Loyalty and devotion were not written large over their front entrance, but it might just as well have been so. That was what life in the household meant, anyway.

So Gamma watched Nairee's pretty change of clothes go into a case and put on her other special clothes for the drive. Bright blue jeans and a short coat went onto her girl's back. It all gave Gamma an ingenuous pleasure.

When Nairee brushed and combed her hair till it rippled in bright waves with the light shining through it, Gamma really smiled her pleasure. *Her* girl was going off for a party, looking lovely, and feeling happy. All was well in the best of this world of the quaint bush home called The Patch.

An hour later Bash came for Nairee and her case. He was driving one of Geko's pickup trucks. It was blue and the sky was blue and Nairee's jeans and coat were blue. Her eyes were no longer gray-green. They were blue-green like the younger shoots of the spinifex, and the young buds on the gum trees that followed the track along the creek bed.

10

GAMMA. QUAINT, LITTLE GAMMA STOOD BY THE SLIP-
rails and waved them off. The pink and gray galahs
saluted the pickup's departure, rising in chevron formation from the big baob—the homestead tree—and
breaking into shrill screams of excitement. In the
horseyard Dandy Two did a race, a mane-shaking
around the fence. The smaller of the finches fluttered
around their ten-by-ten cage then clustered together in
a deafening silence. Disapproval, of course.

"Easy to see you're home and in the right place,"
Bash said. His sunbrowned, wrinkled face was beam-
ing. He did not once turn his head. "The darn things
know you already. What you got, Nairee? A magic
way with you, or something?"

"No. A charming nature," she quipped back. "Only
a few days home, but they know already I'm the one
who feeds them."

"Charming?" he humphed thoughtfully. "That's
strictly for the birds!"

Nairee's laugh, even to case-hardened Bash, was
like silver bells in the bush shadows.

"That's exactly it," she said. "They *are* birds, and I *do* feed them. And love them."

"What about Dandy Two? Can't call Dandy a bird. How did you manage that circus demonstration *he gave* in not more'n a few days?"

"I talk to him. I say the right things. Gently. And he listens. He knows the feel of my hands already. And now he sees me taking off with *you*, Bash. He knows a lot about *you* already. Next time I see him I'll ask him why was he alarmed at my going off in such company?"

Bash's right hand came off the steering wheel and he wiped his chin thoughtfully.

"You and your animals! And the birds!" he said. "The next thing is you'll be telling me they speak English when they're talking to you."

"No," Nairee laughed. "I'm the one speaking English. They only understand it."

"So that's it, is it? Glad you mentioned it, Nairee. Next time I swear at those flaming bullocks I'm yardin' I'll watch out what I say. Make it twice as tough. That is, since I know they understand my brand of English. That'll stir 'em."

They had crossed the creek now, and the pickup would ricochet its way up the rugged bank to the track leading northeast to Geko station. Then onward to places wild—some barren, some spinifex, some everglade, some tall mesas from whose heights wedgetail eagles kept their far-seeing eyes on all moving things including lizards, marsupials, and little frightened scrub mice. Also occasional broken-winged birds. They passed through a belt of pindan scrub where here and there the blue-flowered beauhinia competed with Nairee's jeans and jacket for first place in the color riot.

Nairee's small but capable hands were clenched so the nails nearly bit into her palms.

"This is my land!" she said, swallowing a lump in her throat. "My country. I'll never go away from it again. As Woolarooka says, '*Sing him* my country!' "

"Well, don't let the elders of Woolie's tribe hear you say it," Bash remarked dryly. "You might get the bone pointed."

"At me?" Nairee laughed, glancing at him. "The tribe are my friends. I sing me *their* land too, *and* my land. I was born here."

Bash glanced at her sharply. "Were you?" he said bluntly.

Nairee's smile faded. *Was she? Wasn't she?*

Here again was that haunting question. Where, and by whom *was* I born?

"Woolarooka found me, and brought me to Gamma," she said aloud. "You all know about it, Bash. Everybody in the district knows. I was on Woolarooka's 'spirit land' so I belonged to her tribe. She brought me to Gamma because I was white and the tribe is black."

"So it was!" Bash said. Then, his eyes narrowed against the reflection of the distant sun reflected off a large limpid waterhole. "Why don't you forget it, Nairee? Everybody knows the story all right. So what! Woolie took you over the creek to Gamma, and the tribe sang you as a girl for Gamma down at The Patch. The little lady was all alone, so the tribe made you Gamma's Girl. And *that*, you've been ever since. Don't bug the tribe because *they know* this country's their country. We're just interlopers. They put up with us. Thank your stars they sang you. I guess you're the only white person any of the tribes from the Indian Ocean to the territory border have sung. Who knows? Some place or other they've got you a pegged-out spirit place."

"Spirit place? The spot where one's spirit came up out of the earth, and was born!" Nairee said, almost dreamily. "A stone in a circle of stones? Do you think I'll really *know* if ever I do find that true place, Bash? The one down by the creek bed is only my make-believe—"

He was half irritated, and in his terse, stolid, Out-back way, concerned for her. Come to think of it, he said to himself, it must be kinda hard on the girl because no one knows who she is, and every flaming two-footed whitey bends over backward to make up for it. Good thing she's a nice likeable piece. And worth it.

"Lookee here, Nairee," he said, not quite answering her question. "One day you'll get married—not too far off, I'd say. And you'll have kids. They'll all belong to you, and you'll belong to them. Guess you'll take Gamma along with you. That makes a whole darn tribe of your own. So quit worrying."

"Okay, Bash. I'm not really worrying. I'm just wondering—"

"Well, you wonder now about how come you must be a nice girl when the whole darn North—well, nearly —is coming out to Geko to welcome you home—just everybody." He pushed the forefinger of his right hand under the broad brim of his bushwacker's hat, and shoved the hat two inches further back on his head. "Home's the key word. You got more homes north of Twenty-six, and west of the border, then any other blighter I ever knew. So, like I said before, 'Quit worrying.' And by the same token quit *wondering*! Jes' live and let live. An' collar one of those station rich boys for a husband. Thataway you'll have diamonds as well as a bunch of kids. Come to think of it . . . Dean Lacey's taking his time decidin' who he'll marry. And half the station owners hereabouts after him for one or another of their daughters. Why not make a pass at him? Big station. Big herds. Biggest homestead north of Capricorn. An' not bad looking to boot. You could win . . ."

Nairee laughed. Bash was as good as a firebrand dose of tonic to her.

"Okay. I'll be good," she said, deliberately ignoring the remark about Dean.

"Better be. Homestead'll be in sight give another half-hour."

Dean Lacey . . . , she was thinking. Why, Dean could have any girl in the northwest for asking, surely.

She thought about him, and in her mind's eye she

could see his tall slim figure. His steel-gray, long-distance-seeing eyes. The way he walked, the step of a man who owned acres and acres. Who couldn't see even *one* of his boundary fences from his homestead roof on the tip of a rise. As if he'd be interested in her? No matter what she looked like, she was only Nairee from The Patch. A nobody!

But sometimes he *did* look. Then he would turn away. What was he thinking on those occasions? *There goes a girl—well, not all that plain anyway. But not for me. Me for one of the pretty daughters of one of the big stations. A quarter of a million acres thrown in for a wedding present!*

Nairee sighed. She wished she could get him out of her mind. She wished he wasn't so often withdrawn. He was striking in any crowd. Aloof or smiling!

Better to think of someone else. Mark! Where are you, Mark? Why don't you help me, like you help lost people? All the animals and birds and trees too. What about *me*?

She was a grown young woman now. And the young chaps at The Institute had liked her. Well, enough of them to give her a good time at the dances. But Mark was never there. Nor Dean . . .

"Guess I'm the age," she said, not realizing she'd spoken aloud.

"The age?" Bash asked, this time pulling his hat down over his brow.

"The age to vote," she said, thinking quickly. "How do we do it out here in the Never-Never? Or do we go to Barlee too?"

"The oldies do it by postal vote," he said. "The overland postie collects them. The rest of us—you too, this time—take a day or two off to get into Barlee Wells and make whoopee. There's always some make too much whoopee, and forget to vote. They get fined."

Nairee laughed. She had once or twice been in the nearest big town, several hundred miles away, when the station people had come in en masse. She knew what their "making whoopee" was like. Dressed up in his policeman's uniform, Uncle Jack would be quietly sitting behind the manager's office door in the pub. He wore his best dress uniform on those occasions. And when he was indoors he carried his best wide-awake hat with its oval Mounted Police badge polished up. Everyone knew he was there. And knew he would come out if he had to. That is, if someone went too far in their "whoopee-making." But no one, when right in Barlee, ever did go quite too far. If they didn't draw the line someone did it for them. All because they knew that Sergeant Jack Allen was there—behind that door—and if he did come out there'd be all hell to pay for someone. Except when an odd stranger came to town and wanted to make trouble . . . Uncle Jack stayed in that chair, smoked a cigarette or two, and listened to the radio news, especially to the football scores. Only when the voting was over and the last of the parties ended, did he emerge and wave all the station people off in their Land Rovers and pickups. And they all waved back. They always did that!

"Good old Jack Allen!" was usually the last of the toasts before they took their long homeward journeys over spinifex, and over the border plain, and dust plain, through the everglades to the creek lands and beyond mesa tops.

Recalling a trip to Barlee one election day years ago, Nairee visualized the girls laughing and the young men with their arms round the girls' waists. She hadn't realized at the time what *voting* meant.

It had been great fun. Like a party!

She had longed to be grown up then.

Now she was just that. Grown up. She looked forward to exercising that first vote of hers. She would go to town on "whoopee" night, and maybe—maybe, there'd be one young man or another who'd put an arm around her. And dance her up the street. If she let him, that is.

As Bash geared down to make the rise to Geko's boundary fence Nairee was happy again. Here she was now, arriving at another kind of party. Geko's welcome-home.

The track up to the homestead gate was a dusty snake of a track. Those already there were out on the bungalow's wide verandah to meet her. They'd have seen Bash's dustball rolling across the land many minutes before.

"Out you get!" Bash said, leaning across her to open the door for her. "This is where you take over, luv. Don't let it go to your head."

It just about did do that.

There were shouts from the homestead verandah—and such waving! Some jumped the distance over the flower bed to run to meet Nairee, waving and calling as they came. "Welcome home, Nairee! Welcome back to the Never-Never! Welcome home!"

It was wonderful!

Better than the parties when she had come home for holidays in the past. Today everyone was here. "But *everyone*!" the voice in her head was now saying as she ran through the cyclone garden gate and up the path toward the people. And it was *people*—not just the Brown family, but others. Children and all. The stockmen had come around the sides of the homestead and were cracking their whips in concert. The dogs—a half a dozen of them all but rioted. Everything was wondermusic in Nairee's ears. Now there was a lump in her throat too, and wetness in her eyes.

"Me! This is me!" Then her arms were around goodness only knew who. Other hands and arms were reaching for her. The children pulled at the waist of her jeans. They called out, "You come home for good this time, Nairee?" "You going to stay, Nairee?" "You coming to my birthday next month, Nairee? I'll be seven. You will come, won't you?"

"Yes . . . yes . . . yes!" she said with a lump in her throat, willing the tears out of her eyes.

She couldn't believe it. She had known it was to be a welcome-home party. But like this? Everyone was here, it seemed. From stations as far away as the border country. And all the stockmen. Woolarooka's people making a hullabaloo with their stamping and the low hornlike commands of the didgeridoo.

All for me? Just me? Oh, how good and kind they all were . . . !

She stooped over a bunch of little children, her arms around them, her kisses on their foreheads.

"What you crying for, Nairee?" a little girl asked, troubled.

"Glad tears," she said, hardly knowing she was even speaking. "*You* cry when you're sad and you cry when you're hurt, and *I* cry when I'm glad. Glad tears . . . I call them."

She brushed the back of her hand across her eyes, then looking up from the path, she could see the grown-ups standing by the rails on the verandah. She looked along the line, not knowing what to say. Then she saw *him*: Dean Lacey. Standing a little apart, not smiling. He just stood and looked across the distance at her, and there was something in his gray eyes. It was something special, important, and *different* as he looked at her.

Nairee was just that little bit dazed. It had to be the welcome, of course. But where had she seen that look in gray eyes before? Had Dean been like that once before? No . . . it was someone else. Perhaps Mrs. Lacey had blue in the gray of her eyes, dusty eyes. Not much expression in them at all. Someone had looked at her with those eyes once. Someone else. Who?

It took almost a physical effort for her to drag away her own eyes. Dean was being a sort-of Svengali. Yet she knew somewhere inside him, he wasn't being that at all. It was something inside *her*. Inside *herself*. Not in Dean, at all.

II

NAIREE STRAIGHTENED HER BACK AND WAVED AGAIN
to the guests on the verandah. "Hullo everybody!"
That sounded weak. "Hullo darlings, and thank you so
much. Hullo Hank . . . and Margaret. Oh everybody.
Just hullo!" She couldn't help it. She just had to brush
the back of her hand across her eyes once again. Then
the children on either side of her literally led her up the
four stone steps to the verandah.

The magic spell—half sad, half wildly glad—was
broken. She threw out both arms and for the next ten
minutes it was all of a kissing game. They all kissed
her. The stockmen—their natural silence lost because
of the atmosphere—kissed her too. And she them. All
of them. Everybody.

Except Dean. He had turned on his heel and gone
around the verandah to the side door.

Then she saw Mark Allen. She had heard over
Bash's car radio that the Ranger had been called out to
a posse of strangers camping by a forbidden loop of
the river. Out after the alligators? Alligator skins
brought a fortune on the black market! Well, Mark
had had to go and see. This was not good country for

strangers. Not at this time of the year with the dangerous cyclone and monsoon season approaching.

Nearly all of them around her now told her of some party, or rodeo, or race meeting that was coming up soon.

"You'll be there, Nairee, won't you?" One and all seemed to ask her that question. Nearly all of them sounded as if they really wanted her to be there. It was important that she be there.

It was all quite wonderful.

Yet in the back of her mind she couldn't help wondering, Why me? What have I ever done that they all should come to this welcome-home!

Some of them had come many many miles. A hundred miles was a flea hop to most of them. Of course it was a party, and parties were rare. If there was a party, or races, or a rodeo, everyone came. Life in the outback was lonely except for these get-togethers. But everyone seemed to suggest that *this* occasion was special. She couldn't quite believe it. She wasn't just nobody, after all. She didn't have a second name—except Gamma's, and that was only borrowed. Yet everyone greeted her as one of their own. Funny, as if she borrowed all *their* surnames too! They were all in denims so she didn't have to change.

One of the stockmen—Bill Blamey from Beelagur Station—took her by the arm, and said:

"Come on, Nairee. We're all in 'off' clothes today. The stockmen are all coming up from the yards. It's cooled off by now. Come and have a dip in the barrel. That's a real nor'wester's brew."

She let him take the cup and saucer that had just been handed to her, and she followed him down the three steps from the verandah. Then at the last step she let him take her arm and lead her round the homestead corner to the group around the barrel.

"One for me and one for Nairee," Bill Blamey demanded with a grin.

"You really want one, Nairee?" Bash asked tentatively. He'd been doing the honors at the barrel since he had relinquished Nairee to the verandah hosts.

"Not really," she said. "Just enough to drink everyone's toast."

"Good scout," someone said, and a kind of cheer went up as Bash tapped out half a glass and finished filling it with lemonade.

As Nairee sipped at her glass and the others tossed their drinks off, she looked surreptitiously around.

Where was Dean now? Where had he gone? And why?

She saw him coming down the three steps of the verandah toward the barrel group. Then, unexpectedly, he was there, beside her.

"I'll drink that for you," he said, taking the glass from her hand.

She didn't quite know what to say. She wanted to look right into his eyes, though she didn't know why. It happened the other way round: Dean looked at her—right into *her* eyes—over the rim of the glass as he drank down the contents. He was saying something by that look, but she didn't know what.

"Mostly lemonade," Dean said somewhat disdainfully of his drink. Then glancing at the stockmen, he added, "You fellers can't monopolize Nairee, you know. She belongs up there on the verandah—please excuse us."

Very peremptory.

He took Nairee by the arm and walked her back to the foot of the verandah steps. She couldn't look at him this way. He was too tall, and his shoulders were wide and powerful. She felt smaller than she really was.

She turned and waved a goodbye to the men standing around the barrel.

She could not understand Dean, nor her reaction to him. He was just another station owner in a crowd of other station owners, wasn't he? Was it because Mrs. Lacey had always, from a dignified distance, been so helpful to her? Did he mind? Did he feel that she was an intruder, a nobody? But then why did his mother do the things she did do for her?

Nairee smothered a sigh. She wanted to enjoy herself and all these people—stockmen and their families. Station owners in their own right. Shed hands. All of them had come here today to welcome her home for good.

They couldn't *all* be just putting on a front!

They couldn't stay away when asked because it would look like snobbishness. Or would it?

Dean took her arm to help her up the three steps to the verandah—this, after all, was the courtly thing to do.

When they stepped on the verandah she turned to thank him. Their eyes met. It was Dean who turned away. His face suddenly became a strange mask, almost as if he were hiding something from her.

What had she done? Or said? There was dismay in her own face now, and she quickly looked down at her feet as if there might be one more step to take. But of course . . . there was not.

Dean turned and walked away without a parting word. This was surprising because generally he was a man of good polished manners.

Nairee smiled and talked to others, as others smiled and talked to her.

They all seem to like me, she thought. I'm sure. Or they wouldn't have come, would they? But Dean came. Then he dropped me like a hotcake!

She was quietly miserable now. She was like that—smiling and pretending till something inside her became so tired, all she wanted—in spite of the great and genuine kindness all around—was to go home. All because of Dean? And so suddenly!

Go home to The Patch! To the birds, and the bush animals, and the goats, and Dandy Two. Mostly to Gamma.

She turned away from the group and looked out across the grass, past the scarlet bougainvillea and the brilliant blue beauhinia, to the track that led to the river crossing then to the by-creek, and the home paddock.

Why did she have to think *silly* about Dean? Why?

There, down that track, was a great ball of dust. It meant someone was coming. A Land Rover came up the lead track at a terrific pace, then it stopped abruptly alongside the other vehicles. A tall man came from under the steering wheel, took off his wide-brimmed Outbacker's hat, shook it, then straightened himself and turned toward the verandah.

Mark! For no reason whatever, Nairee's eyes smarted again.

Mark! She'd be all right now. It was like seeing a guide coming toward her when she had thought she was lost. Salvation—in the form of a Ranger!

A shout of welcome came from someone on the verandah who saw Mark coming. Around the barrel glasses were quickly emptied, then refilled. Someone filled a glass for Mark, and carried it to the top of the verandah steps.

"Here you are, mate! Been keeping it cold for you this last hour. How'd you manage to get here? Someone been shooting crocodiles back of the range?"

"I'll catch them sooner if not later," Mark said with a grin as he took the frothing glass. "They were just campers who didn't look or read 'No Camping.' I moved them on a quarter mile upriver where there's a public camping ground. All amenities. Thanks for that." As he drank from the glass he half turned and looked aroung him.

"Quite a job lot here today," he said. "Where's Nairee? Anybody here seen that girl?"

"Right behind you," Hank Brown said. "All tricked out to catch a feller's fancy."

They were fun-making, of course. But Nairee's spirits were back. Mark often had that effect on her. He sort of calmed her down, then brought the sparkles back to her eyes.

"Hullo Mark!" she said happily. No sad eyes now.

"The last I heard of you, you were heading east to see that no one was shooting wild donkeys round that backaway camp over the range."

"They weren't looking for donkeys this time. Just giving themselves a holiday. Lighting a fire at the wrong time of the year. In the wrong place too. A right fire-hazard lot."

"Did they leave when you told them?"

Mark's eyes momentarily looked like stones. They didn't blink. "They did," he said. "And *fast*. Seems as if some people can't read. Or maybe they just don't want to read."

"How did you know they were there?" .

He smiled easily now. "Same way as one always knows. Birds in the wind wheeling about, but not going anyplace. That told me someone or something was out there. So out there I went." He paused for a moment. "Sorry I wasn't here to greet you when you came in, Nairee," he said, "but I brought you something. Just a little something, and it's injured. Will you take care of it for me? I didn't want to kill it just to put it out of its misery."

"Something?" Nairee said quickly. "What is it? Where is it, Mark?"

"Just take a walk with me round that line of cars. I have it cached away and I don't want the rest of the world watching me undress to get it—'"

"I know. It's down your shirtfront," she laughed. "It's not a snake or a lizard, I hope."

"Wait and see," he said. He linked Nairee's hand in his arm. "It's just there, below my rib cage. Feel it?" She nodded. "Well, don't press too hard. It has an injured wing. The second bird I've brought to you since I came home."

The line of cars was between them and the verandah party now.

Mark threw his hat onto the bonnet of a large station wagon, then undid his tie. "Wouldn't have worn that thing," he said of the tie, "except I was coming to your party."

He undid the top buttons of his shirt. The little captive bird moved around to his back.

"I knew the darn thing would do that," he said, smiling into Nairee's eyes. "They go for safety . . . as they think it to be. Now put your hand over it—shirt and all—and don't let it move while I get the front of my shirt pulled out. Ready?"

She nodded.

"Good. Hold it tight."

One of the guests coming around the corner of the homestead to his car stopped in his tracks.

"For crying out loud!" he said. "Not here and now. Can't you wait till after dark, Mark?"

Mark, his shirt pulled right out now, winked at Nairee.

"Can't wait another minute," he said. "So what's keeping *you*? Why don't you take off?"

"You all right, Nairee?" the newcomer asked.

"Never better in my life," she laughed back at him. "Good."

The unwelcome visitor grabbed something from the front seat of his wagon, slammed the door shut, and went back the way he had come—walking fast.

Mark and Nairee stood stock still. It had been a delicate operation to remove a frightened and injured small bird encased between the shirt and Mark's waistline. Slowly and carefully, Nairee closed her hand round the bird. She could feel the little thing shivering, even through the shirt.

If she had not been so concerned for the little captive she just might have laughed. Her other hand went inside Mark's shirt now! It was quite a day after all!

"What do I do now?" she asked. "I've got it tight in your shirt but what next?"

"Hold on a minute. I'll take my shirt right off. For Heaven's sake don't loosen your hold. But easy does it."

"I won't."

Inch by inch Mark eased out of his shirt, taking care not to strain on the part that was holding the bird.

Shirtless, he closed his hand round Nairee's hand then threw the shirt back. He guided Nairee's hand away from his body—holding the little feathered captive.

"Done!" Mark said. "Now slip your hand out from under mine and I'll hold the creature. You'd better start liking it, Nairee. It had better be worth the trouble!"

They were quite unaware of a trio of stockmen lounging against the corner of the side verandah, watching them.

"Whacko! We're right!" Mark said, holding out the shirt freely, though still encasing the captive.

Nairee stepped back and gave an outsized sigh.

"I was dead scared I'd muff it," she said. "Have you a handkerchief in your shirt pocket, Mark? I'll need something to wrap around the birdie . . . just in case."

"Top left-hand side," he said.

She pulled a large khaki handkerchief from the pocket.

"Now carefully, all over again," Mark advised. "Wrap it high around the bird's neck, while I hold it.

For the first time Nairee could see just what their captive was.

"Why! It's a baby galah! A little *baby* bird! Not long out of the shell!" Her voice was full of pity, as it always was for things small and hurt.

The handkerchief was around the bird, leaving only its damp-feathered head free. It made a choked sound.

Nairee had her back to the men lounging against the upright post of the verandah. She didn't even know they were there. She was only attentive to a poor little wounded feathered creature, its pink and gray feathers flat on its head, and wet.

Mark was now busy pulling on his shirt, buttoning it through, then tucking it in his belt. As he did this he was looking directly at the audience a few yards away. Mark knew instantly what was going through their minds. Their idea of a joke—a good after-dark story.

"Scat!" he said in loud tones. Nairee, caressing the bird, jerked up her head in surprise.

"What? I mean, what did you say, Mark?" All her attention was still focused on the baby bird.

Mark was concerned with something else now. He knew what those knowing chuckles were all about. His shirt was on and tidied up. He was tying his tie.

"Never thought the Ranger had it in him," one of the men said loudly to the others.

Mark walked steadily toward the group.

Nairee was puzzled at the tone of *his* voice, and now by the way he walked—one downright determined step after another. She followed him now, carefully cradling the bird, whose left wing looked as if it might be broken. It did not occur to her that the onlookers could not see what she was holding—or that she was holding anything at all. They stood, feet apart, their bodies equally balanced in a stance typical of those who wait for a fight.

Mark, dead in front of them now, stood in exactly the same way. His eyes held theirs. He did not blink once.

It was a battle of the eyes.

The three onlookers broke first.

"Come on, Syd," one of them said. "Let's get out of here. Hank Brown just might take his gun to anyone starting a fight this day. It's damn-all supposed to be a party."

"Cool it, Mark!" Syd said to the Ranger. "It was all only a joke. How the heck did we know you were juggling with a raking galah? You did say it was a galah, didn't you? Or was it, Nairee? They're two-a-penny hereabouts. Raking nuisance most of the time. Split all the nuts in two before sunup, any day. Sorry—there I've got my foot in it again. Your job as Ranger is to preserve everything in the bush. Good or bad. That so?"

"That is so. I don't mind you having a crack at *me*, Syd. But leave ladies out of it. Right bang smart out of it. Have you got the message? And stop those others making a good tucker-board story of it later."

"You mean . . . ?"

"You know darn well what I mean. Same as what *you* were thinking—alll of you—while Nairee was trying to hold the bird safe inside my shirt until I'd pulled the thing off. You have my message, Syd? Any one of you fellers try to turn this into a talking point when it's Nairee's party . . . then you'll find I can pack the same comeback as you think *you* can when you're throwing a steer."

"Okay, okay, Mark! We just didn't know there was a bird tied up in the shirt." He drew a packet of cigarettes out of his pocket and offered the open end to Mark. "Smoke the pipe of peace, old feller? If it's a party, and that's what it is, let's go and enjoy ourselves. How about it?"

"Right. Thanks, I'll have one of those cigarettes. Next time we meet you have one of mine."

Syd struck the match and held it to Mark's cigarette. While Mark was taking the first draw Syd looked up and found himself looking down the tunnels of Mark's eyes. He applied the match to his own cigarette.

"Guess you like that girl quite a lot, eh? Sorry again, Mark. She's a nice lass. I wouldn't mean her any harm."

"Good for you. Let's go and drink her health. It's about time the corks were popping again."

The two strolled together toward the bungalow's corner, looking like friends—for the time being . . .

Meantime Nairee had disappeared inside with Mrs. Brown. They were searching for the right kind of box in which to cage the wounded bird. A small carton was found and the galah was bedded down in it on a layer of torn snippets of paper.

"I'll leave you to feed it, Nairee," Mrs. Brown said. "The men have the drinks flowing but the ladies will want more tea. You'll find scalded milk in the pan at the side of the stove. You'd better thicken it . . . but only just. Cornflour's in the third cannister on the top shelf of the big cupboard. You can manage?"

"Oh yes, I can manage all right," Nairee said. She was already tearing another sheet of paper into tiny pieces. She didn't add that ever since she could remember, she and Gamma had been attending to sick or wounded birds. Including Mark's white Mitchell with the yellow comb and one broken leg.

Every one of them in that big caged area at The Patch had come finally to live there because first they had been found wounded, one way or another, and had been taken home and nursed, then added to the aviary.

Except for its own parents—if they could be found and identified, which rarely happened—birds that had for some time been caged away from the parent flock could quite often, when released, become the victims of other birds.

Once in a cage, always in a cage, had been Gamma's dictum. That way they stayed alive.

Nairee fed the tiny galah, holding its beak open with the thumb and forefinger of her left hand while her right hand was used to drop the tiny morsels of milk-and-cornflour into the back of the bird's throat. She was so engrossed she did not even hear the wire door open. Dean Lacey was right behind her before she realized anyone was there at all.

She turned quickly.

"Oh!" She was surprised it was Dean; she thought he had gone.

He had been there in Alice Springs when she had arrived. Well, why not? "The Alice" had always been the meeting place for businessmen and station people from north of Twenty-six—whatever their business might be.

When she had actually come home to The Patch he had been down by the creek, barely veiled by the trees. He had just faded away that time, not even called hullo. It oughtn't have mattered, except it did matter to Nairee. There had always been something about

Dean that had attracted her curiosity. And something more? She dared not look *that* question in the face. So tall, so handsone. So aloof. A lord of this ancient land. Something that charmed, yet was not to be defined.

He was distinguished.

Secretly, deep in her heart, Nairee feared that she could fall in love with Dean. Because of his appearance and manner. All the rest of him was a mystery to her.

"A baby bird," she said, smiling up at him. "Its wing is injured. I'm going to take him home to Gamma—'"

Dean raised his eyebrows. As always his voice was soft, yet stirred strange chords of disquiet in her.

"That's asking for trouble," he said. "It's a galah. There are thousands of them about. They destroy the nuts on the trees—"

"But they're so *loving*,'" she said. "The way they cuddle their heads under one's chin. And nibble with their little beaks—their way of kissing. They're real little lovers. Let me hold this one under your chin, Dean?" She lifted the tiny bird from the box. "There you are. Nibble, nibble. Yet they never bite—"

"Take the silly thing away," Dean said unexpectedly. He sounded very nearly angry. "They are rated as pests."

Why so angry?

Nairee met his eyes. "I'll take it away, all right, Dean. Mark has never allowed the galahs to be rated as pests. And he *knows*. He's the Ranger. It's his job to see that as many living things as possible are protected in the bush. In their natural environment."

"I am *not* Mark," Dean said. "I have my own point of view about these things—"

"Of course." Nairee put the bird back in its box. She felt sad, but for the life of her she could not think why. Except perhaps she didn't want Dean to be like this. It wasn't reasonable. She knew some people in the bushlands disliked some of the animals—dingoes, for instance. And certainly wild goats and wild donkeys—anything they could not round up. But birds? Who could wish harm to little feathered creatures? The galahs and all the other types of cockatoo did eat from nut-bearing trees. That was true. But what of it? Humans ate beef and lamb. That meant the death of something, didn't it? She lifted the galah from its box again and pressed it to her neck, giving some of her own warmth to it. And love.

Mrs. Lacey had come down the passage and now paused in the doorway. She turned toward Nairee as Dean passed her before continuing out of the homestead, down the outside steps, then off across the gravel square. He was angry, it seemed.

How strange the Laceys were! Why? Dean's manner today completely baffled her. Why be so angry? And whenever Dean was near her—there only minutes later was Mrs. Lacey! Why?

"There you are, Nairee!" Mrs. Lacey said pleasantly. This was one of the times when she looked the gracious lady Nairee knew her to be, and sometimes even loved. So gracefully tall. When she smiled she was almost beautiful. Her eyes, at this moment anyway, were kind. "You must come and join the others, my dear. It is your party, you know. The other guests will be missing you."

Mrs. Lacey was correcting her, but gently. She did not mind. So often, even when she was a small child, Mrs. Lacey had told her, quite simply, what to do and what not to do and *when* in certain company. She had never been unkind about it. More like a kindly aunt. And yet there had always been an indefinable *something*. A distance, yet a . . . watchfulness. A *caring*. Only when Dean was about did Mrs. Lacey appear, in a nebulous kind of way, to change. It wasn't in her looks or words, but in her manner.

Once, tentatively, Nairee had mentioned this to Mrs. Gray. Mrs. Gray had laughed it off.

"My dear child!" she had said airily. "One can never tell what are the real relations between mother and son when they are in the position to one another as are

Dean and Mrs. Lacey. Beelagur is a very valuable and prestigious station. They carry more cattle than any other station in the Outback north. And Dean's the cattleman. But the station property is Mrs. Lacey's. Her husband's will left it that way. They—each of them—need each other. Dean can't do without the property—which means the land, the waterholes, fences, the windmills. Otherwise he wouldn't be able to run his cattle, would he? And Mrs. Lacey needs Dean's cattle to maintain the property and Dean himself to be in charge of them. It is as simple as that. Do you see? People need each other, especially when it comes to property and wealth which they share."

Yes. Nairee could see that. Quite plainly. But there was still something else, something remote . . . Something not to be defined in words.

There was a loyalty between mother and son, but it was never displayed. It had nothing, surely, to do with a station homestead and a herd of cattle. Perhaps even Dean and his mother didn't know it was there. Nairee had grown up learning every variable whisper of the bush, every cry of bird or animal. Every slither of a lizard. Even of a snake. She was sensitive to nuances.

Woolarooka, like all her tribe, knew these strange "talkings" of the bushland. Perhaps she had taught Nairee when Nairee was too young to remember being taught.

So Nairee knew there was *something* at stake other than a head of cattle, and a station homestead. Some obstacle, some tug-of-war between Dean and Mrs. Lacey.

It was a riddle.

Since she was nine or ten years of age she had all but given up trying to work it out. Except that Mrs. Lacey knowingly kept a distance between Dean and Nairee. Almost forced it.

Here, today at her welcome-home party, Nairee was aware of it again. Such a strange feeling. Something inside her warned her to let it alone. To forget it.

Wipe it from her mind! Other people knew about this distance that must be kept. They *never* talked about it in words. Only in glances, and in tiny message-sending shaking of their heads.

12

NAIREE TUCKED THE BIRDLING BACK IN ITS BOX AND
turned to Mrs. Lacey.

"That's something I'll take back to Gamma from
the party," she said, smiling. "Gamma never *never* will
come away from The Patch. But so long as I bring her
something home she is happy. Did I tell you I brought
her back a handbag when I came home this time? She
made a special belt out of a dog's chain and hung
the bag on it. She wears it all the time . . ." Nairee
broke off. Mrs. Lacy was looking at her so closely she
almost felt embarrassed.

"Do you think that is a silly thing to do?" Nairee
asked, defensive on behalf of Gamma, "wearing a handbag dangling from a dog's chain round her waist."

"Of course not," Mrs. Lacey said. "If it makes
Gamma happy, then it is the right thing for *her* to
do . . ."

Even as she spoke Nairee knew Mrs. Lacey's mind
was not on Gamma. Much less on the handbag and
how it was worn. Her mind was on what she could see
through the window. It was Dean walking away.

Oh bother! Bother! Bother! Nairee thought. Why does Mrs. Lacey always have to watch him? He's a grown man. Probably the most powerful man in the district. He looked and sounded it when he needed to do so. He was master of himself, surely. And of others. His men . . .

Perhaps Mrs. Lacey was lonely. And *needed* Dean to be near her. Was that what it was all about?

Yet in her own heart Nairee was not satisfied with that explanation. Somewhere deep inside Mrs. Lacey was a worry. An anxiety. Nairee had no idea how she knew this. Yet she did know it—like she knew just exactly when the wedgetail eagles would come back from their seasonal flyabout. And the dingoes would start howling from the mesa caves. And the bird hosts would start their annual fly-in from the coastal lands. The snipe from the Swan River would take off for Russia in the breeding season. And fly all the way back with their young, too.

She also knew from long-time observation that when it came to station matters it was Dean who was "king of the acres." *His* were the decisions that mattered.

Could it be that Mrs. Lacey was—as some mothers were—overly possessive of her son?

Oh well! What was the good of guessing, anyway!

All the time Nairee was having this thinkfest she was settling, then resettling the tiny bird amongst the torn pieces of paper in the bottom of the box. She was aware that Mrs. Lacey was still watching her. She gave the bird its last tickle under its beak, slipped the punch-holed lid on the box, and looked up.

The strangest thing had happened. There were *tears* in Mrs. Lacey's eyes!

Actual real tears. She had been looking through them at Nairee's hands tending the bird, then punching the holes and fixing the lid on the box.

Nairee was too surprised to turn away. To act quickly in any way at all. Mrs. Lacey looked up. Their eyes met.

Mrs. Lacey spoke first.

"You are a good kind girl, Nairee. I'm so thankful you have grown up this way. It wasn't a mistake leaving you with Gamma. . . ."

The change was so sudden. And the remark inexplicable. Nairee could not think *what* to think. Let alone what to say.

If Mrs. Lacey had ever had any influence as to where the lost child brought in from the creek grasses was to live, then nobody had ever told Nairee. She had a good kind neighborly friend in Mrs. Lacey. She had tried to repay Mrs. Lacey by doing exactly what that lady had taught her as "correct." Never to sit when an older lady was standing. Always open the door for people older than herself, and not put fruit in a fingerbowl.

But never never in all those years had she seen Mrs. Lacey anything but the well-preserved, firm and gracious, somewhat cold lady. The senior citizen—prestigewise—of the whole area. And this very same self-controlled lady just one moment ago had had tears in her eyes! About what?

"I'm afraid I'm getting a cold, Nairee," Mrs. Lacey said, taking out a handkerchief and wiping her eyes. "Don't come near me. You don't want to take a cold home to Gamma, do you?"

Nairee knew intuitively that this was an excuse.

Dear Gamma! She wouldn't really be alone, like Mrs. Lacey seemed to be. Nairee knew that just about this time Gamma would be talking to the birds.

Midafternoon was always the time Gamma went into the bird yard. Almost one and all of the birds would squabble about which and how many of them would find a perch on Gamma's shoulder. Even on top of that funny little narrow-brimmed white hat Gamma always wore—from the moment she stepped outside the door in the early morning till sundown.

Nairee looked at her wristwatch. About ten minutes from now Gamma would be off down the creek path toward the place where the goats would be gathering themselves into a loose bunch, waiting.

Funny how Gamma always knew when the time came to go out into the bush, and the goats knew the exact time when to come in from it. The dogs inevitably knew too. They would be waiting for Gamma, who would be hatted and armed with a short stick which she liked for company, as much as anything. She never hit anything with it. Not even an old dead tree trunk.

Mrs. Lacey took a step away, then turned back to Nairee again. She was quite composed now.

"Why don't you release that bird into the bush, Nairee?" she said. "Nature has a way of looking after its own."

"Yes . . ." Nairee said doubtfully. "But not one as helpless as this little one. They—the other birds, I mean—would peck it to death. That is what they do to save the injured bird from suffering too much for too long. They give it death . . . quickly." Nairee took the lid off the box and looked down at the tiny, wet gray and pink thing.

"Please, Mrs. Lacey . . . I would like to keep it. Please let me keep it?" she pleaded.

"Of course, my dear. I shouldn't interfere. It is your bird so you must think what is best to do with it."

"Thank you. When it's big enough and old enough to talk I'll bring it over to Beelagur to see you."

"Yes, of course. We must arrange that soon. Now I think we must go back to the others. They will miss you, and that would never do. You are the guest of honor so you have certain duties . . ."

"Yes, of course. I wasn't thinking—"

"Oh, they'll all forgive you. I haven't any doubt about that."

Yes, but will you? Nairee thought. You will be just that little bit angry because I saw you with tears in your eyes.

She held the door open for the older lady. "It was kind of you to be bothered with me, *and* the galah," she said quietly.

Mrs. Lacey touched her arm. "Let us both forget it, shall we?" she asked.

Nairee nodded her head. She had a lump in her throat, partly because of the wounded bird, but mostly because she had seen Mrs. Lacey with tears in her eyes. And she could do nothing about it. Mrs. Lacey would not have let her. This, they both knew.

On the wide verandah and in the huge living room, the other guests were at the stage when they had all but forgotten the reason why they were at Hank Brown's homestead at all. Forgotten temporarily who their guest of honor might be. Or even if there was one.

So long and lonely were the distances between the homesteads on that vast plain of red dust, bushland, and rock breakaway; so occasional were the times when they all could meet, greeting each other like lost astranauts catching up with a space ship, that they had weeks, sometimes months, of loneliness to be redeemed. In as short a time as possible. So the talk and the call of one to another were a concatenation of sound!

Appearing from the outer regions of the side verandah, Nairee realized she should have been here like the others, someone's arm along *her* shoulder, not noticing that time and events, no matter how minuscule, had almost worn the afternoon away. Yet Nairee had been outside too long! She knew it, and was sorry for all she might have missed.

The occasional wafts of wind had slowed to nothing now. The whole wide land was beginning its sundown standstill. The stillness had the mysterious power of bringing conversation to an end. Empty teacups and empty glasses stood about on tables and mantelpiece. Sad disposals at the end of a time.

It was the hour to go home.

People began to say good-bye.

"What a lovely get-together it has been!" And: "Will that damn car get us the fifty miles home without breaking down again?" And: "Good-bye, Beth. Thanks a million, Hank. It was a bonza party. Where's that Nairee—the cause of all the hoo-haa? Why, over there! Come here, dear girl, and be kissed while no one else is lining up for that piece of joy."

When Nairee had been kissed enough for a year, and teased about becoming such a beautiful girl after all that time she had taken to grow up, the guests began to thin out.

The horse riders untied reins from posts. Some already were galloping away into the gold fire of dying day, into distances so vast that any stranger would have given up trying to guess how far they had yet to go before they reached their own homesteads.

Cars, utilities, Land Rovers, and even a few motorcycles added to the din of departure and to the last notes of a party finished out.

Nairee, her little boxed bird in her left hand, was saying good-bye to Mrs. Brown.

"Thank you so much," she said. "It was lovely. I can't really believe it was all for me."

Mrs. Brown had her arm round Nairee's shoulder. "Thank you for coming home for good. It gave us all an excuse to have a party. You *are* home for good, aren't you?"

Nairee nodded. "Of course," she said. "Where else is *home?*" It was meant to be her own demonstration of gratitude and happiness, but strangely a tiny silence fell on the small group of people still waiting to make their adieux. It was as if Nairee had touched something with the shock of electricity in it. Something the few still there understood, but which Nairee did not.

"Where else is home?" Nairee asked again, surprised at the momentary silence.

"Here, of course!" someone said. "But after the bright lights of the city, won't you want to leave The Patch?"

"Of course not." Nairee was quite firm. *"Never."*

"Oh come now!" said a little woman who lived further north near the great river and the cotton fields. "There's no companionship here for you. Not more than two or three young people this side of the rain forest."

"There's Dean Lacey," someone said with a laugh. "One for you, Nairee. How about it?"

A silence fell after that.

"Dean's gone a while back," Hank Brown put in. "Has to bring in the horses. We ourselves have got two new jackeroos from the far side of Australia coming up here to the north soon. That'll be company enough for the girls. And for Nairee. Blow Dean Lacey! You other young chaps had better sharpen up your spurs!"

Nairee was not a simpleton, so she knew at once that the party had been as much a boy-and-girl match-making game for the younger guests as a welcome-home to her.

She did not think of herself as having pride, but something inside now felt bruised, let down. A girl turns eighteen, comes home for good. So the older generation starts having a try at picking the winner who just might take this girl they all loved—to the altar.

They had wiped off Dean Lacey. Why? How would or could they know whether she and Dean Lacey were more than casual friends?

She was old enough to guess what they were thinking along with their mild and joking innuendos, yet young enough to be a little offended, and—well, yes, taken aback.

She did not look around. She also knew that the Laceys had gone. Just *gone*. It hurt a little that they had not said good-bye to her.

Why had Mrs. Lacey gone like that? And not even a wave of the hand, or a whispered good-bye. And Dean too—

"Where is Bash?" Nairee said, looking around. "Bash always looks after me. He's my good friend."

She felt she was speaking foolishly but, for the moment, she was terribly embarrassed.

"Blow Bash," a male voice said from behind her. "I'm taking Nairee home. That is, if she will let me do just that—"

She knew who it was before she turned round. Mark! Oh Mark! Saved again by Mark. Somewhere not far away would be Sergeant Jack Allen. All the world suddenly brightened. She belonged to someone. Funny how she cared so much about that. But she did care. Belongingness. Something everyone needed.

"Oh Mark, you are a dear," she said. "It wouldn't be fair to Bash for him to make that journey twice in a day."

"Who said I wouldn't want to do just that?" Bash's voice came from somewhere between the head and shoulders of the last of the party-makers.

"I spoke first," Mark said. He slipped his hand under Nairee's arm. "Come on, girl," he went on. "Don't keep everyone waiting. One kiss each apiece all round . . . and that's the end of the best party this season."

He had Nairee's arm imprisoned now. She could not have pulled it away even if she had wanted to.

There were more good-byes called. The last of the kisses were exchanged, and Nairee was walking down the few steps to the path, Mark holding her hand and Sergeant Allen, who had appeared out of nowhere, bringing up the rear.

Nairee turned and waved a good-bye with the hand still holding the boxed bird.

"Bye, Bash *dear,*" was her last call.

" 'Bye, the best girl ever," he called back. "Be seeing you soon. Love to Gamma. Take care of that hoss Dandy Two!"

"Oh, I will. I will."

Suddenly the Browns and the last of the guests took up a refrain:

"Love to Gamma!"

That finish brought color to Nairee's cheeks, and a glow to her eyes. How good they all were! They had given her this welcome-home party—the best ever! And they had not forgotten Gamma.

13

MARK TIGHTENED HIS HOLD ON NAIREE'S ARM. WITH the other hand he took the small cardboard box from her. "I'll hold it," he said. "It will be safe with me."

"Are we going in the helicopter, Mark?" Nairee asked, wanting only to make conversation to hide that tiny shade of embarrassment that had come over her those last few moments on the verandah when it occurred to her that she was the only one who didn't have a *real* relative to take her home.

Catching up with them, Sergeant Jack could see the fleeting shadows in her eyes. He slipped his hand on Nairee's arm.

"How lucky can you be!" he said in matter-of-fact tones. "An entire district turns up to welcome you back amongst them! That's something that wouldn't happen to most people. You must be quite a nice person, Nairee! Are you? I've never known this lot out here in this part of the Never-never do that before. And *mean* it."

"Yes, I'm lucky, Uncle Jack," Nairee said, happy again. "I can't be all *that* special . . ."

Mark too had caught the catch in Nairee's voice. "Even the birds are calling in," he said. "Look over there past the boab trees—"

It was the sundown rise of the galahs. They were coming noisily through the air in a magnificent arc of gray and pink plumage. Dozens and dozens of them. Then, almost when they were overhead, they wheeled. The pink feathers were touched with sunset gold. Their plumage made ribbons of glory as they swept away to the south, their collective sundown cries drowning all other bushland sounds.

"Oh, aren't they lovely?" Nairee exclaimed. She had completely, in one brief moment, forgotten she had thought of herself as an outsider.

The galahs wheeled again. The departing sun lit up with the dazzling spread of their wings. They screamed their call before they turned about. It was for all the world as if they, too, were giving their salute to a great occasion.

Nairee felt Mark's hand tighten on her arm and she guessed *he* knew what the galahs were doing and, more important, what they were saying. Or was it all a daydream?

"Uncle Jack," she said. "I don't think I'll ever again feel—well, sort of a nobody. I'll always have the birds, won't I?"

"And Gamma. And the dogs, the goats, the finches, the 'roos, a pack of wild donkeys, and—well, everything including me and Mark. Right, Mark?"

"Very right," he said. "But then, after all, you're never wrong, are you? It was a good party, wasn't it, Nairee?"

"Yes. And everyone stayed to the very end. That is, except for . . ." She broke off.

"Yes, everyone," Sergeant Allen and Mark both said together. Too smartly for Nairee to be taken in. They knew Mrs. Lacey—*and Dean*—had departed first. Before the party was absolutely finished.

She wondered why it bothered her.

She herself remembered and noticed things more,

now she had left school and come back to The Patch for good. And thought about things and people at length. That was because life would be different now. A new life! She was adult and had a vote!

Birds and animals had their pecking order. Nairee thought of each station-owning family in the district. There weren't so many numerically because stations were huge places. Whole districts in themselves.

In this particular area not far from the rain forest, the early colonizing families had taken up their own postures of possession—quite literally, in some cases —before anyone else even knew such places were in existence. Those first settlers were primarily the explorers. They mapped the place for posterity, and received—on lease, from the infant government—a good slab for themselves. Being explorers before they were settlers, they had the advantage of knowing in advance just which, what, and why they mapped and pegged what they had seen.

Slowly over the years the colonizing government became acquainted with what and whom they governed. And charged a fee for what was named in that early Parliament—a lease-hold. Those families which, by inheritances, had more money were able to establish themselves faster. They were already *there* and settled when new adventurers came seeking land. This way the human pecking order came into being.

Now that she was home for keeps Nairee did a lot of thinking about these matters.

Why, for instance, the Lacey family was so much more important than Hank Brown's family. Hank's family had hit upon the best water-holes around for a hundred miles. So he did better with his cattle than most others, including the Lacey family. But Hank wasn't *first* there, so he wasn't, psychologically speaking, permitted regal status and airs of the Laceys. Mrs. Lacey, in the spirit of the Outback, had allowed Hank Brown to take the important role of district giver-of-parties-when-people-came-home-from-afar, or conversely, were-packing-up-to-take-that-biannual-trip-abroad.

Yes, the social procedures were all in order. Everyone accepted the fact that Nairee was being taken back to The Patch by Sergeant Allen and Chief Bush Ranger Mark Allen. Sergeant Allen had been Nairee's official guardian. He had a special role. And Ranger Mark was his son! It remained Sergeant Allen's prerogative to continue a caretaker interest in Gamma's Girl. Most satisfactory to everyone, including the host Hank Brown and his stockman Bash.

14

LATER THAT EVENING, HAVING SAID GOOD-BYE TO THE Allens, Nairee and Gamma were left alone, the sole inhabitors of The Patch. Nairee had watched Mark's tall figure, dark against the last light of day, walking away. There was a lump in her throat for which she could find no explanation. Dear Mark. So strong yet so often so gentle. So tall yet so at home with nature's smallest creatures. So much the guardian of all that flew or crawled or raced across the bushland of the Outback!

Nairee told Gamma all about the party. Gamma kept nodding her head with approval. It did not occur to either of them that in the ordinary world of ordinary human beings Gamma, too, might have been at Hank's homestead. Like everyone else in the district, the Browns knew that Gamma would never have gone. Gamma rarely went anywhere. It was part of her quaintness.

But when it came to a wounded bird or animal or reptile, then Gamma was no longer retiring and quaint.

She knew exactly what to do. And went about doing it *her way*.

Now she was all wrapped up in Nairee's captured baby galah. *This* was Gamma's party. It had nothing to do with cups of tea, sandwiches and cakes. Not with stockmen standing round a barrel of beer.

Everything was now moved from the living-room table. A towel was spread out. An imitation nest was made of dried sticks, tendrils from the vine plants, and torn snippets of paper.

Nairee sat on a tall stool at the foot of the table while Gamma took over. When everything was ready, including a bowl of warm water and a sponge made of lamb's wool, Gamma took the little bird from the cardboard box and went to work. Each feather was individually lifted and dried. Nairee had often seen this operation performed, but this particular time things were different. This little bird was only a few days old at the most. It should have been afraid of the human hand. But so adroit was Gamma that the little chick snuggled into the palm of one hand while Gamma's other hand, with a magical touch, wiped each one of those fluff feathers. Then as Nairee had done before, Gamma snuggled the chick under her own chin. First she had knotted a clean flour bag round her neck, then set the bird in one of the folds of the neckcloth.

Nairee knew not to intrude, much as she longed to practice her own little piece of goodwill. The chick burrowed itself into a tight fold of the cloth, and there it remained, clean and dry, warm and safe, all fear gone. No patient of distinguished address and position in a city nursing home could feel safer than the chick, now motionless, was in its new environment. Gamma was queen fairy in her own environment, all right. Gamma was supremely happy at this moment. She was saving a life. Giving herself a new child.

She had one more family to care for.

One week later came Mrs. Lacey's invitation to Nairee for a visit to Beelagur. The invitation suggested that Nairee might like to stay a night or two. It was an annual invitation to which Nairee had been accustomed ever since she had turned twelve.

Everything that Mrs. Lacey did in her walk through life was according to the book of good manners and etiquette. So her invitation was addressed to Gamma with the added hope that Nairee also would be able to come. This, though Mrs. Lacey knew as well as Nairee and Gamma knew that the little gray-haired lady of The Patch never willingly stepped beyond her own domain. And Nairee and Gamma knew that she knew, and that the invitation was meant for Nairee. But at least it had the outward semblance of being correct. Etiquette had been observed.

Nairee's suitcase was brought out again. She took out the best of her pajamas, and underclothes—to the pleasure of Gamma, sitting in a small cane chair in Nairee's room, making exclamations of delight at all the pretty things. Some of them she had seen before, but each sight of something new brought a nod and a smile. There was a frilly blue blouse. And *red* shoes! Gamma was shaken with surprise that anything so colorful and with such heels could possibly be worn at all—let alone by Nairee who, like her, spent her days at The Patch in solid flat-heeled footwear. Shoes for house parties or even for dances would never stand up to the hard use along the rough tracks to, from, and round The Patch. These new shoes, though puzzling, were magical to Gamma. Did they wear such things at Mrs. Lacey's homestead? she wondered.

Nairee was going to Beelagur by The Patch's small utility, which she could drive herself and which had recently been gone over and gassed up by one of the mechanics from Hank Brown's outstation.

When the moment arrived for her to set out she was almost as sorry to leave Kissa—the name given to the new baby galah—as she was to leave Gamma.

"It's only a few days," she said. A fact which Gamma already knew, of course.

"You go and have a good time, Nairee," Gamma

said. "Woolarooka will come and keep me company as soon as she knows you're off——'"

"Of course she will!" Nairee mused a while, for the umpteenth time, on how Woolarooka and the rest of her tribe always *knew* when something was about to happen. So often they knew details *beforehand*.

As she drove over the creek, skirted the everglades, headed—generally speaking—north by north east till she came to the track bend, she knew Woolarooka and her kind were about somewhere. Maybe knowing exactly her route by the movement of the birds, and by fast-moving marsupials too. *They* made the upper tips of the grass to bend in the truck's movement of air, maybe just a quarter mile ahead of her. Now, as ever, the land spoke. Man became aware of what the wind in the trees, the birds, and animals in the bush already knew. "Something going east," a stockman a mile or two away would say, and give no explanation for his knowledge. The others with him knew anyway.

Beelagur's head stockman was at the boundary gate to meet Nairee. This also was a ritual among the inhabitants of this mesa land.

As she came nearer the homestead, almost within *cooee* of it, Beelagur's native tribal population appeared along the stockyard fence. They had their "better" clothes on, and their broadest, most gloriously white-toothed smiles wreathed their faces.

" 'Ullo you, Nairee. How you bin? You bin stay with that fella Gamma at Patch, alla time now? Finish school? Eh?"

Mrs. Lacey was also—as good manners dictated—at the ready for her visitor. She stood tall and cool and correctly dressed, just as she would be if it were the governor's wife who was coming to visit.

Irrelevant courtesies that had died for other people a century ago were still impeccably enacted by the mistress of Beelagur. In her book there was only one way to behave—and that was the way her mother and her mother's mother before her had behaved. Your home is your castle, be it in the bush or on the southern plains.

Nairee's status as visitor wiped out temporarily the history recording her as a foundling child, picked out of the bush by Woolarooka, then a young aboriginal woman.

Though Mrs. Lacey rarely smiled, when she did, as now, it was something quite beautiful. Her oval-shaped face and pearly teeth automatically invited a smile in return. So Nairee unconsciously smiled in a quite joyous way. Her eyes shone at their gray-green best.

"Here I am!" she said happily. "It's ever so good to be at Beelagur again." She kissed Mrs. Lacey's proferred cheek. It was cool and soft, that cheek. For some extraordinary reason, at that moment Mrs. Lacey's eyes and the softness of her skin reminded Nairee of something—someone else. But of what? Whom? Of course, she said to herself. I've been here so many times. And Mrs. Lacey always meets me on the verandah, like this. I remember exactly how it is. The same welcome. The same way. That's all it is!

But was it?

She did not have time to pursue the thought. Dean's blue-heeler dog came around the corner of the verandah at racing speed and all but threw himself at Nairee.

"Oh Jex, darling," Nairee cried. "You remember me, don't you! You never forget—" She bent to pat then rub her hand along the dog's side right to the end of its wagging tail.

"Jex never forgets anybody," Mrs. Lacey said. "I'm especially glad he remembers you, Nairee. . . . Oh, here comes Dean. You'll have to forgive his dress, Nairee. He's just brought in the cattle from the east paddock."

Dean's firm-booted tread could be heard coming along the side verandah. Mrs. Lacey had not finished apologizing for his dress when the man himself came round the corner.

Actually his appearance was just what it ought to

be, Nairee thought. His familiar tall and lean body, much like that of most men used to handling cattle in the north, looked so lithe and strong. He wore the usual khaki shirt and riding trousers. His hat was the wide-brimmed nor'westers' mustering hat. In spite of the fact he'd been at a dusty job he didn't look dusty himself. He took his hat off with one hand and with the other brushed his sleeved arm across his face.

"Hullo Nairee," he said, just barely smiling. Nairee's heart told her it would have been a bigger smile if Mrs. Lacey had not been there. But her head told her to be satisfied with the small and not the big if that was the way it had to be.

"Hullo Dean," she said, careful with her own smile too. But she could not banish the look from her eyes which was questing, and just a little sad. It would have been all glad if Mrs. Lacey had not been there.

Realizing this, Nairee felt quite dreadful for a full minute. She fell silent almost like a shy girl—which she was not.

"Oh Dean, you are in early," his mother said. This could have been a protest, but against what Nairee would not even guess.

"Kim Drew came over from Wellton and gave us a hand," he said. "We've left the cattle in the outer paddock and we'll finish the cutout tomorrow—if the weather holds."

There were signs of an early Wet, and any day now the rain could start. Dean looked at Nairee again, and this time he really smiled. It warmed her heart.

"We have some good stock horses this cutout, Nairee. You'll enjoy it—"

"Everything depends on the weather," Mrs. Lacey said somewhat hastily. "Dean . . . go and clean up. We'll have tea in about ten minutes." She moved toward the open door. "Come along, Nairee. Cook made a special cake for you this morning so we must go and do it justice."

～～～～～～～～～～～

15

INSIDE THE HOMESTEAD ALL WAS AS COOL AS IT WAS stately. Though by no means rare, it was still a notable house. A long, wide, high-ceilinged passage went straight through the middle of the house from the front door. It was what had come, by later comers, to be called "Colonial style." This was because the early colonists and settlers had built high and wide, like this continent they had come to inhabit. A wide verandah all the way around. The rear part of the house was built of wattle and daub, and was now mostly covered by timber paneling inset with gravelstone. As the homestead was only a short distance from the breakaway country, small melon-sized rocks for building were not hard to come by. But they were of many shapes. The main rooms were so wide and the ceilings so high they gave the whole the impression of a very large homestead. From all sides, because of the verandah entirely surrounding the house, whatever was coming or who going could be noted long before the hoofbeats or hum of an engine was heard.

Nairee was to have the "visitor's" room this visit.

This demonstrated very clearly she really was grown up now. Mrs. Lacey had pronounced by gesture! Nairee knew from childhood that this visitor's room was always kept blinds down, for special people. Thus elevated, she thought she had better mind all the little "this" and "thats" Mrs. Lacey had taught her over the years. "Never raise your voice when indoors. Actually, in fact a lady should never raise her voice at all. Not even for a winning horse at the rodeo, or a long stayer at the rodeo."

"Apologies from Dean," Mrs. Lacey said when Nairee, hands and face washed, dress replacing shirt and jeans, hair brushed, entered the dining room where afternoon tea was set out on the long table. "Being Dean," Mrs. Lacey said, "he had said that nothing short of a shower and a complete change would get the dust out of his system. So we'll go ahead and have our tea together, Nairee." She sighed as if Dean's ablutions were a major complication. "Mary will probably give Dean his tea on the side verandah," she continued. "As you know dear, the men are frightfully busy at cutout time. They'll drive the prime animals down to the northern highway, and from there they'll be trucked across the river—on the way to Wyndham."

Nairee was disappointed, but covered it behind a polite cough. It sounded very much as if Dean would hardly be here at Beelagur at all. Was he going all the way to the coast with the cattle?

Mrs. Lacey noticed the disappointment in Nairee's face. She herself had the appearance of someone thinking hard, then changing her mind. About something worrisome?

"Would you like to watch the cutout, Nairee?" she asked, quite gently. "Dean could tell the men to find you an appropriate mount."

Nairee's spirits rose. "Oh yes! I'd love that. Our cutouts at The Patch are so small they almost don't matter. But when it comes to more than a hundred beasts—well, that's different, isn't it? How many do you expect to send away?"

"A hundred and fifty this month. More later in the season if we can foresee a long enough break through the Wet. This lot is the first from our Brahmin stud."

Nairee was delighted now that she knew she would be allowed to join in the cutout. Amongst Brahmins too! She wondered how the blue-heeler dogs bested *them*.

There was no sign of Dean when Mrs. Lacey and Nairee had finished their tea. Mary reported she had made tea for Dean on the side verandah, but he had not come in. Jacky the roustabout had told her the men were having a "spot of trouble" with the cattle just brought in. Obviously Dean had been called out to solve whatever problems were besetting man and beast out at the far paddock.

"Can you amuse yourself—perhaps in the garden— for a while, Nairee?" Mrs. Lacey asked. "I simply must go down to the cottages. Two of the women are sick. Obviously they both ate something, or *both* wouldn't be sick, would they? I must go and investigate."

"Of course," Nairee said. "But could I help . . . if there is anything I can do?"

"Not just at the minute, anyway. If I need help I'll send someone up for you."

Mrs. Lacey was reaching for her sunhat from a wall peg on the verandah as she spoke. It was the same garden hat Nairee had often seen her wear when she had come to Beelagur, over the years. Maybe it would never wear out. "Leghorn straw," Mrs. Lacey had explained to her once. "It gets shabby but never wears through. I don't know what I would do without it."

Maybe one day get another one, Nairee had thought quietly to herself. Now, watching as Mrs. Lacey put the hat on, she added a rider to that thought. She is too fond of it ever to let it wear out completely. Mary, the housekeeper had once confided to Nairee that when that old Leghorn hat went, Mrs. Lacey would go too. At the time of that confidence Nairee had hoped nothing dreadful would ever happen to this notable headpiece. She was older now, but the hat didn't look any older at all. It had always been old, anyway. The way Mrs. Lacey put it on—both the lady and the hat looked the same as far back as Nairee could remember.

It had once been Nairee's dream to wear that kind of hat exactly as Mrs. Lacey wore hers. A long pin through the crown and through a nob of its wearer's hair. Then tied down with a piece of a silk scarf under the chin.

As Mrs. Lacey donned the hat, theen went down the wooden steps of the verandah, Nairee realized for the first time just *what* Mrs. Lacey's role was to her. *An example.*

Those shopping trips in Adelaide. The plays to which Mrs. Lacey had taken her. The musical fiestas. That whole series of wonderful events—in the Queen City, Adelaide. Affluent, generous, and example-setting —Mrs. Lacey was trying to repeat in Nairee the person she herself had been when young. Or make her *like* that person anyway. A Mrs. Lacey. Certainly not a Mrs. *Dean* Lacey, of course. Dean must be being kept for someone else. A careful barrier was erected between Nairee and Dean. Very careful, but very much there.

But why?

Mrs. Lacey didn't want her son, the heir to Beelagur, marrying a *waif*. Was that it? Yet how to account for the tutelage in the right manners, the right attitudes?

Nairee leaned against the house wall and looked out over the kitchen garden, past the homestead verandah, and the stables. She was watching for Mrs. Lacey's return now.

When that lady did in fact come around the timbered structure of the stables Nairee had once again that strange knowledge of a special relationship.

It wasn't because she had seen Mrs. Lacey today,

and many other days over the years, wearing that hat and looking as she looked today. It was some essence. Something as strange as seeing a fairy ghost walking through the grass at the bottom of the garden. But *Mrs. Lacey* was coming toward her walking across the gravel. And fairies, if there were such people, didn't wear hats at all. Much less a hat like that old but useful and shady leghorn, tied neatly to its owner's head with a faded pink scarf-like veiling.

Mrs. Lacey came up the three steps of the verandah, taking off the hat as she advanced. She smiled at Nairee before she spoke. And Nairee found herself returning that smile with something like conspiratorial ease. As if they really *did* understand one another. Which they didn't, of course.

She blinked hard. What an extraordinary set of sensations! Maybe she was a bit sunstruck herself.

Yes, that was it. Definitely it. She hadn't put her own hat on each time she had gone out of the shack back at The Patch since she had come home. She had overlooked the cardinal rule that dictated that one never *never* NEVER went anywhere without a hat when north of Twenty-six. Never mind your complexion. Just think of your life. Sunstroke north of Twenty-six was a punishment meant for fools.

"They have a rogue steer down there," Mrs. Lacey said. "Heaven only knows how they brought that mob in without a stampede."

"What will they do with him?" Nairee asked. A rogue meant a bullock which tried to battle for a leadership position while a mob was on the move. If he won it against the other animals and stayed in the lead, he would lead here, there, and everywhere. All over the track. No straight controlled line for a rogue! Usually the stockmen had to keep such an animal outside from the main herd. By whip, will, or cursing, when a mob was brought into the homestead paddock for the cutout, the first animal they had to separate from the rest was the rogue. He had to have a yard of his own. And he was equally determined *not* to.

Nairee instantly forgot her curious daydream, and now came back to earth with a little excited jump.

"Who cut him out?" she asked eagerly. "Who yarded him in?"

"Why Dean, of course!" Mrs. Lacey said, taking off that hat and hanging it on the wall peg. She had her back turned to Nairee and did not see the sudden light in Nairee's eyes when Dean's name was mentioned. Nairee had twice before seen Dean handling a "wild one." He was a master on horseback, and a wizard with the stock whip when he was handling something difficult. The whip end never touched the animal, yet infallibly it cracked—like a pistol shot— no more than an inch behind the creature's ear. Sometimes two inches off its rump. And this, while hunter and rebel were both on the move.

Turning, Mrs. Lacey did not miss the shine in Nairee's eyes.

"I think you'd better take that middle room down the passage, dear, instead of the front one," Mrs. Lacey said out of the blue. "It's more homey. We'll have dinner at seven—as usual."

Nairee's spirits dropped a little. Rarely when she was invited over to Beelagur did she have the front glamour room. Dean's study was on the other side of the passage. To take the middle room now meant she would not see his light on, late at night. It was companionable to know someone was there—across the passage.

Oh well! It didn't really matter did it? Or did it?

For the next half or three quarters of an hour Mrs. Lacey had what she called "things to do." Nairee knew that time was likely to be passed in a deep cane chair in the sewing room listening to the short-wave radio. Mrs. Lacey loved the short-wave. She could listen in to foreign stations as well as to Radio Australia. This, she had said more than once, was how she knew what was going on in the outside world. She also managed thus to keep out of the cook's way.

Nairee took a shower in the white porcelain-lined

shower alcove. The checked cotton dress she slipped on over her head was a replica of the one she had worn all day, but looked neater and cooler than the earlier one. The heat was so intense it was almost a must to take one or two changes of clothes wherever one went. Cottons were the order of the day for man, woman, and child. Windows and doors were open in every room.

When she was ready Nairee came out of her room, and walked quietly along the passage. Mrs. Lacey would be busy listening to whatever was going on in the world. Meantime Nairee would while away half an hour watching the sunset.

16

NAIREE NEVER GREW TIRED OF WATCHING THE SUNSET in tropical Australia. Even a lifetime with it never accustomed her to its wonder. A flaming red sky with the trees silhouetted against it was not to be believed except you knew it was real because you were seeing it.

Then Nairee saw the black silhouette of a man on horseback framed against the glorious picture.

She knew at once it was Dean coming in. She was a horsewoman herself and would know Dean's seat anywhere in the world . . . or so she thought. That straight back. That hat with the brim pulled slightly down to shade his eyes. He was walking his mount and he had that curious but noteworthy habit of keeping his left leg thrust forward—in a straight line.

Her heart warmed. She was watching "the master" coming home for the night! Soon he would have his shave, change, and join them at dinner.

After Dean and his horse had passed around behind the stables she went back into the house and briefly joined Mrs. Lacey by the radio.

For some reason she could not even explain, she

felt guilty now. As if she had been peeping in quiet places that belonged to others. He had had as usual that "king of the acres" look. She wondered if he *felt* like that? How did he feel at all? He was silent more often than not. To hear him whistle, or to hum a note or two of a tune like Mark Allen did, was unthinkable.

Oh, I wish . . . I wish . . . she thought. She went quietly back to the verandah again. What did she wish? She couldn't put a name to it. Not now, anyway. Maybe later, or even another day. At home, when she was feeding the birds or giving the shacklike homestead at the Patch a cleanup.

She started when she heard footsteps on the verandah coming from the passage. Mrs. Lacey.

"Nothing newsworthy on the air now," she said. "Just overseas cricket by way of the satellite." She slipped her hand through the crook of Nairee's arm. "Cricket," she said. "Sometimes nothing but *sport*. Especially on Saturdays."

"Seeing something going on in another country while it is actually going on is rather wonderful though."

"The extreme wonder of the world, I suppose." Mrs. Lacey was looking far down toward the stables as she spoke.

"No sign of Dean, yet? Station men always work by the sun, never by their watches. You are taller than I am, Nairee, when you stand on your toes. Can you see him coming?"

"Uh . . . that is no," Nairee said, then felt guilty.

"Well, you are looking into the dying rim of the sun, aren't you?" Mrs. Lacey said. "You'd never see anything but sunset looking that way. The sky's too bright."

Nairee blinked. She wondered why she didn't automatically tell Mrs. Lacey that Dean had come in to the stables a few minutes earlier. It was too late now. She bit her bottom lip and had to fight not to feel thoroughly wretched. Such deceit! There was no *reason* why she should not have spoken up. It was too late now. Strange, but she had been *afraid* of admitting that she had been watching Dean ride in against the sunset.

Yet the truth was all over her face in a pink flush. A part of her own private sunset.

She was here. At Beelagur. But she wouldn't see much of Dean.

She knew that in advance.

Why? For what reason?

And she didn't see much of him. He wouldn't be in for dinner, he said. He was going over the range to Sanderson's place. Maybe they'd have a game of chess tonight, so he wouldn't be in till all hours.

Mrs. Lacey looked as if Dean's going over the range pleased her. Yet there was a visitor here! Well, Nairee supposed, *this* visitor didn't matter that much. Yet somehow—was it a sundown murmur? A turned head? Or what? She had the sorry feeling that Dean was going over the range just because she herself *was* here. Silly, because at the back of her mind she thought Dean did like her just that little bit. Something in the air when he was near her. Or she near him. That turned head—

Nairee was used to being mystified by all these strange moods of the Laceys. But she was older now. Not just because she had a vote, either. It was because of the college dances, and sometimes sports competitions, that she had learned a little of how a young man sometimes turned away from a girl. Or a girl sometimes did the turning away.

She had picked that up quite early in her school life. Boys could be more shy than girls. At least, some of them.

But all this was not the case with Dean. Mrs. Lacey was actually *pleased* that Dean was going off over the range. Why? "I haven't been over your particular part of the range since I was about ten or twelve," Nairee said, amazed at herself for speaking. "Will you take me sometime, Dean? In the daytime, I mean?" She swallowed hard because with only a tiny turn of her head she saw Mrs. Lacey reflected in the old mirror on the back wall. Mrs. Lacey—in the mirror—shook her head to Dean. Ever so slightly. Meaning, of course, No. Don't take her.

There was a little sprite in Nairee's makeup. And sometimes it could get angry. Very angry. It did just that right now.

But she was a guest in the house, so she must mind her manners. She not only loved the old homestead but its four generations of Lacey history spelled out in all kinds of old but beautifully framed photographs, and in ornaments here and there along the mantel shelves in each of the day rooms. She loved its history. She often wondered if only those first pioneers who had crossed unmapped ranges and water courses and vast spinifex plains for the first time could come back just for a little while and see how well their descendants had carried on.

"We're rounding up brumbies in the next few days," Dean said, changing the subject of his impending departure from Beelagur. "I'll select a special one for you, Nairee. My men are hard riders, so when you've mastered the brumby—well, then you can ride with us. Not easy, mind you. It's breakaway country east of the mesa tops." He actually smiled as he spoke, and he looked at Nairee. *Right* at her.

His smile stirred that odd chord in her heart. She smiled back almost as if they were swapping secret thoughts.

Dinner was a slow and graceful meal, as it always was at Beelagur. They talked of this and that, yet said nothing much at all. When Nairee was a small girl visiting Beelagur, Mrs. Lacey had taught her the gentler, more graceful manners of an older generation. She watched herself very carefully now as she sat at the table with her hostess. For at least the hundredth time she wondered why the elegant and starchy Mrs. Lacey had taken so much trouble with her. Just kindness to an orphaned child? It had to be that, because there could not be any other reason. Leastwise that

Nairee could see or understand. As she had grown, she had come to realize that Mrs. Lacey, and of course Dean, stood in a special situation in relation to the other station owners. The early Laceys—the first colonials—had pioneered the area. In each generation there had been a son to carry on the tradition. That particular son had married someone from the top pioneering class of good families. Those people were always the aristocrats of the district. They effortlessly maintained this role.

Nairee could see that Dean would naturally follow his forebears. He too would marry an aristocrat.

And she, Nairee, was a nobody. Just a *nobody*.

She had long since learned the antidote to such feelings. She told herself she was *Gamma's Girl,* and without her, Gamma would have nobody at all. That was a statement of fact, and she was proud of it. People coming through the area from time to time would ask the then-small girl who she was . . . even if they already knew. It was to see that chin go up, and the gentle voice declare: "I am Gamma's Girl."

Then she would toss her head. This was yet another way of saying "I am *somebody*."

That night, her first at Beelagur this season, Nairee went to bed early, as did everyone on the station. And she slept the sleep of the just. She didn't even think about Dean . . . whether he had come in or at what hour. All she wanted on waking was to see the sunrise over the red ironstone range in the east. At The Patch sunrise was always seen through trees. Here at Beelagur, there was no leafy veil to soften the brilliant colors. It was as if the world on the other side of the mesa was on fire. On this side, the flat-topped mountains were in purple shadow.

Tourists, newspapermen, and artists came two thousand miles to see the sunrise over this northerly range of Outback mesa. It surely was one of the wonders of their world. First there was light, then a pink glow. Then the whole horizontal line of mesas lit up along

their crags, like a running fire, leaving purple shadows
in the cave cracks below. The crags stayed silhouetted
purple and black against this fiery glow. Here and
there a ghost-gum, white-trunked in ordinary daylight,
lifted black arms like a statue against the fiery red of
the coming sun.

As the sun climbed up in its sky, the eastern plain
with its pile of broken stones was a wounded red. And
there was vast panorama of broken half-mountains,
and barren deep gorges. Only for a few minutes was
the world like this. Then, with the sun risen, the sky
was suddenly a no-color. Not white nor red nor blue.
Things began to move across the ground, dingoes
slouched toward their crag holes. A wedgetail eagle
would spread its enormous wings against the horizon.
The rock hideouts and the earth changed color as the
little beasties, the lizards, a myriad of unnamed birds,
the bullocks, a kangaroo here and an emu there, an
alligator in a rock pool, turned the whole world into a
living, moving, noisemaking thing.

It was morning.

Time for breakfast.

In the kitchen Cook rattled pans; out by the stock
rails the stockmen shouted and cracked stock whips,
as they bunched the cattle and directed them into lane-
ways. Down in the cottage village, a few hundred yards
from the homestead, the house staff stirred. Padding of
feet up the back steps, clang of a milk pail set down
suddenly. In the kitchen the teacups rattled.

Nairee had woken at sunup on this day. By the time
the plain was flooded with pure light she had had her
shower and put on her morning "casuals": blue jeans
and a many-pocketed blue denim shirt. She had her
riding boots in her hand as she went down the long
passage to the verandah breakfast table. In that short
time the silence of the wonder world outside had van-
ished completely. Members of the house staff were talking, grumbling, or clattering dishes.

Mrs. Lacey was at the breakfast table before Nairee.
"How did you sleep. dear?" she asked. Before any

answer could come she delivered herself of the day's news. She had listened in to the transceiver's early-morning call, and a thousand miles out here in the wilderness she knew what was happening in London, New York, in Perth Western Australia, and the price of beef cattle in yesterday's sale yards, on the north-west coast of the continent.

"The men came in with the horses at sunup," she said as she passed Nairee the wheat biscuits, then the sugar and milk. "There's a mount for you, dear. The mount Dean told you about last night. Woolarooka said you have ridden it before. Roan—"

"Woolarooka?" Nairee asked quickly. "When did she come in?"

"Before you did yesterday, my dear," Mrs. Lacey said with a smile. "She went out last evening with two other lubras to see Dean's men and the one-time brumby Dean had marked for you."

"Wouldn't it!" Nairee said, pouring cereal into her plate. "Wherever I go—excepting when I was at school—there goes Woolarooka. I sometimes wonder what things would be like without her."

"You mind?"

"Oh *no!*" Nairee said quickly. "I love her. It's just that it is always a wonder to me. How does she always *know* where I am at any particular moment in time?"

"Count your blessings, my dear. One thing certain, no harm will ever come to you while Woolarooka is around."

"I know," Nairee's spoon was halfway to her mouth. "She found me, didn't she? So according to the law of her particular tribe, I belong to her. To all of them, I suppose—the whole tribe, I mean."

There was a hubbub on the brown clay ground below the verandah railing.

Mrs. Lacey and Nairee glanced at one another.

"Here she comes!" Nairee said.

"Here she *is*," said Mrs. Lacey. Then turning her head a little, she called: "Come up out of there, Woolarooka. But for goodness sake leave those pups out there. Too much noise."

"Awright, Miz Lacey! Every time you have Nairee I come too, eh?"

"Yes, you come too," Mrs. Lacey said in a tone of voice that was mildly bored. "You caught your horse already?"

"Yeah. I come up all along that creek bed. That fella Dean got one more horse with his big Red Fire fella."

"Yes. He had Red Fire in the stableyard last night. Red Fire knew just as well as you do, Woolarooka, that one extra yarded from the mob meant there was a visitor up at the homestead."

Wookarooka laughed, a high shrill sound coming out of a red mouth that looked too big for her face.

"I bin know yestadee Nairee come up here, Miz Lacey. So I find my horse—this one I got very fast maybe I call 'im Yarto. Bin fast like the wind, this one."

Mrs. Lacey pushed back her chair and stood up. This was the signal that breakfast was over. The kitchen girls came out to collect the used dishes and their noisy greeting to Woolarooka was one big din.

"I don't know what they're all saying," Nairee said with a laugh. "Every year when I go away down south I forget the words."

"You come bin stay all alonga here alla time now, Nairee," Woolarooka said. "You best get ready to remember betta. Eh?"

"Yes, Woolie, I'll do just that," Nairee said, laughing. Mrs. Lacey had pushed back her own chair and gone to the edge of the verandah. She blew a kiss to Woolarooka.

"Miz Lacey?" Woolarooka said. "Okay Nairee come along now? Dean, he wants to get rid of that horse too many so he can run others along the creek paddock, eh?"

"Yes. Off you go, Nairee. Don't forget your hat. If you go by the water track you'll burn badly."

"I'll get it now." Nairee was making toward the passage door and still talking as she went. "You don't mind my going out now? I'd like to help you a little?"

"No. You go along with Woolarooka. You only have a day or two here. Make the best of them."

Naiee's spirits were high now. Though the conversation between the others did not convey all that was meant she knew from past visits that it was quite expected of her that she would go off with Woolarooka. See something of the roundup, and the cutting out, see which horse was to go this way and which one was to go the other.

Dean would be out with the stockmen and the mob. It was so much more exciting to be here at Beelagur when there was to be a cut-out . . . of either horses or bullocks. If she already had had her hat in her hand she would have thrown it high in the air. Behind that screen of a still face and clear, unblinking eyes, Mrs. Lacey was a darling, after all.

17

IT WAS A RIP-ROARING DAY AS ARE ALL CUTOUTS OF horse mobs or cattle on the bigger stations. There were so many more cattle than on a smaller holding. And more stockmen and at least one or two more dogs.

Most of the cattle dogs were blue-heelers. Part kelpie and part a rare breed of lesser collie. Bash, of Geko station, always said that when faced with a mob of cattle, a blue-heeler was more intelligent than man. Dean Lacey, when he heard of that remark, set his lips in a hard line and said: "Bash ought to know. He measures everyone by his *own* degree of intelligence."

When that story went the rounds of the cattleyards Hank Brown, Bash's boss, had reciprocated with: "Dean Lacey would know. Bash's level of intelligence is on a par with the best stockmen in the district and that includes the owner stockman"—meaning Dean—"along with the blue-heeler."

That story, as it wavered over the district like a light wind bending the tussock grasses over the land, brought a promise for all: "Since Geko station lot had come off best in the duel of words, they'd shout the loser—Dean Lacey—the biggest round ever at the Pub of Pubs next time they, their cattle, and the dogs, met on their way to the coastal sale yards."

Nairee had learned, as a growing girl, that a yarn that gave way to universal laughter was what made the Outback a friendly place for all.

Nairee had a wonderful day down at the stockyards. The air was humid to the degree that perspiration poured off everyone's face, warning that somewhere not too far off the coast, a cyclone was brewing. The pace had to be faster, and therefore more exciting as each separated mob was corralled in for the night. Horses pounded like minor thunderers. Men shouted, stockwhips cracked. The dogs, including Dean's blue-heeler, raced and snapped at hind cattle legs until each individual horned head, or humped-back Brahmin, was yarded through the right gate.

Woolarooka, though not young now, could match the men racing her horse up the sides of the mob. With the horses yarded earlier and in a different section of the main yards she was superb. An untidy rider, slipping this way then that on her mount, her clothes bunched on one side and flying loose, almost like dark sails, she was one with the mob. Her black hair streamed over her face, but she did not seem to need eyes. She drove her mount in against the sides of the jittery moving column of animals, so they hedged away from her just enough to keep the side column moving. Every time she got a frisky animal forced through, the stockmen gave her a shout. If anything, they enjoyed Woolarooka's contribution to the yarding as much as any part of the day's activities.

When all was over and gates clanged to, they gave her three cheers. And three more for Nairee, riding behind Woolarooka.

Nairee was physically tired but the prospect of more excitement at the final cut-out kept her restless. It was not only excitement that warded off sleep that night, but discomfort from the increasing heat and humidity. She had thrown off her bedcover and was now only half awake, battling with the twisted sheet. Then came a sense of foreboding.

At some point in the small hours, she woke up and

did not have to turn her head to know what was wrong with Beelagur's world. It was pitch dark outside. Not even one star twinkled through her window net.

From far far away, probably somewhere off the coastline, there came that occasional ominous rumble. Short and deep-sounding. A moment later the sky outside her window lit up in a sheet of light.

Oh no! Nairee thought as she scrambled out of bed and, barefooted, went to the window. "It is coming after all!"

Last night, just as she had been going to her bedroom, she had heard Dean come in from the stables for the last time. Mrs. Lacey had said, "The news on the air warned us that a cyclone was well out to sea, and no sign yet of turning inland. But we should batten down in case."

"I couldn't do anything about the last lot of cattle except turn them loose," Dean had said. "I wasn't going to do that on a mere warning. I shan't go to sleep. I'll sit up and do the account books. I'll call you if the cyclone breaks through, but as yet I don't think it is likely. Its direction at nine-thirty was south by southwest . . ."

Nairee, wearing thin pajamas at the time, had been coming from the bathroom. Dean turned and looked at her. It had been hot and humid enough then, and Nairee had only draped her cotton dressing gown over her shoulders.

"Oh!" she had said. "I didn't know anyone was in the passage. It is hot and I've just toweled myself down. Is anything wrong?"

"Damned cyclone!" Dean said, pushing the long finger of his right hand up under his hair. "Go to bed, Nairee. We'll call you if it turns inland. Get some sleep while you can. It's all hands to the front line if the blasted thing moves inland. It is moving at seventy kilometers to the hour, and if it hits at all it should hit further south as far down as Karratha."

"Yes," Mrs. Lacey agreed. "Go to bed, Nairee. Batten down your shutters like a good girl, please."

"Of course," Nairee said. "But let me help you with the other windows. I'll start at the kitchen end—"

"No you won't, my dear." Mrs. Lacey was very very firm. Her eyes took in the slim lines of Nairee's body under the flimsy pajama shorts and gown. "You'll be called if you are needed."

Dean smiled at Nairee, and it was a real smile now. It said, *Go along. If anyone else forgets to call you . . . which is most unlikely . . . then I will.*

Mrs. Lacey had turned away, but she now glanced over her shoulder. Though not close together, Nairee and Dean were smiling at one another.

"Oh. Go to bed, child!" she said. Not unkindly, but as if she might be irritable and suddenly very *tired*.

Perhaps she was just that.

"Good night, both of you," Nairee said, turning toward her own door. "I hope that cyclone won't happen." She did not look at either of them, but went through her own doorway, and quietly closed the door behind her.

She hung her towel on the railing by the verandah door.

How dark it was out there tonight! No moon and no stars. The black heavens had a purple tinge along the western sky. A dark dark purple. A cyclone's banner. Was it turning south, or wasn't it?

There'll be a blow from that cyclone somewhere, she said to herself. The thought of Gamma . . . *if it comes* . . . But Gamma had suffered cyclones many a time. She knew what to do. When Nairee had been engrossed in "education" down south, someone had always gone to see how Gamma was making out. One or another of the male inhabitants had traveled miles and miles down one or other of the tracks to "bring that ratty old girl in."

Nairee turned off her lights and went to bed. She feigned sleep so well that when Mrs. Lacey, a silent shadow, turned the door handle and peered in her room, she found only silence. Nairee obligingly had made a hump of herself under the sheet—no blankets, of course. The night was steamy hot, but Mrs. Lacey would see the hump against any lighter world outside the window. She would know all was well with Nairee.

Nairee fell asleep without meaning to. It wasn't until now that an ominous rumble, and great flash of light disturbed her. Animals, birds, and everything that crept, walked, or moved in any way, responded in a creaking or fluttering or thump-thump way to that mystery of striking light Old Man Fire-Fire was making at intervals across the western sky.

Damp with the heat, and startled by the flashes of light more than the rumble, Nairee threw off her sheet and pulled on cotton jeans as fast as she could. She tied her hair back, then flung on a loose blouse as she wondered what her role was to be now that the fierceness of the whirling winds told her a cyclone was bestirring the land. One thing she did know was that the cyclone would be on its way south down the Indian Ocean and that it might wreak havoc in the coastal areas. But surely not inland here at The Patch or Beelagur?

Anyway she just had to go and see.

Even before she reached the end of the long passage and opened the door, she knew just what was happening.

A sound was pitting the silence like tiny nuts falling to earth. Then there was a long swish and a heavy continuous, muted, but formidable, sound of water falling from the sky.

Toward the front end of the passage, Mrs. Lacey's door opened, and a shaft of light streamed out. Mrs. Lacey was pulling on her dressing gown as she came into the hallway.

"It's the rain!" she said. "Now it has started it will go on for days. Even weeks. The Wet."

Nairee unlatched the back door and pulled it inward.

Outside it was pitch dark except for the downward movement of sheets of rain.

Further back along the passage, Dean was emerging in shorts and a short dark nylon coat.

"That kind of rain means we'll have it for days," he said. "Floods again, I predict."

"Better than the east-coast cyclone itself," Mrs. Lacey said. "It has turned inland off the Queensland coast. It will bank up the river waters right across the north."

Nairee was standing within a foot of the doorway leading out to the rear verandah.

"It's coming down in sheets," she said as she looked outside at a wall of water coming straight down from the blacked-out heavens.

Dean started through the dayroom leading to the north verandah. Mrs. Lacey and Nairee followed. Mary, the housekeeper, and her two side-helps were already there.

"The big creek will flood," Mary announced flatly.

"Is flooded already," one of the help girls said, equally flat.

"Possibly," Mrs. Lacey corrected her. "If it goes on for days we will be housebound."

Except for those few remarks, the little group from the passage was silent. They were each thinking the same thoughts, punctuated with a more dismal one. Would they be flooded? If the rivers in the east bank up, too, how much and how high would the water come? It was an anxiety with which they all lived in the times of the Wet.

Dean disappeared down the verandah steps and leapt across the deep pool now swirling around the landing. He was off through the downpour though none of the waiting ones could see him go, or his direction, because of that wall of rain.

"He'll have gone to let the horses out," Mary said. "The stable ones, that is . . ."

"The stable ones?" Nairee asked. "Not the yarded ones?" She was alarmed for Dean because of the extreme darkness. It was as if he were going out to nowhere.

"He knows best," Mrs. Lacey said shortly. "If he lets the horses out of the home paddock it will be because he knows they can better fend for themselves in their own free world."

Nairee wanted to say, *Sometimes they can, but not always.* She didn't dare. In any case there was the roundup to go through again. And the cutout. And the yarding. All over again, in knee-deep mud.

She could not bear to think of those animals out in that terrible downpour. She had to think about Gamma too. Gamma would have gone out into that storm. She would bring the birds into the shack. The little crying animals too. The dogs would be inside. But the goats? And the donkeys and the cow and the two horses?

Useless even to think about them all. They were shut off by this wall of falling water. Not only Gamma's family, but Nairee's family too.

Mary turned and caught the expression on Nairee's face. She knew the girl well enough to know she was not worrying about Beelagur and its occupants. It was The Patch that concerned her. Far from home, and unable to do anything about it. The water was no longer just rain, it was a moving wall coming straight down from on high—and could possibly keep that up for hours. Even days.

Don't you worry, Nairee," Mary said quietly. "Woolarooka went hours and hours ago. Before it started. She knew what was coming."

Nairee felt tears stinging her eyes. Tears of gratitude for Woolarooka.

One day someone would ask, "Who looks after Woolarooka?" Useless to ask.

"Oh well," Mrs. Lacey said, as if unmoved. Which she was not, only completely self-controlled. She turned to Mary. "I think we will make some tea. Tea for all of us. Dean will be in again soon. If not, put something warm—soup, I think—in a thermos for him. We must keep calm and do something other than worry. Tea for all please, Mary."

18

❧❧❧❧❧❧❧❧❧❧

IT WAS IN THIS MANNER THE WET BEGAN EARLY THAT
year.

The steady solid downpour went on over the next
twenty-four hours with no signs of abating. Nairee
knew well enough that someone other than Woolarooka, somewhere further away, past the grasslands
and the rain forest, would be looking in to see how
things were going with Gamma. Nevertheless she worried. Imprisoned at Beelagur, lovely, comfortable and
picturesque though it was, made her restless, so she
did what she could to help Mrs. Lacey and the kitchen
girls at the homestead.

Once again Nairee was beguiled by the large
framed photographs of Laceys of former generations.
Two of the gentlemen were on camelback, the rest on
horseback. They wore the clothes of the earliest generation who emigrated to Australia.

"How ever could they wear those heavy clothes? Or
go on wearing them?" she asked Mrs. Lacey, putting
down her damp wiping cloth to stand back and gaze
thoughtfully at a large photograph in the dayroom. It

was of a party of men, each bestride a magnificent
horse, and clothed in heavy twill riding pants, a shirt
with collar and tie beneath a topcoat, and a pith hel-
met.

Even Mrs. Lacey smiled a little. "It is a wonder
they didn't die from overheating," she said. "But
they didn't, and they would rather have died then be
seen by their servants—because that was what their
stockmen were in those days—in an open-necked
shirt, no tie, and the denim trousers or shorts of today."

Perhaps as much to occupy time, Mrs. Lacey began
telling Nairee the history of every piece of silver, old-
fashioned ornament, and even certain pieces of furniture that must have had a great antique value because
they had been brought to Australia by the first of the
Laceys. Aware no longer of being imprisoned by a
wall of rain, Nairee fell under the spell of history.

"Do you remember that little tin trunk full of postcards you used to save when you were a girl?" she
asked Mrs. Lacey. "I think you said you loved them
so much you brought them to Beelagur when you were
married. Are they still in the back room?"

"Yes. I long ago moved them from the old trunk to
the bottom drawer of that old cedar chest in the same
room. Would you like to go through them for me,
Nairee? There might be silverfish and other destructive
wogs amongst them by this time. Would you take a
damp rag and check them for me? We must *do* something. *Keep* busy."

Nairee was delighted to have something to do that
was entertaining in its own right.

"I'm going to pull out the sewing machine, and make
up curtains from that new material I bought when last
in Adelaide," Mrs. Lacey said. "Mary's room has been
crying out for new curtains for I don't know how long.
I don't suppose Dean will come through that rain from
the stables until he has to come for food or sleep.
We have the homestead to ourselves."

Even as Nairee began to lift out the dozens and

dozens of postcards and old photographs from the bottom drawer of the chest, she had a thought that was nearly a hope that if not Dean, then some other visitor might find his way through the wall of water to the homestead. While Mrs. Lacey had been talking she had heard—or thought she had heard—a faint whirligig sound that just could be a helicopter.

Mark! she wished. Mark could radio-talk from the air in that noisy thing. He might have news of Gamma. The homestead radio was in the same room as the sewing machine. Mrs. Lacey would hear if he called. Fantastic of him to be out there in that unrelenting fall of water! He would have been out since daylight. But then Mark was always brave. A Ranger had to be brave. Alligators in the river beds, snakes galore inland, wedgetail eagles cruising down from their aeries to investigate with killer claws and beaks anything that flew, walked, or even rode horses near their own heavenly domains.

There were the human marauders who, in the name of science, zoos, or overseas buyers came in to take away the creatures living in all the wild inland northern areas. As Nairee took her damp cloth of 230 spray she thought of all the little finches and gaily colored parakeets, not to mention her beloved pink-and-gray galahs that some quite awful people captured and placed, still living, in cardboard rolls disguised as magazine containers to send them with friends or relatives who were traveling overseas to take to bird fanciers in return for a very good price.

Sitting cross-legged on the floor before the open drawer of the cedar chest, Nairee lifted out dozens and dozens of postcards.

It was a fascinating occupation as she looked at each card—some of them actually old photographs—that had belonged to Laceys in other times.

Where were they now? All those people who had signed their messages of greeting and goodwill on the backs of those cards? Some cards carried stamps and postmarks of other countries. It was hard to decipher the post dates—the cards were so old now. But Nairee did find several from the nineteenth century. They must surely have belonged to Mrs. Lacey's parents or those of her husband.

What stories—history in fact—these cards could tell! She wished she had the courage to ask Mrs. Lacey about some of them. But above all things, Mrs. Lacey respected privacy, almost to a fault.

She remembered having previously seen before the card she was holding in her hand. Long, long ago—when Mrs. Lacey had let her, then a child, "play" with the cards.

The ink was faded on the back of the card and Nairee could not read the several lines of message. But the signature was clearer. It read—*Caroline!*

As Nairee read the name she unconsciously said it. *"Caroline."* Why did it give her a strange feeling? The picture on the other side was of two lovebirds, beak to beak in the "kissing" pose. Perhaps that was why she, Nairee, had taken special note of it. Only someone very close to Mrs. Lacey would have sent a card with so intimate a picture on it.

Or was she, Nairee, guessing? And guessing *wrong?*

Yet the name Caroline meant something to her. What? She did not know anyone at school whose name was Caroline. And no one she knew here in the north of the Outback went by that name. Yet there was something familiar about it.

Or was she dreaming it all?

Without thinking Nairee put that postcard aside on the floor a foot away from the other cards so that it lay there very lonely. *Apart . . .*

Apart?

Then Nairee remembered where she had seen that name written before.

Those lonely graves, somewhere at the back boundary of every station up to fifty or a hundred years old had that little forlorn railed-in yardage. Always on the outside boundary. The most distant.

In more than a hundred years of landholding, people

had died, of course. A fatal illness, an accident. A stockman thrown against a boundary fence. A faithful aboriginal bush-tracker. They were buried there in those sad little railed-in squares where they were most at home. By their own station property.

And so with Caroline.

Even as she looked at the card again Nairee knew she would not ask Mrs. Lacey about it. Mrs. Lacey was by nature a very reserved person. She rarely if ever spoke of any of her relations. Not even of some few living ones who resided down south.

The cards Nairee had wiped with the cloth were all set out in rows on the floor now. The fan whirling round in the ceiling had earlier dusted them off. She began to sort them into classes. "Down South" pictures into one group. Trees into another. Northwest animals and birds into a heap of their own. Homestead pictures she felt must take pride of place, so she put them in a neat pile at the head of the line.

She was deliberating where to put pictures of the homestead outbuilding, and the staff, when she heard footsteps coming down the passage. Heavy-booted steps.

The door opened and Mary put her head around from the passage.

"A visitor to see you, Nairee," she said. All smiles. "Fancy coming in this rain! I didn't even hear the buzzer for the water noises—"

Nairee scrambled to her feet and quickly put away the pictures.

"I'll be there in a minute."

"No you won't," a male voice said. "You know me. I never wait."

Mary's face was gone and *he* was there.

"Mark! Oh, Mark!"

For the life of her Nairee had no idea why she wanted to cry. She wasn't homesick. Never here at Beelagur.

But he had a fine grin on his face and his arms extended, so Nairee went straight into those arms.

"How ever did you come through the rain?" she asked, a little damp about the eyes.

"The whirligig. It never lets me down. Just brings me where I want." He didn't wait for her to ask why he came. "Guess what? I've brought Gamma too."

"Oh *no!*" She was incredulous, but delighted. She drew herself out of his arms. "Did anything go wrong? I mean, at the shack? Not blown down, or anything? The animals?"

"All serene, and Bash's offsider is there looking after things. Brown from Geko signaled me I'd better come and fetch Gamma. The rain is not just local, Nairee. The rivers, lakes—the lot—east in Queensland are flooding like never before. Then add a cyclone crossing the east coast—to ours out here in the west.

"But a northeast cyclone never gets this far, Mark?"

"No, and this one's fizzled out too—except it brought the tropical rains and they *haven't* fizzled out. I don't think even its remnants will get this far, but what it has done is stimulate our own atmosphere disturbance here on this side. Hence the rain . . . Eastern rains bang-on, and our own western winds at gale force offshore. Right between the two, we have deluge and flood!"

"Floods?"

"Sure thing." He kissed her on the forehead. He had never done that before. Not *that* way. It had the strangest effect on Nairee. She felt frightened. Of Mark! Oh, never never ever! It was a token, that was all. But it did mean something. Or didn't it?

A lock of Nairee's hair had fallen fringelike across her forehead. Mark lifted his hand and pushed it back. She thought he might have been cajoling a child, and she wanted to stamp her foot. Just like a child. Then she wanted to bury her face against his shoulder. But she did not. Not this, or anything else to draw herself closer to him. She wasn't afraid now. Only shy. Her heart was beating too fast.

"Oh Mark, please let me go. You are hurting me . . "

He dropped his arms abruptly. "I'm sorry, Nairee. I didn't mean to offend you. Cross my heart. It was just that I thought you were alarmed because I've done the Never-Never thing—bring Gamma out of her cocoon." He paused, looking right down into her eyes. His own eyes were very serious. "The creek is up . . . which wouldn't matter so much, except the forecast is bad. Even battened down, Gamma couldn't stay on at The Patch alone."

"But the birds? And the animals . . . and Woolarooka?"

"Last seen, Woolarooka was up in the fork of a tree telling me in mixed aboriginal and Australian to get Gamma out of there, and go to heaven. Heaven being —to Woolarooka at that moment—any place on earth that wasn't The Patch. Her way of saying 'haven' of course."

Nairee felt limp. "Let me sit down," she said. "Mark, that has never happened before. Why *our* creek?" She was down on the low stool she had previously put before the cedar chest. Her vagrant lock of hair fell across her forehead again, and she peered up through the strands of hair at Mark.

He stood, his legs slightly apart and his body balanced evenly between them. As he looked down at Nairee, his grin was kindly. And something more which she could not define!

"One thing in this world is certain," Mark said. "That is that *nothing* is certain."

"Are you trying to tell me something has gone wrong at The Patch?"

"No, I'm not. Hank Brown is sending two of his stockmen down there till the flood is over?"

"Flood? But the creek has never ever flooded up as far as the home paddocks and the shack."

"And it hasn't flooded that way now. It's the eastern tributaries of Great River that are flooding. The rain out there is twice what it is here. So the 'all precautions' rule has gone out across the north. I was at the creek, and am now here as part of my job, Nairee. It is all a matter of precaution only. I care for the menagerie at The Patch as much as you do."

Nairee was up on her feet and at the door by this time. Mark walked across and held the door so she could not open it.

"Nairee?"

"Yes?"

"I, do have a job to do."

"I know. I'm sorry, Mark. Thank you for bringing Gamma in. I hope Mrs. Lacey won't mind."

"Last seen, Mrs. Lacey was heading for the kitchen to see that Mary and Company were taking suitable care of the latest visitor. And Nairee . . . ?"

"Yes?"

"Regardless of your feelings for me as of this moment . . . if the flooding of inland rivers as well as at Great River continues I just might need your help. Yours and that of every other grown person in the district." His voice was serious.

He still had his hand on the door so she could not open it. He was waiting for a promise, and it had nothing to do with Gamma.

Nairee relented. There was something about his eyes as they looked into hers. They held an expression that did something she could not define. She was legally grown up now. Did that mean things between her and Mark were different? The "play days" gone?

Oh Mark! she thought, I would do anything . . . anything for you. But I wouldn't sacrifice Gamma or the welfare of The Patch to anyone. Anyone at all. You see, I can't. I owe them my everything. I don't belong to anybody, except to Gamma. And to my birds, and to my everything at The Patch.

Even as she stood there returning his gaze, she thought of seeing Mark across the tarmac at Alice Springs and how she had surmised he'd come to meet her—someone of her own! Then he had turned and followed the police posse guarding the little Asian

Prince. He hadn't been there for her at all. Oh Mark! she thought. If you only *knew!* I'm everybody's guest, but nobody's very own. Like "Caroline" written in scroll letters on a grave out there by the boundary . . .

She was a little frightened by her own train of thought.

"What is bothering you now, Nairee?" Mark asked, in a voice that didn't expect an answer. His dark-blue eyes were looking into her face. Then he glanced toward the cedar chest where she had been turning over the old postcards and photographs. He saw the little photograph she had put out on the floor . . . separate from the others.

Nairee's eyes followed him as he took a few steps across the floor and picked up the orphaned card. He looked at it, turned it over and read the name on the back, then looked up quickly at Nairee.

"Where did you get this?" he asked. "Are you worrying about something?"

"I found it," she said. "At the bottom of that pile of old photographs. I think it had been stuck to the elderly lady one—the lady holding the parasol. Did they really carry parasols up here in those days?"

It seemed to Nairee that he breathed out as if he were relieved about something.

"Yes. I guess they carried parasols," he said, slipping the card in amongst the others in the drawer. He straightened up and turned back again to Nairee. She thought he was not only being tidy, but had some other, unspoken reason for hiding Caroline's picture amongst dozens of other cards. "Parasols," he went on, "were the kind of thing those pioneer colonists used in England, before they ever came here. They soon learned that the wide-brimmed Stetson—for the men or ladies —was a better thing in this climate and terrain. You can't ride a cantering horse with safety while holding a dainty umbrella." There was a smile in his eyes now. "For that matter, you can't push your way through the trailing stems of bush trees with one hand out of action trying to shield you from the sun."

Nairee laughed. The atmosphere between them was easier now. "I suppose not," she said.

"And I suppose you've forgotten Gamma," he said with a teasing grin. Nairee's right hand flew to her mouth.

"Oh Mark!" she said. "Whatever am I doing? Please let me get by you? I'll run."

And this she did. She did not once turn back. Had she done so she might have wondered why Mark went to the cedar drawer and sorted through the cards where he had placed "Caroline's" picture. He lifted it out of the pack and slipped it in his side pocket. There was no one there so it did not matter to anybody that, as he walked to the door, he shook his head. Not once but twice, as if something out of place and time had happened. And he was not happy about it.

19

GAMMA WAS ALREADY AT HOME IN THE KITCHEN seated on a chair at the end of the enormous wooden table. A white tea cloth was placed in front of her and Mary was preparing a revivifying cup of tea.

"There you are, old lady!" she said, setting down a plate of buttered scones behind the teacup. She knew Gamma well enough—as everyone did in the district —to know that she did not mind whether they called her old or young. The tea and the scones spoke their own reassuring language.

The wire door flew open and Nairee came running in.

"Oh Gamma!" she said. "I'm so glad Mark brought you. I don't have to worry being away from The Patch now the rain has started. Are you dry? *All* dry?"

Gamma only nodded by way of reply, then lifted first the cup then the largest of the scones to her as Nairee dropped a kiss on her forehead and began patting and feeling the old lady's clothes all over.

Mary burst out laughing. "I've felt her already. She's quite dry. Mark had a scrappy old plastic cover he'd wound round her. I've put her shoes outside the door, and Doreen has gone to fetch her some shoes from the outhouse. They'll be big enough and do for the time being."

Gamma sipped more tea and took another bite of scone. Nairee sat herself down on a kitchen stool by the side wall, clasped her hands round her knees and tossed back the vagrant fringe of hair across her forehead while she sought for words.

"Oh Gamma!" she said at length. "I'm so glad you're here. Did you feed the animals before you came?"

Gamma nodded her head to Mary. "You tell her," she said. What was meant by this was that Gamma had already told the kitchen girls whatever was necessary for all to know, and then returned to her usual taciturn state.

"Seems like she was fixing everything along with Bash from Geko when Mark dropped in. Between them, Bash and Mark fixed that menagerie up. The only unmanageables in Gamma's absence were the two birds—one with a leg in splints and the galah with a damaged wing. And Ratter the kelpie. He's outside and Dean's put a chain on him. He's out of the wet. Bash took the two birds back to Geko with him, and my guess is that it was over Woolarooka's dead body."

"*Not* dead," Gamma said, "Woolarooka's gone for the goats."

"Thank goodness for that." Nairee brushed her lock of hair back again. With great tenderness she removed Gamma's canvas hat from the old lady's head, and hung it on a peg near the fire. Then with her fingers she brushed Gamma's hair into a state of tidiness. During the operation Gamma continued alternately to sip tea and take nibbles from her second scone.

In the midst of these attentions Mrs. Lacey came through the door. She pulled out a chair and sat at the side table by the wall.

"Oh there you are, Gamma," she said in her firm voice. "Dean sent a message that you were here." She looked around the large homey kitchen. It was the biggest room in the house—which said a lot, for other rooms in Beelagur homestead were the largest in any homestead north of Twenty-six. "Where is the Ranger? I understand he brought Gamma in. I'd better thank him, I suppose. The water must be high out that way near The Patch. I've always regarded the Ranger's chief duty was to the birds and animals, and other creatures of the bush."

"That's me," Gamma said. Mary and the kitchen girls tried hard not to laugh. After all, Mrs. Lacey was now present. They had to mind their manners.

"You're the pick of the lot, old lady," Mary said. "So I guess the Ranger had to lift you first."

"Lift?" asked Gamma, puzzled.

"That's what that helicopter does," Mary said. "Lift you up in the air. Over all that drenched land. How was the water, Gamma? All over the land, eh?"

The old lady shook her head. "Everywhere," she said. "Only trees growing out of water. Like a big lake."

Nairee finished refilling Gamma's cup with tea. She was so thankful that Gamma was here, safe from the rising waters, that she had a lump in her throat, and found it difficult to say anything at all.

Now she swallowed.

"May I pour you some tea, Mrs. Lacey?" she asked. "Or shall I make a fresh pot?"

But where is Mark? she said to herself.

"Yes. Thank you, Nairee," Mrs. Lacey said. "I think we might as well have a fresh pot. I'll have it in the dayroom with the Ranger. I think he's out viewing the seascape with Dean. Make the tea in the big pot, there's a good girl. I'll call the men in."

Gamma gave more pleasure than she knew by the delight she showed when taken into the big visitors' room. She had been in other homesteads, notably Hank

Brown's at Geko, but not one as thickly carpeted as Beelagur and certainly not one with a big befrilled double bed. This was a room generally reserved for Mrs. Lacey's more-than-special guests. The ones who came but rarely. The State Governor and his wife who had come twice in the last five years. Once a professor of zoology, and more than once the State Premier. It was now being offered to Gamma because the water outside had risen to the verandah level on the bedroom side of the house. Much more of it, and it would begin to creep in under the outside door and who knew how much higher.

Nairee was a little anxious that Gamma, so used to the four small, tiny rooms at the shack on The Patch, would be overawed. She stayed a few minutes longer than Mrs. Lacey. She wanted to comfort Gamma in case the little old lady was afraid of such vastness. Also to unpack the canvas carryall into which Mark had packed all the clothes and odds and ends that he calculated Gamma would need if her stay was longer than shorter.

"Oh . . . look at this! Look at the flowers on the curtains, Nairee! Where do you suppose flowers like this grow." Gamma was fingering the long ceiling-to-floor cretonne curtains with both wonder and admiration. "I haven't seen such curtains, not even when I was a girl in the coast town."

"They come from England, that's why," Nairee said. "And you haven't ever been in England."

Gamma wrinkled her brow thoughtfully. "No," she said. "I don't think I have, have I?"

Had she? Nairee realized she knew so little of Gamma's background. Where had Gamma come from before she married and set out with her husband to conquer an acre or two of the inland bush? Gamma hadn't minded having no relatives, had she? How she and Gamma both had a background of mystery. If Gamma *did* know Nairee's background, she didn't tell.

Oh bother, bother, bother! Nairee thought as she unpacked Gamma's holdall and placed her folded nightie under one of the pillows on the bed. How tiny Gamma would look in that huge bed!

Why were her own spirits so low now? It must be the rain, which now enveloped all their world. Over at The Patch as well as here at Beelagur. Much more and they would be under water. Mark must have felt that way or he would never have snatched up Gamma and brought her out of the creek lands. It would have had to be a forcible evacuation. Gamma never left The Patch willingly.

Well, Gamma *had* left it now, and nothing disastrous had happened. There she was, bouncing up and down on the edge of the bed, *enjoying* herself.

Had they all been wrong all these years in treating Gamma as someone "different"? All the time there might have been someone fun-loving and gregarious under that shy, mostly silent manner.

After three days and three nights the rain stopped. Just stopped. It was as if someone up there in Heaven had turned on a waterfall with a tap, then turned it off.

Now there was no taking Gamma back to The Patch. The land was flooded. Drowned.

The men came and went from the outstations to the home paddocks and, for food and rest, into the Beelagur kitchen, the verandah enclosure, and even the rear store rooms. There was mud everywhere. Dean's blue-heeler dogs were everywhere too. The sky was an overroof of gray and the station powerhouse had ceased to function, so lamps and candles were everywhere.

The only person who was absent was Mark. He hadn't even stayed overnight the day he had brought Gamma in.

Nairee never remembered feeling sick to her stomach before, but she felt that now Mark had gone. What good could he possibly do out there along the rain forest? Or anywhere else for perhaps a hundred miles. He'd not be able to see anything for the rain.

The next day the rain stopped yet Mark did not come.

Meantime the outstation overseer had rigged up a dummy aerial to connect up the radio with something —anything—in the outside world.

Dean, after much fiddling and juggling with wires and coppercoils in the ceiling was the first with news of the outside world. In Wet, there was no big cyclone off the northwest coast. Except for a small outward-wheeling cyclone, the Indian Ocean had been no more than a whirl of winds. It had been a cyclone off the Queensland coast, a thousand miles away, that was the main cause of inland floods. The consequent disturbance of the air currents had brought the rain to this area of the Outback from the north and west. It was much worse out east. The force of the winds had been so great they had driven the waters of the rivers and their tributaries inland, onward, and westward, flooding all the land; even as far inland as the sand plains, then southwest to and across the northern part of the Simpson Desert.

Alice Springs, in the very center of the Outback, was not spared. The dried out bed of the Todd River was in full flow for the first time in years.

The mighty land was awash. A great inland lake rose across the desert lands and suddenly . . . there was a sea. An inland sea. Rivers and creeks, their courses lost in their swollen currents and vast spillover, could not now be mapped. At Beelagur, the homestead was surrounded by water . . . still swirling slightly and somewhat receded, but threatening nonetheless.

Where—out there in that paralyzing mud sea— was Mark?

Nairee dared not show her concern because in this great unique land there was a rule of life. There had to be or no one would survive. No complaints. No fears. Heads up, chins out and a will to survive and help others to survive.

"The water's down a foot now, Dean," Mrs. Lacey

said on the fourth morning. "Is it time yet to make a dash for Mount Overall?"

"Yep, I'm going out today. I'll take the roan and a packhorse. Roan knows the stony track well enough to find her footing and a way to the high ground. The water will probably be no more than stirrup high along that track. And it's sinking already. The rivers and lakes will be flooded for some time. Possibly weeks.

Through the time of the rain Gamma had sat in the dayroom and played Patience. First with one deck of cards, then another. The humidity had been such that everything one touched was damp. When the second deck of cards lost *their* patience and began quietly to fall apart, Mary fetched her very best "Spring Flowers" deck and insisted Gamma continue her pre-occupation with winning against herself while all else around her was worry and concern.

Nairee sat quietly by, and watched. Gamma certainly was a wizard with those cards!

"Mark Allen will have a busy time," Mrs. Lacey said to Nairee as she came into the dayroom. "The radio is back to normal, thank goodness. He gave his 'honor bright' call, earlier. Seems he's reported into his headquarters. There are several island formations created by the flood. The bush animals have all taken refuge on the higher lands in the lakes. But there is nothing there for them to eat."

Nairee appeared as if she had not heard. She could not speak anyway because of the lump now in her throat. Those poor animals!

This was the first time Mrs. Lacey had spoken of Mark in such a friendly tone. That, too, caught Nairee off her guard.

Mostly Mark had been "that Ranger," and under ordinary circumstances, Mrs. Lacey might have used Mark's radio call "honor bright" as the target of a sarcastic jibe.

"He'll do something about the stranded animals," Nairee said confidently.

Mrs. Lacey poked a wayward strand of hair into place with her index finger. She looked directly into Nairee's eyes as if she, Mrs. Lacey, were considering something.

"Well," she said at last. "He has called for all able-bodied men, and competent horsewomen. They have to take their own mounts, of course. And a substantial tucker bag, rolled rug, and ground rug. The usual outcamp clothes, of course . . ."

Nairee was already on her feet. "That's me," she said decisively, her chin up.

"I didn't like mentioning it," Mrs. Lacey said. "I thought you might feel like this. But don't be too impulsive, Nairee. You have Gamma here . . ."

And Dean and the stockmen would be contribution enough for Beelagur, Nairee thought, then was ashamed of herself. After all, Mrs. Lacey was being kind enough and was more than willing to give Gamma shelter for the duration. And, of course all the Beelagur stockmen would be out with horses, each animal carrying small sacks of rations, their own chaff and bran, and goodness only knew what else of Beelagur's stores. But then so would every station far and wide be doing something likewise.

Nairee wished she was eight again, instead of eighteen. She longed to please Mrs. Lacey and do the right thing in Mrs. Lacey's eyes. Yet she knew, and she knew that Mrs. Lacey also knew, that a "call for rescue" was a command anywhere in the Outback. It was a tradition handed down from the early days of the pioneers, and was not to be denied by any able person in any later generation.

Nairee was already edging toward the door. Then she hesitated. She looked from Mrs. Lacey to Gamma, and saw that Gamma was smiling over the top of her card-filled hand.

"That's my girl!" she said. She looked down at the table and carefully placed the Knave of Hearts under the Queen of Spades, then looked up at Nairee again.

Mrs. Lacey had gone thoughtfully toward the door.

"You wicked old lady!" Nairee whispered laughingly into Gamma's ear. "You're cheating. But you be good while I'm gone." Then standing up straight, she gave Gamma the circled index finger and thumb's signal. She blew her a kiss then followed Mrs. Lacey through the door.

As they walked down the passage Mrs. Lacey touched Nairee's hand.

"I know you knew I didn't really want you to go, Nairee," she said in a troubled voice. "But it is the rule of the country. All hands. We must all obey it. I have to bow to that. But, please Nairee, do take care—"

"I will. Of course I will," Nairee said lightly. Then as she glanced at Mrs. Lacey she swallowed whatever her next words might have been. She had never before seen an expression such as Mrs. Lacey was now wearing. It was not only that Mrs. Lacey was concerned for fear Nairee would do something rash, like get herself cut off from the other people in some backwash. They would all be going out there to the swollen lakes, to the creeks, and even to Great River. But there was something more. Mrs. Lacey looked sad. Even *defeated*. But about what?

Nairee slipped her hand in the crook of Mrs. Lacey's arm.

"I've been out before," she said. "Please, please don't worry. I've been out with the rest of the people to big bushfires . . . and they're ever so much more dangerous than floods. I can swim, and swim well too . . ."

To her surprise there was something of a lump in her own throat as she spoke. She knew Mrs. Lacey was fond of her. Of course she knew that. How could she not know that—when she thought of all the things Mrs. Lacey had done for her over the years. But why now that look of impending tragedy?

Mrs. Lacey had not answered.

"Are you worrying about Gamma?" Nairee asked. "Gamma won't worry. Not one little bit. God made her with the faculty never to worry. If you will let her play with the cards she will keep busy—in between eating and sleeping—all day."

She glanced at Mrs. Lacey again.

"Did you know that once, when a whole bunch of card-playing gambling men were coming through, they ended up by telling Gamma, who never spoke one word to them and won every set of games, that they'd give her a thousand dollars a week to go along with them. Of course, they didn't quite mean that. What those men really meant . . . and they were professionals . . . was that Gamma could cheat better than they could cheat. Oh dear! What am I saying? Gamma's not really a cheat. She just practices it, for fun, but never tells anyone . . . just so she can win at *something . . .*"

They had both stopped in their tracks, dead in the middle of the passage, and stood looking at one another. Then Mrs. Lacey patted Nairee's arm. "Yes, I know, dear," she said. "We all know about Gamma and the cards. She will be quite happy here. It is . . . just . . . It is just that I'm very fond of *you,* Nairee. I wouldn't want anything to happen to *you.* Take care for my sake. *Please* . . . Gamma is a very old woman, you know, Nairee. In a way you really belong to me . . . I mean belong to me, *too.* I mean to everybody up here in the Outback . . ."

The incredible had happened. Mrs. Lacey was fumbling for words. The dignified, sometimes reserved, and almost always aloof lady of Beelagur was pleading. Her eyes, looking into the very depths of Nairee's, were *really pleading*.

Nairee let her hand slip down Mrs. Lacey's arm.

"Of course!" she said. "Of course! But I must go, mustn't I? The call was for 'all out' wasn't it? No able-bodied person can refuse to go. And I'm able. Very able. I can handle any horse. And Dean will give me a good one. I know that. I'll tell him he has to watch out for me—for your—I mean, for Gamma's and your sakes . . ."

Nairee felt awkward. She too was embarrassed. When Mrs. Lacey saw this, she suddenly straightened up, dropped Nairee's hand, and said, "Go along, child. Do your best for the animals. Stay near the Beelagur men. I'll send Dean a message. Blaise, our number-two stockman, is in the kitchen. He'll get your mount for you. And take stores. On your way out to the river let Blaise go in front and I'll tell him to keep a 'tie' on you."

"Yes, thank you! That would be a help." Tying her mount roped to Blaise's would be a farce, she thought. But she would agree to anything Mrs. Lacey asked. She herself was still in a state of puzzlement. Never had she seen Mrs. Lacey look and sound as if she had momentarily "lost her cool." Mrs. Lacey wasn't like that. It wasn't possible. Obviously, there was some deeply hidden reason. But what could it be? What could it *possibly be*? Had something odd happened in the last day and night? Something alarming? But if so—*what?*

Nairee was certain of one thing: Whatever call Mark Allen had sent out, he would not have let alarm creep into his voice. It wasn't in his character to be scared.

Oh Mark! she thought. Oh, the calm and security of Mark!

She went about the business of getting herself into her rain slicker, then finding a rainproof cap from Mrs. Lacey's collection in the cupboard on the side verandah and a pair of riding gloves with the finger sheaths cut off. She thought no more of Gamma and the cards. Nor about Mrs. Lacey. Not even of Dean who, according to Blaise, would come to the junction of Two-way Creek to meet her. She thought about Mark, and about security. And about "honor bright," which was the radio call Mark used to identify himself.

"Oh Mark! Why are you so safe? And why do I

want something safe just this minute? *Honor bright, this girl is coming!*" Yet she longed to see how Dean would take her arrival.

I'm one awfully muddled girl, she thought. Two men! Which one? Oh! bother, bother bother! Think about the marooned animals! That's more important.

Twenty minutes later Mary called out from the kitchen verandah that Blaise, with an extra horse on the rein, was at the verandah rail.

Nairee ran into the dayroom and kissed Gamma lightly on the forehead. "I guess I'll be back in a day. Well, some time!" Nairee said.

"Don't you come back here till all those creatures are safe and sound," Gamma said, not looking up. "If you see Woolarooka, or Mark, ask them how my goats are doing? Did they all come in? Did they behave themselves so they could be got up on the high land?" Never had Gamma said so many words in one go.

"And the horses! Not to mention Hee and Haw, the donkeys," Nairee said lightly. She was sure enough not only of Woolarooka but of Woolarooka's tribesmen who would come down the track and see if all was well at The Patch. If it wasn't well, they'd fix it. This had all happened before, and everyone knew what to do— when and how—when the rains came and made torrents of the tracks and lakes of the creek beds.

20

WITHIN MINUTES, SADDLE BAGS LADEN WITH DOG BIS-
cuits and thermos flasks of hot drinks, Blaise and
Nairee had slipped the tie ropes, wheeled about, and
were pounding through the mud of what, before the
rains, had been the track down past the stables. They
went up the rise, then out onto the track north to the
swollen creek and Great River.

There was no sign of Dean or the other stockmen,
so Nairee assumed all hands had gone to the rescue.
In these situations, only one stockman remained behind at the station to act as guardian and man-of-all-
work, and to help the homestead women if need be.

Though there was still a gray sky above them and
the air was heavy with moisture, it was a good day for
traveling by horseback. Blaise had brought in two
mounts that had a touch of the American quarterhorse
in them, and could go anywhere, anyhow. No mud
could suck down their strong back legs, no fallen trees
could be a barrier. They could round or jump anything at top speed, without endangering the rider.

Neither Nairee nor her escort spoke once they had
shaken their reins and cried, "Go boy go!"

167

The heat and the humidity were distressing, but had to be endured. The keen eyes of the riders told them when to rein in their mounts so the humps of spinifex in the miniature lakes of water across the unseen track did not tear their forelocks.

Nairee and Blaise rode without stopping till they came to the first lookout man at what once, before the flood, was a fork road. He signaled them down.

"You take the left line to Two-way Creek," the lookout shouted at them. "It's under flood water. Mark and his Rangers are out thataway. Dean Lacey's rounding up the fellers coming in from the west."

"How's it going?" Blaise shouted back.

"It's going. But we'll never save everything. So far as we know from the walkie-talkie, every man's out from every station. Some of the women who can ride it are out too. Glad to see you, Nairee. Keep ahead and you'll strike the first lake. It used to be, a day or two back, the Lizard Creek. Bit of an island in the middle of it and the fellers are fetching the animals off it to mainland so they can feed.

"Right. We're on our way," Blaise said. Nairee waved her hand. They were high in water and mud now, but Nairee knew the way. Blaise let her precede him—"So I can fetch you up out of the water if you fall," he remarked, lugubrious as was his nature.

As they neared what had become a big lake they saw that the verges were a network of valleys and ravines. Which way now?

Then they saw someone approaching. Because of the rounded cap pulled down over the rider's eyes Nairee could not see who was coming. Then the cap came off, and the rider called to them.

It was Mark.

" 'Ho," he called. Then as he rode up, he shook his head in a kindly way to Nairee. "I had a hunch you'd come, Nairee," he said. "That is, if the Beelagur lot would let go. Welcome to the flood. Hullo there, Blaise! Thank you for coming along."

He had reined in his horse and now turned in the

saddle to point back in the direction from which he had come.

"There's kangaroos galore caught on that island in the middle over there!" he said. "Along with the wallabies, of course. They won't drown, but they'll die of starvation if we don't get them off. Some of the chaps have made rafts. Blaise, you could lend a hand there for a while. They've brought ropes, and tackle. There are probably more wallabies than we can see at the moment. They're down in the spinifex. There's two aluminum boats brought out from Geko. Hank Brown's running them. You'll have to leave the big euros to the rafts. There's nailtail wallabies along with the sandy wallabies. They're fast and don't want to be rescued, so you'll have your work cut out."

"Right. I'll get down there amongst the fellers right away," Blaise said. He wheeled his horse, and together they ploughed their way through thick mud toward several men who were cutting down tree boughs. Others were roping the boughs into rafts.

Mark swung himself from his horse onto the large humps of rock where Nairee had reined in her mount. He stopped looking and sounding like the official Ranger now. He took Nairee's horse by the chin strap, and looked up at her.

Mark's eyes were glad, yet seemed to be questioning. Looking at him, Nairee had the almost crazy wish to slide off the saddle and into his arms. She flushed because she did not know how to control that something in her. That very strange something. She'd never had this before! Why now?

"Oh Mark!" was all she said, then quickly collected her wits. "It is so sad for the 'roos. We won't be able to save them all, will we?"

"Doubtful. Further back there's a dozen islands. They're formed by the waters of the creek dividing round rock humps and then becoming three and four separate creeks. They're animals caught on every one of them. Reptiles and alligators too . . ."

His questing gaze changed, and he smiled as he

looked up at her. "We won't put you amongst the alligators," he said. "They take knowing. Ever tickled one of those things? Or a crocodile, for that matter?"

"No. But I do know that experienced hunters go amongst them unharmed. Have we got any of those men along with us?"

"Not yet. But they're coming out by helicopter. We'll leave those fellers to them. Experience is more valuable than any amount of courage."

"Can I come down, Mark. Here? I mean. What is the depth of water. I've my waterproof boots on. . . ."

"When you go to Beelagur you go all prepared?" he asked lightly.

"Well, actually Beelagur is rigged for any emergency. The boots are always there. They're not really mine."

"Everything waiting for you?" There was a curious note in his voice, and an inquiring look in his face.

"Well, yes. I mean . . . well, why not? Beelagur is always rigged for any visitor, and any emergency. It is a very well-equipped station."

He held up both arms as if to lift down a child.

Nairee swung her right foot over the saddle, leaned on the left foot, and came down into his arms. She was a little bit embarrassed. But not Mark. His eyes were laughing at her.

"Featherweight. Like a child," he said.

"Is that what you think I am! A child?"

"Sometimes," he said. His smile became broader. He patted her on the back. "A nice one, though."

Blaise was scraping the mud from his boots on a sharp-edged rock.

"Come on, you two," he said, not looking up from his boot-scraping. "What are we here for? Operation Noah, or sweethearting?"

Nairee said, "Operation Noah," too quickly. Mark turned back to his own horse.

"Follow me," he called over his shoulder. He gave his mount a slight kick with the heel of his boot. "Step your mounts in this one's hoofsteps. That way, you'll keep from begging."

The "moment"—if it was that—was gone. Like puffs of down in a gentle wind.

They set off in single file. Every now and again one horse or another slipped a hoof on the scattered flat wet stones that once had been a track. The heat and humidity enveloped them again. It was like a turkish bath.

As they came through to the clearing on the verge of the first newly made creek flood, Nairee was appalled at what she saw. Before her was a wide sweep of swirling water. Old legs and fallen tree boughs jammed the irregular bays of this new lake. One-time creatures of the bush floated downstream, lifeless. Round one tree that was still standing a few feet out from the bank, the water swirled and eddied. At the east end of a flood-made bay were two aluminum rescue boats, and a flood tractor. Even as they rode up, the flood tractor moved off. Two men in one of the boats started to cross the swirling water to an island of heaped-up dead tree debris and a flat-topped outcrop of dull red rock. Further upwater were dying trees, their foliage drooping in the water. On the nearest point of the island one of Hank Brown's men was in the act of catching a euro with a net.

Another man Nairee recognized was a well-known dogger. He was in full chase after something brown and fast. It had to be a dingo.

"Oh spare him!" Nairee almost cried. "He's an animal too—"

Blaise shook his head. "The dogger's probably been after that same dingo for half the season. He's not likely to have any mercy now."

"Mark?" Nairee pleaded.

He shook his head. "The dingo or the sheep?" he said. "The dingo doesn't eat everything he kills, you know. Kills for the love of it."

"Yes, I know," Nairee's voice was so low Mark did not hear her. She went on praying the dogger's shotgun was too wet to function. The dingo reached out of sight between two high flame-colored ironstone rocks that stood side by side at the head of a rock tumble from the mesa tops.

There were sounds of men coming from all over the flood-made island.

They didn't have to keep as quiet as in a normal dry-time hunt. They made the strangest noises shooing the smaller marsupials toward the nets.

"If we leave them there, they'll starve," Blaise commented. "When the creek goes down we'd get nothing but carcasses floating down, and fouling first Two-way Creek, then the Great River."

They tethered their horses, and all three, laden with the food packages from the saddlebags, were ploughing their way across drier patches toward the main camp standing on a hump of higher ground, just a hundred yards this side of the main water stream.

"Your job is to light a fire if you can, Nairee," Mark said. "Your best chance of finding dry enough brush is if you hunt under those overhanging rocks by the far cliff edge. Look out for big lizards. Make a fire large enough to dry off more wood, especially the short pieces. We'll need them for a campfire tonight. Right?"

"Right," Nairee answered. But she was disappointed. She had wanted to do what the men were doing: save animals. The men ought to be able to feed themselves. However Mark was the boss and each had to get on with his or her allotted job. "They also serve who only cook and wait."

Blaise took her mount along with him to tether it beside his horse on a small dry, upland some hundred yards south of the end wall of the mesa.

With as good a will as she could muster Nairee set to work to make the best wet-weather fire ever. First she made a cavelet of rock, then gathered stones to construct a wind tunnel leading to it. Then came the stacking of small twig wood, and bigger logs just above the wind tunnel. Then she added bark and bigger lumps of wood on top of that. A dangerous fire this, in dry weather, she thought. But not in the Wet. She hunted around for flat plates of rock, and as soon as she had made a circular flat area around the fire-to-be with them, she collected all available pieces of bark from the inside bark shield of sapling trees. She set these on the flat stones to dry out entirely and so make coals to feed the small wind tunnel. This last would warm and dry out the back and sticks. These in turn would then dry out the smaller pieces of wood. After adding the larger wood, she would finally have made a first-class bushman's campfire.

There was no early blaze, but small warmth begat more warmth which passed up to the bigger pieces. These led to the small logs, and so to a classic campfire.

Nairee stood over it and rubbed her hands with pleasure.

She had seen this done by bushmen before. Now she had done it for herself!

How did I come to remember how it was done? she asked herself, then answered the question: That's what comes of being born in this land—one just *knows!*

This thought led to another: How do I know I was born in this land? Maybe I wasn't born here at all?

But I was! That little circle of stones with the stone in the middle! According to the aborigines, that small spot was *her* spirit land. Out of the spirit land a child was born. The aborigines believed that. Woolarooka had told her. But it wasn't true for white people, was it? Or was it?

Nairee brushed the back of her hand across her eyes. There's always more smoke with damp wood than with dry, she thought.

But there was not anything that could damp down forever those old, nagging question: Who am I? Where did I come from? For no reason at all, she thought of "Caroline." That "grave" with the circle of stones and a stone in the middle. Why was Caroline's "spirit" token the same as her own? What had she to do with Caroline? That postcard photograph from Caroline was forty years old! The postmark said so.

Heavy boots were clamping through the bush. Nairee turned and looked at the man coming toward her. It was Bash from Geko.

"Brought some beef from Hank," he said, unrolling a piece of canvas and letting huge thick slices of beef make a pile of themselves on a flat rock surface. "Have got another lot in my back saddlebag," he added. "Enough to keep us all going till Hank gets here. Back at Geko he's having all hell bringing the cattle into the homestead paddock. Water's nine inches deep thereabouts. But good news. Guess what?"

His grin was endearing.

"The water's going down," Nairee said with a laugh.

"You bet it is. Those flaming stockmen round our place started screaming mad at the cattle, and the water took fright. Won't be more'n two inches by to-morrow. Guess who's comin' up the east track faster than a bunyip?"

"Hank!" Nairee said.

"Easy seen you're a newcomer to this here rescue operation. Hank's been out since daylight. Worse'n him—the one coming along any minute now. Expects the best cut of beef; he never had anything but the world's best in all his life!"

"You wouldn't be talking about Dean Lacey, would you?" Nairee asked, looking balefully at Bash through the strands of hair that had fallen across her eyes.

"Who else? You wouldn't be falling for him or anything like that, would you Nairee?"

"Why not?" Nairee said, just to be prickly.

The fire was crackling now so she didn't hear the moccasin tread of Mark the Ranger as he came through the bush from the direction of the lake.

"Why not indeed?" said Mark, not quite as lightly as he intended. "But it's fire and food we're mostly concerned about this minute. Glad to see you, Bash. We've taken off a dozen kangaroos and as many wallabies. We'll have to give up at sundown. Can you be here at daylight? We need all extra hands available."

"I'm here right now," Bash said, "and I stay. I brought you beef."

"Marvelous," Mark said. "I'll give you a hand to grill it, Nairee. The men are just about done for this day. I'll call them off—" He half swung away, then turned back to Nairee. "Dean Lacey has his own men out on one of the other islands. I think they've rations of their own. He sent a message up they'd make their own campfire.

"That will help!" Nairee said, mostly because she couldn't think of anything more natural to say.

"You've been a guest up at Beelagur," Mark went on, kicking the first of the coals together in the fire. "Do you think you should join his lot? They've probably brought provisions for you too."

Nairee stared into the tree leafery because she did not know what to say. Why was she at a loss when with Mark? Or when she was with Dean, for that matter?

Bash saved the day for her.

"Well, seeing she's made a real bushman's job of this fire I reckon she ought to be allowed to enjoy it," he said. "What's more important, Hank singled out the best cut of this here beef for her, himself. 'Bash, old fella!' he said. 'Give that there particular piece to Nairee with my love. Tell her I'll see her come morning. And tell her, 'Take care an' keep safe.' All that he did indeed say, Mark. Not a word wrong—"

Nairee laughed, and her sad shyness went skyward with the curls of smoke rising from her very own fire.

"Bash darling!" she said. "You tell lies. But such nice ones. Thank you."

Mark smiled now as he kicked more bark into the fire.

"Keep the fire at coals later, will you, Nairee?" he said. "The large black bucket over by the men's pack saddles is half full of salt beef. We'll put it to cook slowly most of the night. Right?"

"Right!" Nairee said. Salt beef wasn't as bad as it sounded. It was local slang for corned beef and could be as delicious as any other. A big hunk just had to simmer slowly for four or five hours.

Mark took his horse by the chin strap and led him off toward the thicker bush. He was about to "count the catch" and call the men in for tea. As Dean Lacey came along the side track they stopped to talk for a few minutes. Nairee forgot what she was supposed to be doing as she too stopped work, and stood looking at them.

Dean slid off his horse and was facing Mark as they talked. Mark, ever vigilant, kept glancing this way and that, as if waiting for someone to arrive. Or the sight of some lone and frightened animal on the run.

Dean was just slightly taller than Mark. Nairee had noticed that, aad folded the knowledge away in the library of her mind, a year or two ago. An inch perhaps? She wished Mark was the taller of the two. What did it matter? Then as the two men finished their conversation, Dean turned and sprang up on his horse again. He wheeled around a tree, splashing as he went through several inches of mud and water. He galloped off through the bush without turning his head. Nairee watched him as he went. He was a magnificent horseman.

Where was he going? And why didn't he wave his hand? Well, why should he? After all, he'd seen her in his own homestead not so many hours before!

Mark walked back along the path in his slow balanced bushman's gait. He mounted his horse, then without a wave of his hand or a last word of cheer, he walked his horse away through the heavy slush toward "the lake." He was deep in thought. What had he and Dean said to one another? For the first time Nairee wondered why she seemed almost, not consciously, to compare the two men.

21

❧❧❧❧❧❧❧❧❧

ROUND THE CAMPFIRE, WHEN THE REST OF THE RES-
cue party came in, the men talked about the riskiness
of the new land forms.

What they now called "the lake" had been, before
flooding, a long wide dip in the land. The island upon
which so many bush animals were marooned was in
normal times a hillock to which the land quietly swept
up, uninterrupted by anything but a narrow creek bed.
Sometimes there was water in that creek, but sometimes when there had been too harsh a "Dry," it was
bare. Rounded ironstone rocks were its pebbles.

The creek would normally be similar to the one below the paddock at The Patch. There was a web of
such creeks all over this part of the land below the
mesa range. They had little water in them, except in
the Wet. They overflowed their banks only when
Great River flooded downstream. The river held back,
then later pushed onward across the land, the waters
flooding in from a hundred creeklets webbing the
down side of the moutains to the east.

This evening the older of the men were full of stories, mostly anecdotes of previous floods. The women —besides Nairee there were two others, both from Hank Brown's station—helped with the grilling and serving of the huge thick slabs of prime beef. Later they went about setting up a kind of camp with the leather-lined ground rugs for those tired enough to snatch some sleep in the eerie silence and stillness of the Australian night.

Somewhere back toward the mesas, Dean Lacey's men had set up their own camp.

"No women around for us," they had said. One had dared a further remark that earned him a tree nut fair and square on his head. "Keep the women away after sundown," he had said. "They dream out aloud."

Blaise, the Beelaguur stockman who had brought Nairee out with him, also defected. He whispered to Nairee as he took off, "Gotta keep sweet with the boss, luv. I kinda belong to Dean's camp—willy-nilly."

"Of course!" Nairee said. "Sleep well, Blaise. I'll see you in the morning. It'll be cold salt beef for breakfast, but well cooked by then." He blew her a kiss, then followed Dean and the rest of the Beelagur party into the dark trees.

Watching him go, Nairee had the feeling of being a castaway. Or was it deserted? She was temporarily attached to Beelagur. She was their guest. Or was she? Shouldn't she be with them? To which party did she belong? "To whom do I ever belong?" she asked, more of herself than of others.

From across the dying coals of the fire, Mark caught the shadows in her face. He caught her softly spoken words too.

"You belong to me, Nairee," he said lightly. "I'm boss here. Right?"

"Fight you for her," said Bash, also awake and listening. "No Nairee, means no breakfast for any of us. Best camp-maker in the Outback."

Mark and Bash jestingly made shadow punches at one another across the dying coals.

"Nice to be you, Nairee," Gertie Evans, housekeeper from Geko, said. "Seems like you belong to all of us."

How kind they were! These bush world people were her people. Why did she worry? Or was she only *wondering*. Something quite different!

The darkness came down quickly as it always did in that tropical land. The coals from the fire were dampened down. The under rocks and the ground under the fire would stay warm for some hours yet —the big pot of salt beef had been set on the center rocks where the warmth would keep it simmering for hours.

It had been a hard day for the rescuers, and for the latest arrivals as well. Each and all rolled themselves in their ground rugs and soon lay sleeping. They were not unlike the tree logs which the monsoons of yester year had broken from the trees and left lying on the ground in a crazy desolate pattern. Right now, it would have been hard to distinguish which was log and which was a human being had some visitor from Mars dropped by to take a look at this part of Planet Earth.

Yet, for all the trials of the flood it was a perfect night now: silence except for the occasional drop of a nut or slither of some creature on a night errand.

Sometime in the night a stranger did come by the now-deadened fire and the quiet sleepfulness of the party. Stakes sharpened by bush knives had been driven into the ground, and mosquito nets had been set up to shroud the sleepers. All of them out in the wilderness this night had had previous experiences of damp humid camps. Mosquito netting was a must. Cicadas came out along with the haziness of the no-longer-hidden moon. They played their continuous clicking rhythms uninterrupted through most of the night. But the sleepers slept the sleep of the just, and of the very tired. Except one: Mark Allen did not more than doze lightly. Having spent all his adult life ranging the broadlands, the high hill mesa country, and the rock-strewn ground floor hereabouts, he slept with one ear tuned to the night sounds of the bush and one eye not quite closed.

Mark always knew, once he was in the bush, be it day or night, just exactly what its animal inhabitants were doing. Which creatures were asleep, like the birds on tree boughs and in tree forks, and which animals were, quite naturally, on the prowl. A frightened cry of pain in the night, and Mark knew that brer dingo was abroad—killing more than he really needed for sustenance. Killing for the sake of killing.

On those occasions, come morning, and the washing and eating chores over, Mark would take his gun, and then traveling on foot, would not give up till he found that killer dingo.

Only a very experienced and cunning tracker could find a killer dingo. Mark was both experienced and cunning.

On this particular night, Mark woke from his half-sleep when his listening ear had heard *something*. Or was it someone creeping round and about the bush? For quite a while he lay with his eyes open but did not stir. But he *listened*.

No dingo this time, but the crack of a stick, the pad of a horse. Then the slow slither of a body to the ground. Two steps taken by that human being, and Mark *knew*. All else around were sleeping soundly so he spoke softly. No need as yet to waken anybody, least of all the women, and Nairee.

"What the hell are you up to, Woolie?" he asked. His voice was just loud enough to carry the short distance to be heard by Woolarooka.

Woolie, for it was Woolarooka all right, came to the Ranger's ground roll.

"That you, Mark, eh?" she whispered. "Gamma, she all right up there at Beelagur. But where you put Nairee?"

She sat down cross-legged as Mark unrolled himself and sat up.

"Over there. That pair away toward the big tree.

What you want Nairee for? Something gone wrong at The Patch?"

"No, everything are right and good. Maybe I didn't know which one was at Beelagur, and which one be here, eh?"

"You knew all right, Woolie. What's worrying you anyway? What's it matter who is where?"

"When Nairee go to Beelagur I go along sometime, maybe little time. Jes' to make sure. That all ri', eh? First I went, then the blackfellas tell me the big storm coming so I better go back to Patch and see about ol' Gamma. Then Gamma come up Beelagur. So what I do, eh? You tell me, Mark. What I do? Dean Lacey, he gone down here alonga you-all. I don't like it. I gotta keep watch. You know all about Caroline, eh Mark?"

He was sitting up by this time, so he took a packet of cigarettes and matches from his pocket. He lit up, then blew little rings.

"Here, have a cigarette, Woolie. You watch that smoke too. One blowout and it's gone with the wind. Like Caroline. You can't call the smoke back, and you can't call Caroline back."

"Yeah," Woolarooka said slowly. Then she took a cigarette and lit it. She blew the smoke through her nose in a long stream. "Like you say, Mark. Gone with tha' wind, eh? Only there ain't any wind tonight. And Dean Lacey—he's up around somewhere. You can't go blow him away, Mark. Him and Nairee both here in the dark. Sometime before up there at Beelagur, she look and look at him. At Geko that time of the party too. I think maybe she like him pretty much, eh?"

Mark was thoughtful. He looked now at the dead coals of the fire, and he drew on his cigarette. He again blew out little rings of smoke.

Suddenly he was just a little irritated by Woolarooka, even though he had always been grateful for Woolarooka's devotion to Nairee and old Gamma. She was a godsend all round when it was a matter of keeping an eye on The Patch. Mrs. Gray, the social worker from across the state border had said long ago, to both his

father and separately to him that the welfare department would never have allowed Gamma to be there
alone if it had not been for Woolarooka.

But what now with Nairee?

And Dean Lacey! He stubbed his cigarette out and
threw the butt amongst the dead coals of the fire.

If he didn't want problems on his hands in the middle
of Operation Noah he had to do something about
Woolarooka. But what?

"What name you give the milk cow back there at
The Patch, Woolie?" he asked.

"Ah, that one name Pele. She's greedy, that one.
Another one coming on that name Paldi. She come on
good bime-by."

"For crying out loud," Mark said. "Pele and Paldi at
The Patch. Seems like the place is taken up with p's."
Woolarooka was sure she understood what he meant,
but experience advised her to pretend not. She loved
this Mark almost as she loved Nairee. But she knew
he had the 'all-seeing eye' when it came to things and
beings in the bush. Life was much easier if she just
played along pretending not to understand. Me and old
Gamma, she thought, we're a pretty good pair when
it comes to hearing and seeing all, but not blinking our
eyes, not saying anything.

Mark's smile was suddenly endearing, and sadly
Woolarooka admitted he probably was reading her
thoughts just as he read the lay of the land, the curve of
the tree leaves long before even the weatherman could
foretell the coming of a cyclone.

"Hobble that nag of yours, Woolie, and come and
camp down the other side of the fire." He heaved himself up from his blanket and thumped off toward the
tree by which the men had bundled the ground rugs.
Those not already taken were in one pile, neatly
stacked under one very large waterproof cover.

He heaved out a rug and carried it over to where
Nairee was sleeping. He unrolled it within a few feet
of Nairee.

"You brought a rug up there on your horse, Woolie?

Good! Well, bring it over here, and doss down. Brer dingo is out and about tonight, but even he won't dare near the camp while you keep watch. Okay?"

"Okay, Mark, but I are not afraid of any dingo taking a walk round this way. All he do is run for the rocks. It's that other fella. . . ."

"Name no names, Woolie. Everyone lying about might be shut-eye, but that doesn't say they each and all have plugs in their ears. Now *scram*. I want some more sleep myself."

Light-footed though Mark could be he was not as silent as Woolarooka. "G'night Woolie," Mark said softly from his distance. "Thank you for coming. I'm glad you're here, but get back to The Patch in the morning. There's animals and birds there that'll need feeding."

"Okay, boss," Woolarooka said sleepily. "S'long as I know you got Nairee up this way and she's not down the bush with that other lot."

Mark snorted to that. He had had no sleep the night before. He'd been rounding up the rescue volunteers, then up again with the first glimmer of daylight. What bothered him most was not Woolarooka's fears for Nairee. It was that there were still animals on the "island" in the lake, waiting to be rescued. Especially the euros. Several euros were there to his knowledge. They'd have to be brought off . . . if only for the sake of the future kangaroo population thereabouts. No males and there'd be no new kangas.

There just wasn't time to think of the wallabies, the dingos, cats, wild goats, and lost wild cattle; lizards, snakes, and all things that crawled. It was hopeless to save all. But men, boys, and now some women all must work at doing their best to save them. Chasing them into nets was the only way. A sixth sense told him that that water was receding. But too slowly to suit him. Even now, in the dark of night, the heat was barely endurable.

He had to plan ahead for the morning. At first gray glimmer of daybreak, breakfast for all. If one or another of the boys were awake before him he hoped to goodness they'd remember to build a campfire in an already made crater so that breakfast for all would be over and done with quickly. The huge milk buckets acting as billies must be washed and washed again, the first lot of boiling water thrown out; then a sluicing and water for the camp tea. The women knew to be extra particular about that. An outbreak of fever would be a fear in everyone's mind. Nairee's job would be to throw more of those steaks on the hot grilling rocks.

Sleep would not come. His thoughts were crowding sleep out.

Why the hell had Dean Lacey decided to take his men and camp away from the main camp? Still being the early pioneer! Never keep all your men together in one posse. Raiders in the night had spears. Those days were dead and long gone, but somehow the Laceys never forgot.

His mind went on and on. There was so much to think about in the morning. It was not only the rescue of the animals that needed organization. There was the organizing of people and the camp. All had to work in threes; no one ot get out of sight of at least two others. The danger was, of course, not of other people, but of becoming lost.

Why in Heaven's name had Dean Lacey taken it on himself to split up the party. One party was more efficient. Manageable!

All around him were the sound of people sleeping, softly or noisily, according to their individual habits. That rhythmic snore beyond the baob tree had to be Bash. He had his own resonant way of snoring.

꙰꙰꙰꙰꙰꙰꙰꙰꙰

MARK SAT UP SUDDENLY, VERY WIDE AWAKE. HE'D heard a sound. Footsteps in the bush approaching quietly accompanied by an occasional tiny crack of a dried stick when a boot stepped on it.

Very very deftly and silently Mark lifted himself first to a sitting position, then a standing one. He was so silent and smooth about it even Woolarooka, a natural gifted bushwoman, had not heard him. Boots off so he would not make the mistake the intruder had made by stepping with hard leather on a stick.

Mark slid away, no more than a shadow, but one choosing other shadows, to shield him. He leaned, straight and tall on the bottle-shaped trunk of the baob tree. He was too good a bushman not to realize whose that was. A streak of light from a moon four-fifths hidden by thunder clouds, threw the intruder into relief against the bush.

Another shadow, silent as only a bush aboriginal could be, slowly stood up from the ground rug on the other side of the campsite. Mark, shielded from the frail moonlight now filtering past the storm cloud, stayed statue-still. Woolarooka would handle this one, he knew.

For it was Woolarooka. A shadow herself now, she moved round in a half-circle, and came up alongside the intruder who had not known she was there till she touched him on the arm.

Quite clearly and somewhat noisily he started.

"What the hell . . . ?" It was Dean Lacey's voice.

"You come up here and wake up alla people," Woolarooka said. "What you want, eh? Wollarooka fix it alla same, awright for you, eh? You want cuppa tea? Some in thermos—"

"Get away with you!" Dean said, not quietly. "I came up to see if Nairee was properly camped down. She is staying at Beelagur and is in my charge."

"Okay at Beelagur," Woolarooka said with a comforting tone in her voice. "Maybe up here near lake. Nairee alla same belonga Mark's camp, eh? He look after her pretty good like when some other time she goes camp with him longa bushfire time."

"Camp with him?" Dean was startled out of his whisper and his voice carried to the boab tree.

Mark, in fact, thought it was about time he emerged from his listening post. He walked quite naturally now as he moved toward Dean.

"You wanting something, Dean?" he asked.

"Yes," Dean said in his most station-owning voice. "Nairee is our guest at Beelagur. I have a responsibility—"

"Of course you have," Mark said pleasantly. Woolarooka's keen ear told her Mark was angry, but that just as he was hiding this same anger, Dean was too aloof and self-absorbed to detect it. She pretended to be surprised at Mark's shadowy appearance from the other side of the boab tree. She had known where he was all the time.

"You there Mark, eh?" she said, still very softly. "You bin look after Nairee okay, eh?"

"I look after all my campers," Mark said bluntly. "Including Nairee." If there had been light enough an onlooker might have detected a bright anger in Mark's eyes. He understood very well what was on Dean's mind. "There are two other women here, and if Nairee or anyone else is wanting for attention there are people of both sexes sleeping on either side of the campfire."

"Exactly," Dean said. "They would all know my position as to *responsibility*—'"

Hank Brown's head emerged from the shadows of his rug.

"Oh come off it, Dean!" he said. As a fellow station owner—though not of such an illustrious property as Dean—he could speak to him as an equal.

"You there, Hank?" Dean said evenly. "I did not see you earlier. This changes things if you are around—"

Nairee was well awake by now. She lay on her ground sheet without stirring. She had overheard the conversation and was now lying puzzled as to why so many people seemed to be concerned as to which campfire she slept by. She knew that Woolarooka was bedded only a few feet from her. And that there was Mark and then now Dean talking almost as if they had proprietorial rights over her. In one way it was an engaging thought. She wasn't only Gamma's "nobody" and Woolarooka's "care," after all. Two men! Wow!

She was somebody in her own right because the grass kings of the outback were arguing over their rights to watch over her. Even dear old Hank Brown had put in a stake. That made three. Better and better! Hank sounded as if he were all for Mark being in command. And not Dean.

Mark was the National Ranger anyway, wasn't he? Woolarooka touched Nairee's arm.

"You wake up, eh Nairee?" she said in a whisper.

"Yes, Woolie. Why are they arguing about me?"

"You are lucky, Nairee. Three fellas . . ." Then she dropped her voice. "I think I go'n' see what's all about," she said.

A minute later she was near enough to the men to

overhear them. But she was not sharp enough for Mark. He too had the bushman's listening ear.

"Woolie . . . clear out! Or else!" he said.

"What you say all about Nairee?" she demanded, glowering balefully at Dean. It was too dark for him to read her face.

"All I want is peace and a good night's sleep in this camp," he said very weary. "For Heaven's sake go back to your rugs, both of you. Woolarooka, if you can't sleep peacefully here, take yourself off to Dean's camp." He paused, then added, "Dean's just departing that way himself. He'll guide you."

This did not fool Woolarooka. She knew as well as Mark himself that she was quite capable of finding her way anywhere in the bush, possibly even better than the two men now standing as black shadows by the baob tree.

"You fella want to argue, and me not here to know?" she asked cheekily. "All about that girl Nairee. Why don't leave her quiet with me, eh?"

Dark though it was, she knew that Hank Brown, leaning up from his rug on his elbows, was taking in every word. One or two of the other men lying in rugs rolled here and there about the campsite were now also sitting up.

"For goodness sake," one of them said. "Can't you all get to sleep! What goes? Everyone's awake and noisy. And at this hour—"

"Some girl keeping you awake? Eh, Dean?" another said.

There was sudden silence. It was against the law of the bush to talk about women when women were nearby. The two Geko ladies were asleep. Only Nairee and Woolarooka were awake. But that was enough for Dean.

"Get yourself out of that rug, Nairee," Dean said, his voice full of authority. "I don't like you sleeping here without proper arrangements for privacy. Hurry up. I'll take you to my camp."

Mark did not say a word. Instead he walked around

what had earlier been the camfire. He stopped over
Nairee and drew her up to standing position, his
hands holding her shoulders steady as she kicked
away the ground rug.

She stood absolutely silent, for almost a minute.
All those who were awake listened too—in silence.

She did not comprehend the nuances of this silence,
while all waited for her answer.

No one thought of the foolishness of the moment.
Here was a rescuers' camp by a flooded river, on a
barely moonlit night. A young girl was almost on the
brink of taking the wrong turn at a two-way junction
into the shadows. Into the bush?

Mark or Dean? Dean or Mark?

Why had she to get up and go anywhere, anyway?

Yet beneath these layers of conscious talk a little
wakeful night bird was singing in her heart.

Dean or Mark? Mark or Dean? Which? But they
both cared, didn't they? She was at what might be a
crossroads in her life, yet did not quite comprehend it.

At college, other girls—or young women, as they
were called by the lecturers—often talked about their
prospective dance partners, and whether they were
drawn more to this one than that. Nairee had listened with just that little spark of envy of any girl who
might have *two* partners about which she might ex-
press a preference. She herself had had a relatively
happy time, that was true, but her heart was in her
home and her home was in the far northwest of the
great Outback. So she didn't have to make choices.
She had had a mild and titillating hero worship for
Dean Lacey because he was very handsome, especially
on horseback. He was truly a great horseman. For
Mark she had had a real love—of the well-known
comradely-next-door-neighbor type. Or was it something else? She wasn't sure because now she was
eighteen and grown up, and had only a hollow in her
heart. A sort of empty space.

Yet suddenly, in the middle of a flooded land,

shadowed and shrouded by the inimical bush, and hushed by the stillness of night, she was discovering she was important to two men. She admired one and loved the other. So what did that mean? What did that give her? The exalted feeling of being argued over—by *two* quite outstanding men. She felt as if she had been awakened by a blow on the head. But not by a stick. It was Woolarooka, and a gum nut.

"Look, you lie down and go to sleep, Nairee," Woolarooka was saying.

But a new Nairee had been born that minute.

"Not on your life," she said clearly. Then being in a certain cloud-happy way, she overlooked the meaning of her words as she added, "Which will I sleep with, Woolie. Mark or Dean?"

She didn't really know how loudly she had spoken, and was not conscious that she had neglected to add, "in whose *camp*."

Only on the top of a snow-clad mountain and in the heart of the great Australian bush when the floods had stilled, could there be *such a silence* as fell on that campsite at that moment.

It took Woolarooka's fierce pinch, together with at least thirty seconds, before Nairee woke up from her trance, and realized what she had said.

No one, of course, could see the deep red flush that dyed her face; her throat, arms, the small of her back too.

Hank Brown and his offsider simultaneously came to her rescue, Hank from a few yards off the other side of the now-deadening fire, Bash from further along but on the same side as where Mark was standing—a statue, it seemed.

"To hell with either of them," Hank said lightly, joking too. "Come over here by Gertie, Nairee, and bring that darn fool Woolie with you. Move out there, Bash. All the ladies along this side. Fetch the ground rugs when you've finished gawping—and though I can't see it, I know that's what you're doing. Mark, old man . . . move off a step or two, will you? I need a bit more space for Nairee's rug. Can't have her on those flaming coals. It'd only take a kick or two in her sleep to bring them into flame again.

In his busyness, Hank had by this time got himself close to Dean.

"Clear out, you blithering fool," he said to the master of Beelagur. "Meantime, forget it—"

"Forget it?" Dean said. He actually was grateful to Hank for taking over the situation. He himself was for the moment at a loss. He knew quite well that Nairee had not meant what her words had said. He also knew "campfire talk" when men of the bush were far from the station yard.

Forty-eight hours and Nairee's question would have become an offer. The impossible had happened. The Master of Beelagur and the well-loved Nairee of The Patch would become the objects of prying questions, and the subject of casual chatterers.

As for Mark . . . , Dean thought. Well to hell with him. The Bush Ranger was not an owner of several million acres. It would be interesting to know how many of the rescuers, rolled in their rugs like logs here and there near the campsite, heard, and how many who would hear about it later.

Dean delibereately stopped thoughts of Nairee and was now contemplating the delegation of responsibility between him and Mark. In any Outback area one or another of the top station men always—and in the course of things—took a leadership role when the Outbackers had to wrestle with the elements, hard times, and other dangers. Lost travelers, dingos, wild men, and storms and drought. All had been attended to by him—Dean Lacey. Men expected it. Damn it all! He had had to risk his life now and again in some bushfire terror. And flood fear—he'd thought nothing of it. The men of this part of the Outback expected it of him. When one owned major property in a district, then one had a sense of responsibility for the well-being of the whole district. The Ranger's job was to look after the creatures—snakes, kangaroos, and wallabies.

These last ate out the grasses anyway, and so menaced the well-being of cattle—each unit of which was worth money. Big money, if the grass season had been a good one.

The situation had lost its origins and Dean Lacey had forgotten—in his thoughts of pride of place—that Nairee had said something bordering on the foolish.

While Dean had this rush of thoughts concerning himself and his own prestige among the campers, Mark stood in complete silence, his weight divided evenly between his legs, his arms folded. His eyes were cold stones.

There was a long silence during which no one moved—not those still rolled in the rugs on the ground, nor those standing.

It occurred to Hank Brown, who was as bush-canny as any one of them, that by some Ranger strategy, some extrasensory powers, Mark was actually controlling the silence. Hank knew only too well that the Ranger had to have, or train himself to have, those extrasensory powers that informed him where and why some bush animal, or a human being, was lost or in trouble. *What* was that cry in the night that came from the broken rock-glowing ridges of old mountain ranges? *Whose* was that desperate call from across the flatlands dotted by hundreds of anthills, some three to six feet in height? *Who* was screened from view behind those termite castles?

The Ranger had to know it all. His job was to rescue and save those in need. Unconsciously Mark carried his acquired gifts of insight over into his ordinary civilized contacts.

In a moment, Hank Brown knew, the silence would break and Mark would move. He had to do *something*. It was necessary. One of the two protagonists —Dean Lacey or Mark—had to establish his leadership. Once and for all. There was the little matter of facesaving too.

Nairee unthinkingly had triggered them off through

no deliberate fault of her own. This situation had been brewing for years. Ever since Nairee had begun to grow up. Which of them was to stand guardian over the girl? And why? Did either of them really know why it was important? Hank knew. Gamma knew. Old Sergeant Allen, the Outback policeman, knew.

The only eligible girl in the near part of the district, with a stigma to her name?

Hank would have shaken his head if someone nearby had suggested such a thing.

"No!" he would have said, and was now saying to himself. "There's a lot more to it than that!" But Hank Brown would never tell. "Not on your life! Never!" He was actually talking to himself. When Mark made a move Hank silenced his thoughts.

"Nairee," Mark said. "You do understand? We need you in the morning at first daylight? Can you make it? Make up the campfire too? What about the salt beef? It's tricky to cut up. Needs that extra long sharp knife in the tool box . . . You've done it before, of course . . . when we've all been in camp . . . ?"

Hank Brown, safe in the darkness, was really smiling now.

Clever! he thought. Getting the girl in on a "duty call." Making a thing about being needed in camp. Wiping out the way the poor girl had put it . . .

He threw a nut with Hank Brown expertise and it just touched Gertie's ear. The moon, still pale and sickly, glanced a shaft of light through a hole in the dark rain cloud. Hank saw Gertie turn her head toward him. Maybe she was a mind-reader too.

"Nairee, pull your ground rug up and come and sleep alongside me," Gertie said, very bossy and not to be denied. "That way we'll wake one another, and be up the same time. Before daylight I reckon, but we can get a twig fire going to light up for us. . . . That suit you, Mark?"

"Yep," Mark said briefly. They all knew that with

one word Mark was settling all questions. Whether he was mind-reading or not he knew how to help Dean Lacey back on his pedestal. "Thanks for calling up, Dean," he said. "It takes both of us to keep a watch on two camps. I hope your men are all right down the slope. Would you take charge of the east side of the hump behind those baob trees from now? I haven't enough men and we need to start pulling the rest of those animals off the island soon after daybreak. Should be all over after midday."

Dean Lacey, conscious that the others were all awake, knew that now was the time to drop the subject of where Nairee belonged. He was too conscious of his own dignity to keep up a scrap with Mark Allen . . . whatever his private thoughts.

"Right!" he said, as if nothing untoward had happened. "I'll give you a shout if we need one of the boats. We have enough nets, I think." He turned on his heel. Over his shoulder he said a loud "Good-night all!" Half a minute later they could hear only the crash of his boots as he thrashed his way through low bushes and wet grasses.

23

NAIREE, AWARE THROUGH THE LAST FEW TENSE moments that she had made an unforgiveable gaffe, was grateful to both men, and to dear old Hank Brown too. Somehow they had all three saved face for her. They had done it by drawing attention to themselves. Probably they had now wiped the whole thing out. The silent listeners in their own rug rolls would, she hoped, be thinking only that Dean and Mark had barely noticed it. They had busied themselves making plans for the morning. Or so she thought.

Only Gertie, Hank Brown's housekeeper from Geko, seemed to be amused. She almost giggled as she helped Nairee straighten out her ground rug and start to settle herself in.

"Where's Woolarooka?" Nairee asked.

"Gone bush!" Gertie said as she herself snuggled down into her rug. "You have everyone else looking after you, Nairee. I guess Woolarooka doesn't like competition. She's off to tell the outposts of that flaming tribe of hers that the white man 'plurry all

fix their things okay.' " With a last soft laugh she
patted Nairee on the shoulder and finished with: "For
the sake of all those wretched animals, not to mention
the salt beef for breakfast . . . let's get to sleep." She
turned over on her side, and presented her back to
Nairee.

Nairee wanted to ask if anyone knew where Mark
had gone, but she didn't dare. She was three quarters asleep anyway. She would think about tomorrow. Time enough then.

She pushed her hair back and pressed her cheek
down against the folds of her rug. Somehow, for no
specific reason, she suddenly felt warm and wanted
and happy. *Two* men? That was a bit ridiculous, of
course, but it was nice to dream about. To *pretend,*
so long as she didn't fool herself too much.

The silence of the great Australian bushland settled
over all. The tree-dragons, great bush lizards that they
were, neither crept nor crawled. The whistling ducks
did not whistle, and neither did the bush tortoise slither
along its way. They were almost ghostly silent. All the
night creatures were still and voiceless.

Just as Nairee was about to doze off, there came a
rustling noise, then a thump beside her. Her thoughts
came back from the eerie bushland.

"Oh Woolarooka," she said, almost cross. "Do you
have to make all that noise? Where've you been
anyway?"

"Best you keep quiet and go to sleep, Nairee. You
got plenty work to do in the morning."

"Yes, I know. But that doesn't tell me where you've
been. Snooping around?"

"Okay you got a temper on, eh?"

"I had a beautiful temper on—the nice quiet kind
—till you started slithering into your rug. Just where
have you been?"

"I been see everyone down by Dean Lacey's camp,
all awright."

Nairee was exasperated. She had never before felt

quite like this about Woolarooka. She'd been having such a beautiful self-woven dream—

"Dean can look after himself. *And* his men . . ." she said crossly, forgetting that in the bush silence talking might be heard by others, could even wake them up. They hadn't had time to get into a deep sleep yet.

It was Mark Allen who sat up.

"Is anything the matter with you two?" he asked.

Woolarooka pushed Nairee's head under her rug.

"'Son'y me, boss," Woolarooka said. "I jes' come back from that camp down there other side of the big rock. They're all gone asleep now. Maybe Dean go for some walkabout round the place. Best let him be, boss. He's bin gone way down other side of the water. He's bin feelin' better now."

"If you don't go to sleep, Woolie, I'll go turf you down all along Dean's camp," Mark said. "Then you both can keep up this night time prowl. In company with one another. Keep quiet now. Spare the rest of it for morning."

"Okay, boss!"

Nairee heard only a few muffled words of this midnight dialogue. She sighed and turned over in her rug. She wished she could understand why Mark, usually so gentle and kind, was angry just now. Something was happening to her. Mark and the night and the veiled moon and the silence of the bush all seemed to be laying gentle hands on her heart, which seemed to be beating twice as fast as she had ever experienced before. She was high and happy, yet she wanted to cry. Was it because she was eighteen and adult now? Was this why the world seemed changed . . . and *not* because of the storm and the flood.

Ah well! She'd better go to sleep then, hadn't she? And forget it! Forget *everything!*

Woolarooka, while talking to Mark, was very aware Nairee was not yet asleep. It wasn't for Nairee to know there had come to Gamma's creek a stranger

from the east. Dean did not tell Mark of the visitor—
even if he knew.

But Woolarooka knew. Some of her people were
moving almost silently about the bush. Their sounds
were the sounds that warned of a stranger's approach.
Stranger? They weren't wearing their emu heel-cuffs
which they always wore when they were really threatened.

So they *knew* who that stranger was. Where from,
and where going!

24

NAIREE WOKE TO THE GRAY JUST BEFORE DAWN.
She did not know what had awakened her. Certainly
neither man nor woman from around the fire site.
They were all rolled tight in their rugs.

She lay with her hands propping her head up. No one
was moving. Then why did she wake?

She listened. Then as she listened she knew.

There was no rain noise. Only the flutter and move-
ments in the big gum tree just the other side of the
baob.

"Birds . . ." she said to herself. Stealth was necessary
now. She was not going to wake Woolarooka, that
pest among humans, for anything. She, Nairee, was
tired of being bullied by the old darling. She was
eighteen plus and grown up, so she was going to do
what she wanted to do, and blow dear darling
Woolarooka for now and ever. Well, maybe, anyway.

Inch by inch she crawled out of the rug and then,
careful not to cause some fallen leaf or twig to crack
under foot, she stood up. She moved over to the spot
near the baob where Mark had been standing last night.

It was good to be treading in *his* footsteps. She'd learned a thing or two about stealth, and silent walking from Mark himself. And from the aborigines too. "Walk in the other feller's foot marks. Any rustling of leaves and crackling of dried leaf sticks would all have been done before—by the first one to walk through wherever it was you were following."

Out of the rugs, her blouse on, straightened and smoothed down, her slacks pulled on, she moved forward toward the baob. She was determined to see what was going on in the tree boughs behind the big bottle-shaped tree trunk.

Vaguely she knew that most people would ask if she was out of her mind—gliding about in the bush when everyone else was stealing as much sleep as possible before a hard and fast day's work. But then most people didn't know—or if they knew they didn't really quite understand—her love of the bush birds. Gamma would have known, but Gamma wasn't here.

Actually she felt adventurous, and if anyone had suddenly asked, "What on earth are you doing, Nairee?" she wouldn't have been able to explain. All her life she had done as she was told . . . or at least done as she was asked. Even Woolarooka was given to ordering her about! But not now, not this minute anyway.

Nairee wanted to see which early-morning birds were making that racket in the big tree. She was going to find out, and nobody was going to order her back to bed . . . not even though bed was only a rolled rug on a waterproof ground sheet, hard by half a dozen other people, some of them snoring.

Underfoot it was damp, puddly. She ran her hand around part of the baob's trunk. It was wet too. But the rain had stopped, though the air was laden with moisture—like a land-borne cloud. Birds, dozens of them, were out and about, pecking very noisily.

All was well in the bushland and the team would be able to get dozens of hungry animals off that island out there in the storm-made lake.

It was going to be a wonderful day and she, Nairee was first up to see it! That is, after the birds had come to gabble about it.

"Galahs!" she said blissfully. Then she thought of the little bird at The Patch. No one there to care for it in its little wooden box on the shelf of the lean-to at the back of the shack.

Now from the east a line of bright light eased along the mesa tops like fire running along a single line. Dozens and dozens of galahs were racketing about like nothing on earth except themselves at their most demonstrative. Looking at them where they perched along the straight tree bough stretching from east to west, was like looking at a circus. Holding on by their claws, they swung heads down then swung upright again. They nodded at one another, talked at one another, and even took a friendly nip at one another with their curved beaks. Some cleaned under their pink-and-gray wings while others showed off by dancing up and down.

One bird gave the signal. Then, with a silence-shattering screech, they all took off. The sky was a glorious rainbow of color, the air an orchestra of bird talk.

Nairee, motionless beside the baob tree, stood and watched. The sun was half over the mesa top now and the world had gone from dank gray to fire-light. The dawn picked out the raindrops on leaves and low-growing bushes. The storm-ridden land sparkled with millions and millions of water diamonds, patterned with long shining slivers of gold where the sun rays shot linelike across water pools, and leftover lakelets.

Nairee felt that surely there was nothing more wonderful, more glorious, than a sunrise over wet bushland.

Nairee heard stirrings in the camp behind her. Surely there were enough people there near Great River to save the rest of the animals marooned on the island. What about her own birds and animals at The Patch? In her fantasy dream she forgot they had been taken to Geko for care. She wanted to feel they needed her.

What about the little wounded galah? How could it fly off to find seeds? It was only a baby bird anyway.

She turned and, soft as any of the most silent bush beings, began to thread her way in between wet bushes to where the horses were tethered. At best, Gertie could get the fire built up and breakfast going. At worst they could get their own breakfast. All of them! Men as well as women! Which "duty" called? The human kind, or the birds?

So blow the humans! "Oh my birds and oh the goats, and Hee and Haw and Dandy Two. *Listen. Listen for me! I am coming!*"

Within minutes Nairee had saddled the horse she had ridden from Beelagur, a chaff bag for its breakfast slung over the pommel. The stirrups were long in their leather straps but she did not stop to shorten them. If they went through water or unmanageable bush she could stand in her stirrups. She liked riding that way, anyway.

If they called to her from the camp she did not hear. She was listening only to the sound of her mount galloping over dead and wet spinifex bush between old burned-out blackened stumps, and through the wet green swish of beauhinia and wattle scrub.

Marvellous how her mount, having only carried her once on this visit to Beelagur, felt the tang of her wish to haste. It was as if he, like her, had foresaken the human race and was off against time to save the bird and animal denizens of The Patch.

In no time Nairee came over the low eastern horizon to the flat stretch of grassland sweeping toward the creek. She was less than a quarter of a mile from The Patch when she saw from a distance that there was something odd in the vicinity of The Patch.

A thin curling spiral of smoke reached heavenward from near the back of Gamma's shack.

Nairee reined in, but before she lifted herself to a standing position in the stirrups she told her horse exactly what was bothering her. She was sure he understood, for he too had thrown up his head, shaken it against the cheek straps, then blown a rumble of air through his nostrils and lips.

"Someone's there!" she said, settling stiffly back in her saddle. "But who?"

From all around, the able-bodied were at the animal rescue camp. She scanned the sky—no smoke signals. That was odd—and a little alarming!

What goes on? she asked herself. She had never known her world to be so still and silent. She herself had deserted the rescue camp. Maybe that was a bad thing to do. Was it? Wasn't it?

Where were Woolarooka's tribe? Nairee's bush-trained ear and other senses told her something strange, even foreign, was hereabouts.

Too late to turn back. She must go on now. She must look to her home. Gamma's home. There was no one else to do this, was there? Not a friendly aborigine in sight or earshot.

Her mount stood as still as the rest of the world. Nothing moved . . . except a streak of smoke curling skyward from behind the little house.

"But why are *you* alarmed too?" she said to the back of the horse's neck. "You don't belong here. Or do you? Are you the mount Dean rode the day he came down by the creek? The day I came home? Then what is down there that's so alarming?"

She never remembered being frightened in the Outback.

Well, she wasn't frightened now—only anxious. Something quite different was afoot.

She lifted the reins and slapped them down on the horse's neck.

"I wish I knew what your name was," she said aloud. "Dean did tell me when he brought you up from the stables . . . back there at Beelagur. Or don't *you* remember?"

It comforted her to talk to the horse. And it comforted him. He took a few steps forward, then moved from a trot into a canter.

"That's right, boy," she said. "We'll go and see. That's what we came for, wasn't it?"

She talked to him, and at him, all the way down the gentle slope to the wired fence of the goatyard. But the goats were nowhere in sight. There was new grass lying about in the yard. Someone had put food down. Today. The loose stalks were green and fresh-looking. Had there been signs of the tribe she would have expected that. There was grass lying in sheaths on the ground in the donkey and horse yards too. But they were gone too!

And no dogs. Silence in the sheep pen. Then she remembered. Hank Brown had told her someone had gone down from Geko to take the animals up to Geko for shelter, when it was decided Gamma should go to Beelagur.

Relief flushed over Nairee when she thought of that. But why had she forgotten that? Maybe her alarm had caused her to fear where there was no cause for fear.

Then what was it that was wrong with The Patch?

She reined in again at the edge of the footworn patch that led to and from the creek.

Then, she saw him. A man. A stranger, down near the creek.

He was tall with wide shoulders. A powerful-looking man in the distance whom she did not know.

She walked the horse to the wire enclosure, then slipped down from the saddle. She tied the reins securely to the top rail of the trellis, just past the goatyard. Then she walked steadily and slowly down the footpath toward the creek.

The man had seen her coming and began walking away from the creek up the slope toward her.

Perhaps he had just come to The Patch to take shelter from the cyclonic rain and winds?

Be polite. Welcome a stranger. Nairee could hear the voice of the Outback speaking to her. *Rule one: No stranger is ever turned away.*

He'd made a small fire in the outhouse, so apparently he hadn't gone right into Gamma's cottage.

He had nothing in his hands.

As he came nearer she could see how wet his boots and leggings were. His sombrero hat too. Over one arm was a wet-weather oilskin that apparently had kept the rest of him dry.

She stood quite still now, right by the path into her own vegetable garden.

As he came nearer he smiled a little. He was brown in the way all white people who live in the tropics get brown, and stay that way for the rest of their lives. Even when very old they were still rugged and brown. The Outback left its mark forever on those who dared it in their youth.

So he's a bushman, Nairee thought. No one ever harms anyone in the way-out places. That is a moral law. Out here we need each other to survive!

He was near enough now for her to return his tentative smile.

" 'Morning, stranger!" she said politely. "You have been caught in the storm?"

He was looking at her closely. Taking in every inch of her. Her face, her whole being. Yet he wasn't being offensive. Perhaps it was because he had not seen a white woman . . . or even a white girl hereabouts. But that was absurd of course. Maybe he hadn't seen anyone like *her* round and about here. Yes, he'd been a victim of the storm: the wild fury of the cyclone.

"I live here," Nairee said. "This is my home. I've been away, staying a few days on a cattle station." She waved her hand vaguely in the direction of faraway Beelagur.

She thought he might be middle-aged, but it was difficult to tell. His eyes were blue in a sun-faded way, but he was quite pleasant in his manner. Yet he was still looking at her—with *curiosity*—as if he had never seen anyone *like her* before. He was taking her in. Her height, her hair under the cap. Her hands. Her feet. Everything about her! Why?

She thought quickly of all sorts of odd reasons as to

why he should be looking at her almost as if he were mesmerized.

"Yes. I know you live here," he said. "They told me at the store. The Camel . . . they call it. Hard by the black stump. They said the girl's name was Nairee?"

"Yes. It is my name," Nairee agreed politely. "Did they tell you I lived here with Gamma. My grandmother . . ."

"*Your* grandmother?" He sounded surprised. Yet doubting, in a quiet, hidden way.

"Yes. My name is Nairee Peech. I live here with my grandmother—Mrs. Peech."

He was really taken aback now. But relieved in some strange way, as Nairee could well see. But about what? She could hardly harm him in any way, could she? She was only a girl of medium height. He was big and strong. She wasn't scared of him, though. They were alone in the wilderness—the two of them—but she felt quite friendly if she felt anything at all. Down south in the city, and even at the C.A.E. one did not speak to, or become friendly with strange men. There was thought to be a risk that they might harm you in some way.

Yet, in the bush, right by her own home, she *knew* he was not here to harm her. She just *knew*.

"Shall we go inside and make a cup of tea?" she asked politely. Welcoming a stranger.

"That would be grand," he said. "Actually I took shelter the last two nights and most of yesterday in that storeroom at the back. Lucky you didn't lock everything up. It was a pretty bad blow, but not like the old days. That wind could whirl the place flat . . . the way it would come across from the west." He broke off because he could see the girl was startled.

"You've been here before?" she asked. "I mean . . . you said something about the wind and the storm in the 'old days'. When you were here *then*, did you know my Gamma? Do you know the cattle stations past the mesa?"

He nodded. That was all.

She turned and started to retrace her footsteps toward the house.

"I'll put my horse in the stable paddock," she said over her shoulder. "You come on up to the kitchen. I can put the kettle on the primus stove. . . ."

"Okay!" He nodded as he walked behind her. She could hear his footsteps. It was an Outbacker's slogging walk, slow, rhythmical, and implacable. Sometimes, down south, she would hear that tread along the cemented footpaths of Adelaide, and know a bushman had come to town. She had felt the twinges of homesickness then. Something in her went out to the walking stranger.

He comes from the Outback, she would say to herself. Then she would long for her own stretch of bushland. Spinifex, beauhinia, and the old old land too. The red ironstone gorges. The wilderness.

She already liked this stranger. "Old enough to be my father." Then that old old question bothered her again: But I don't have a father, do I? Who am I?

Inside the cottage, she forgot about this. She welcomed the stranger in, suggested he take a more comfortable chair at the end of the kitchen table.

"It's not a big kitchen, is it?" she said as she reached to the shelf at the side wall, and brought down a bottle of methylated spirits.

"Big enough!" he said.

"Did you have a big one when you were out here, all those years ago?" she asked, trying not to sound too curious. She didn't look at him because she was now attending to the primus, then filling the kettle with water from a tap over a bowl at the far side of the window.

He'd taken off his broad-brimmed bushman's hat and put it where the men always did—on the rung under his chair. The rung that held the legs equidistant from one another.

Yes, he was a bushman, all right. She could see that by the way he did things. It did not once occur to her to be concerned about his presence; here was a stranger and it was the custom of the bush to give a stranger cover. And food to help him on his way.

"Oh, my golly yes!" he said. His thoughts were still with the relative sizes of kitchens. "A real whopper of a cookhouse. Off the end of the homestead verandah. Could have been a ballroom."

"Near here?"

"If you call fifty or sixty miles 'near.' Then yes, it was near here."

He took a flat tobacco tin from his shirt pocket, eased the slim packet of papers from under the lid of the tin, and began to roll himself a cigarette.

Nairee took ryevita biscuits from a packet. The bread would have gone moldy from the heat and humidity that followed the rain, so she did not even open the bread box.

"I'm staying at Beelagur," she said. "And Gamma's there for shelter. So I'm afraid there are not any fresh stores . . . like fresh bread."

"Beelagur!" he said sharply. "You staying there?"

"Now the rains have stopped I'll be coming back here," she said. "Out there to the east—the waters from Great River were pushed inland into the creeks and claypans. They flooded, and all the men from everywhere are rescuing the animals from the new-made barren islands so the animals can get food."

"Yes, I know," he said. His voice had gone back to normal again. A little too normal. He sounded almost cagey. Nairee sensed he did not want to talk about places like Beelagur. So she told him about the storm waters and the two camps of men rescuing the animals by the flow-off from Great River.

When she spoke of Mark and his role as Bush Ranger he just said, "The Ranger? Ah yes! That would be his job."

"And Dean Lacey from Beelagur too," she said. "He's out there too. . . ."

The kettle had boiled quickly and she now put powdered tea in the cups on the table.

"Ah . . . *Dean Lacey*. . . !" he said.

There was a strange note in his voice. She looked at him quickly, over the water jug, but there was nothing in his face. It wasn't even so nice a face anymore. It looked buttoned up and the tiny muscle at the side of the jaw bone near his right ear was working overtime.

Well, she was making him tea. Making him welcome too. *Welcome stranger*! But no . . . he wasn't a stranger to the mesa country. He had said so.

"You sound as if you know Dean, and that you don't quite like him?" she said gently as she pushed the sugar bowl toward him.

He said thank you to the tea, then put sugar in it and began to stir. But he did not look up.

"No I don't . . . I mean I didn't like him," he said. Then he did look up, thoughtfully, at Nairee. "We don't much like people who don't like us," he said. "Do we?"

"I suppose not." Nairee was thoughtful too. There was something sad about her visitor now. A look of something lost. A past not to be regained.

"Don't tell me if you don't want to," she said gently. "I suppose it happens to most of us. Some like us, and some don't."

He looked up at her, directly into her eyes now. There was something she could not quite understand in *his* eyes. They were searching . . . as if he cared what she thought. Or wanted to know what she thought. It was all very strange. But then so was their meeting, here at Gamma's place with seemingly no one else in the world about.

Someone was coming. Nairee's bush-trained ear had caught the distant sound of a horse galloping. So did the bush-knowing ear of this stranger. She saw that he too was listening. The fingers of his right hand were drumming on the table. His eyes were very nearly anxious.

He's an Outbacker all right; Nairee thought. She knew intuitively that horse and horseman were coming here—to The Patch—and not bypassing it on an errand to the Camel store at the far stretch past the creek's bend.

"Someone is coming," she said. "Will you excuse me while I go and see what is wanted."

She had already risen from her chair. She went through the door, out of the shack, across the walkway to the goatyard fence. Through the wire netting she could see the horse and rider coming down the track.

It was Woolarooka. Nairee felt half amused, half cross.

Can't I ever go anywhere, even to my own home, without someone chasing after me? she asked herself.

Woolarooka and horse came around the goatyard and the rider slid off her mount almost at Nairee's feet.

"So what goes with you, Woolie?" Nairee demanded, not very politely.

"You got a temper up, eh?" Woolarooka demanded. "Well you jes' put it down. Mark wants to know why you run away, eh? Why you come home here, eh?"

What's it got to do with Mark? Nairee wondered, but something glad in her sang a little. Mark cares, she thought.

"The animals . . . and the sick birds . . ." she began.

"I told you they be all fix up when Gamma went to Beelagur. You got that fella Sam in there? I know because his horse is down by the creek."

"You know everything, don't you, Woolie? I didn't even know his name was Sam. I didn't ask."

"His name is Sam," Woolie said flatly. "Mark—he turn on that radio he's got an' Miz Smith at the Camel tell him Sam gone up the track to The Patch."

"Oh? And . . . ?"

"Mark, he say, 'You get to hell outa here, Woolie, an' go see Nairee is all right, okay. Bring the li'l sweep back here quick sharp, okay?' Maybe he come himself if I take longa time."

"Nice to know what he calls me in between times," Nairee said scornfully. "All I did was come home to The Patch. *My* home."

"An' start talkin' to that fella Sam? Eh?"

"He is a stranger, and so is welcome, Woolie. He is very correct in a nice way. I like him." Nairee was being the dignified hostess now.

Woolarooka was not impressed. "You jes' doan know . . ." she began.

"She doesn't know all, but what she does know is quite correct," the stranger's voice came from the gravel path behind them. Woolarooka darted her head around past Nairee's shoulder and her eyes grew large as they stared.

"You come back?" she said, not welcoming. "What for you come back, eh?"

"Mind your own business, Woolie . . . No. I take that back. It is your business, isn't it?"

"Too damn aw-right," Woolie said fervently. "You make trouble, eh?"

"No. I just came to see. When I've seen all I'll go away again."

Nairee had half turned, and now was looking first at one and then the other, sensing a mystery but not wishing to say anything just yet. Later, when she knew Sam better. Well, maybe. Was she possibly afraid of what she might learn?

For the moment it was just a matter of a cup of tea for all, including Woolie. After all, Sam wasn't the first person to make a sentimental trip back to the bushlands from whence he had first come. There had been stockmen come and go at both Beelagur and Geko, over the years. There had been would-be explorers and occasionally botanists or zoologists in search of unique plants, animals, or insects for the national records. And, of course, the dam builders who wanted to do something about the waste waters, in flood times, of Great River and its tributaries.

Nairee settled temporarily for the likelihood that Sam had once been in these parts as a stockman. That face burned dark brown, those horseman's horny hands —and that manner of walking! It would all come out, maybe over the next cup of tea. All he was doing was making a sentimental journey.

Reluctantly Woolarooka agreed to make a third at the tea-drinking rites around Gamma's kitchen table

꧁꧂꧁꧂꧁꧂꧁꧂꧁꧂

25

FOR ONCE NAIREE FOUND HERSELF IN THE ROLE OF mistress of The Patch. As she poured tea, she watched with a smiling interest the continuing exchange of baleful glances between Woolie and Sam. They weren't likely to settle down to friendliness. She could see that. But it didn't occur to her that there was something deeper and more serious than disinterest or mere dislike, between the indigenous tribeswoman, and the brown-burnt traveler come again to the bush.

It was only when the sound of yet another horseman coming down the stock track was heard by all three of them, almost simultaneously, that the whole atmosphere changed.

Now it was Woolie and Sam who were on the same side.

"Who's that?" Sam demanded of Woolie.

"It's that Ranger fella, Mark Allen," Woolie said. "He come to find out where Nairee run away. Maybe he doan remember you. Maybe he do remember. Best you go walkabout. Quick, fella."

Sam had pushed out his chair, and was standing up.

"I'm going," he said to Nairee, ignoring Woolarooka now. "I'll come back and see you another day." He had lifted his hat from under the chair and clapped it on his head before he reached the door. "This fella Mark is the mounted policeman's son? Eh? Well, I never did care for that policeman, anyway. Took my rights from me, he did. I'm off."

And he was off, in the quickest exit Nairee had ever seen.

She stared at Woolarooka across the table. Woolarooka was giving nothing away.

Sam had not even said Thank you for the tea. He had simply gone.

"Did he do something wrong once?" Nairee asked Woolarooka.

"Once, by white man's law—maybe. Not for black fella. Well . . . maybe."

Woolarooka was now clearly of two minds about Sam. She sat huddled and worried as she stared at Nairee. Meantime Nairee went first to a window, then to the outside door. Her head was tilted back as she looked up at the sky.

"No smoke writing," she said, turning to Woolarooka. "Where's the tribe, Woolie? Why aren't they talking?"

"They all go help take animals off the island up river," Woolarooka said, shrugging. "They know awright Mark is coming. You know what, Nairee? They jes' minding their own business. Like this one Woolarooka. Maybe sometime Mark tell you awright about this one—Sam . . ." The little old woman sank her chin on her chest and gave herself up to sadness.

"Woolie! Woolie! What is the matter? What is it all about?"

"Doan you ever go away, Nairee. You stay here with old Woolie. I ain't got no chile but you."

"For goodness sake!" Nairee exclaimed. "What *is* going on? I won't ever leave Gamma. Or you, Woolie. *Not ever*. Why—"

She didn't finish. The pounding of a galloping horse

had ceased. Booted footsteps were coming along the path with a determination that said Mark was in a hunting mood. Vaguely the girl wondered if Mark had seen Sam's exit. He would for certain have seen the remnant smoke of Sam's outside fire, and would have sensed the presence of a saddled horse teethered to a tree somewhere down the paddock. He, like a tribesman, would have known instinctively that there had been a visitor—now decamped—at The Patch.

It was strange, strange! Nairee was actually just a little afraid now of Mark's wrath. She knew intuitively that he would be angry with her for entertaining a strange man . . . *alone* in Gamma's house.

Why do I have so many bosses? she asked of herself as she watched the door, waiting for Mark's shadow to be thrown across it.

Who am I? Why me? Why this guardianship all the time? What is the secret of it all? Because there is one. Woolie knows it. Mark knows it. Uncle Jack knows it. Maybe Mrs. Lacey knows it. I'm eighteen and have a vote. "Why can't I know about *me?*"

She did not realize she had asked the last question aloud.

She closed her eyes, then opened them again because Mark's footsteps had stopped right in the doorway. She looked straight across the short distance at him, into his eyes, which held hers.

Whatever he might have been about to say, he now changed his mind. She knew that too. The hard, all-seeing expression in the eyes of the Ranger had changed to one of concern. Perhaps even a *tender* concern? He had heard her words and now saw the distress in her face.

He held out one hand.

Intuitively, almost blindly, Nairee gave him her hand. He held it tight as he looked down into her face.

"Are you all right, Nairee?"

She nodded.

"For the duration, Nairee," he said gently, but oh so firmly! "You belong to *me*. Understand? *Me*."

What "the duration" meant Nairee did not know. But there was a world of comfort in this moment. Something inside her let go. She bent her head, then suddenly put it on his shoulder. Tears came. She did not know why, except the way Mark had claimed her, and it had undone something in her.

"Oh Mark! What is it all about? I'm all mixed up. Why? Why *now*?

With his free hand he brushed her hair back from her forehead.

"It's high time you were unmixed," he said quietly.

26

MARK DROPPED NAIREE'S HAND AND WALKED TO THE table. He levered the chair out from under the end of the table with his booted foot.

"Who made the tea last time?" he asked, smiling, as he looked at the empty cups standing about. He sat down and pulled off his bushman's hat. He stowed it, as Sam had done, on the rung under his chair.

Somehow Mark's simple domestic question eased the atmosphere in the room. Woolarooka stopped scowling, and Nairee relaxed in an all-over way.

So they were going to have another tea party, were they? Maybe Mark had already forgotten his epoch-making statement: "You belong to me." All the same the clouds had gone from Nairee's face, and a little bird—a very little bird—lifted its heart inside her and sang one single sweet note.

Mark had said she belonged to him. Mark never—not ever—said something he did not mean. She would be his special friend! Extra special, she hoped, and dared not think further.

She went to the primus and gave it an extra pump to

get that kettle on the boil again, then she took the used cups with their saucers from the table and dumped them in the sink. She brought out three clean cups and saucers and set them on the table, putting powdered tea in each of them. As she brought the kettle to the table, Mark and Woolarooka sat on opposite sides of the table and stared at one another.

Because of her mysterious glad-feeling, Nairee only smiled as she looked at them. She had temporarily forgotten her own defection from Operation Noah and was distressed that she had drawn Mark away from his special duties. But he had come, hadn't he? He would have known that Woolarooka had come looking for her, of course. So he need not have come—

Mark and Woolarooka were still outstaring one another. Each was annoyed with the other, and both, for just a minute or two, had forgotten to be angry with Nairee, for being the cause of all the trouble.

Mark turned his head and looked across at her.

"Thank you," he said as his cup of tea was filled and Nairee lifted the kettle away. "Pour yourself a cup, Nairee. You are going to need it."

"Yes, I will . . ." She was already filling her own cup. "Don't be cross at Woolie, Mark. She only came to see if everything was all right here at The Patch."

Mark's expression had changed. Then he glanced back at Woolarooka.

"Do you know who that man was? The man who was here?" he demanded more than asked.

"O' course," Woolarooka said. "I doan forget nobody. 'Specially I doan forget Sam. You know Sam, Mark?"

"No I don't," he said. "He was before my time. At least my time as a full-time working Ranger . . ."

"Then my brothers back there at the lake tell you, eh?"

For once Woolarooka was one up on Mark. "Well they tell me too," she went on. " 'Sam's coming,' they tell me. 'You better get down there to The Patch and see Nairee's awright, okay,' they said. See?"

"Yes, I see. But why did you come without telling me?"

"Maybe I think you get mad and tell me stay away." Woolarooka could be very forthright when she wanted.

Nairee sipped her tea and said nothing. In an intuitive way she began to feel there was something momentous in the air: something that affected her, but not in a frightening way. Rather in a troubled way. As they drank their tea a somber silence fell over the room, and she began to think that, having lived so long in the bush, *she too* had developed that special intuition that both Woolarooka and Mark had.

She felt it herself. In herself.

A lone rider had been coming from the west. A tribesman, up a tall tree somewhere back near The Patch, had seen the unnatural lift of a flock of ground birds. He had seen the tall grasses bend away from someone. He had watched the progress of that someone riding over and through the open spinifex plain. He stayed in that tree fork and watched the rider tether his horse to a stump, then make his sit-down camp for the night. The native had come down from his tree roost, mentioned certain things to his tribal brothers, then set out stealthily toward that campfire.

He had, when he arrived at his destination, peered through the high grass-trees and between low bush boughs at the camper. He had known who that rider was who was eastering. He had also known why the stranger was coming. This was because nights before, his own tribal brother had been to the inland town of Barlee and come back with the news that Sam was there. Sam had not been there for sixteen years. He told his tribesmen all and everything—Nothing left out.

From treetops they had watched Sam coming. They had known when he stopped at the Camel store. From the Camel, one of them, sent to observe, but ask no questions, came back with the news. *Sam was heading for The Patch. He had turned off at the track fork and there was only one place he could so dexterously be heading for*. There was only the creek. Then The Patch. Long long ago, the tribal elders knew full well, Sam had come that way with a precious bundle. Now, like all white men, he was coming back—to look, see, and make sure—about *that bundle*.

So a runner was sent to speak to the men helping at the animal rescue campsite. Especially to speak to Woolarooka.

When Nairee had gone from the camp Woolarooka had gone after her, Woolarooka knew who Sam was, and why he was coming back. And that was all there was to it.

Talking some silent language to one another over their cups of tea at the kitchen table in Gamma's house at The Patch, both Mark and Woolarooka knew why Sam had come back—and that they must watch out for Nairee.

And also, knew why Mark had said *Nairee belonged to him*.

There was no bush magic about it at all.

❀❀❀❀❀❀❀❀❀❀

27

WOOLAROOKA KNEW THAT ONE OR ANOTHER OF HER brothers would be snooping about the wetland, round the pandanus trees on the far side of the creek. No magic there, either. Just a custom of the tribe that when odd things were happening someone was sent down to see exactly what *was* going on.

So Woolarooka left Nairee and Mark to the last of their tea dregs. She went outside to send wail calls across the dip in the land through which the creek ran its course.

Oolyarra, her youngest brother, tall and skinny-thin like the good huntsman he was, emerged from dark-trunked wind-stripped sapling gums, any one of which looked exactly like him—only they were rooted, and he was not.

"What you yelling at, old woman?" he asked when they came near enough to one another. "What goes on that fella Mark come down to Ol' Gamma's Patch, eh? What Sam come back this way for, eh?"

"Guess he wanted to see Nairee was all right, okay." Woolarooka could be quite airy when she wanted.

"Mark says, please you go up back of lake and tell Dean Lacey he go on be boss till Mark get back bime-by."

Her brother said "Ur huh!" and forthwith disappeared amongst the sapling trees and bush growth. He was eastering as he went to tell Dean Lacey that he was now in the coveted position of being the only boss at the rescue camp.

That would keep Dean Lacey happy, high and mighty, Woolarooka thought and knew Mark felt likewise. But more important, away from The Patch.

Woolarooka shook her head as she tried to think out the problem of Mrs. Lacey being told that Sam had come back.

"Good job that fella Mark come down here," she told the trees and the grasses and the stumps. Her wariness told her to leave Mark and Nairee be. For quite a while. Her instinct to be with Nairee at ponderous moments in that child's life had to be cuffed and collared down.

She shook her head slowly and sadly. Whether it be Mark or Sam, Nairee would be no more "atchina"— her child. "That fella Sam gib it me, her. Now maybe Mark take away."

She was very sad, but it was only a temporary state of mind. She best wanted her child to be happy.

Nairee made more tea, for want of something to do. I'll be afloat with this stuff before long, she told herself. It was a good way of trying to get her mind away from Mark. He sat on the far side of the table and watched her. All was silence—except for the sound of water dripping continuously from the corner eaves overhanging the edges of Gamma's roof. Nairee kept her head bent as she poured the tea into the cups.

"Do I have to drink another cup of tea just to help keep you busy, Nairee?" Mark asked gently. Nairee sensed the note of compassion in his voice, and it was her undoing.

She put the kettle down on the table and looked up.

"Oh Mark!" she said. "What is it all about? Please, *please* tell me? What has Sam to do with me, or Woolarooka, or Gamma's house? It *is* something to do with me, isn't it? You and Woolarooka are being cagey."

He pushed back his chair and came around the table to her. They were both standing now. Looking at one another. There was concern, and something else in Mark's eyes as he looked down into her face.

"Yes, Nairee. But there is something even more important than Sam and his affairs. Look up at me again —please."

She tilted back her head a little, and their eyes met. "*Please* . . ." she began.

He did not answer in words. He bent his head and kissed her on the lips. His arms tightened around her.

"Nairee, I love you, I really *love* you," he said, smiling now because her lips had returned that kiss, though with a certain diffidence. She only half-believed what he had said. "I do," he repeated. "That was what I meant when I said you belonged to *me*. I should have asked you first, of course, but Woolie was in the way . . ."

She had no idea what to say. She couldn't think of the right words. Her heart was racing, bringing color to her cheeks and a wondering light to her eyes.

He was smiling too. He kissed her again, and this time he took longer about it. It said everything words could not have made clear.

"You believe me?" he asked.

She wanted to tell him about the doubts and fears that had worried her for so long. Of course she loved him. She managed to get that out—very, very shyly this time. But mostly she wanted to ask him what had she to bring to him? She was nobody—or was she?

"Who is Sam?" she asked, as if intuitively she knew that Sam's presence had had something to do with Mark now holding her tightly in his arms—not only to show his love but also to protect her.

He kissed her again. This time it was kindly, intriguing, also beguiling.

"We'll be married and build a house . . . somewhere around here," he said. "We'll build it of stone from the breakaway by the mesa range. And Gamma will have a room bigger than she's ever had—and her own kitchen and bathroom if she wants. We'll all three have all the birds and animals. Including the goats and the donkeys. Nairee, dear. Are you listening?"

Her head was pressed to his shoulder but she managed to nod.

"You can't marry a *nobody*," she said after another silence, but not with any conviction. "But now I must know *about me*. I know that you know, Mark. Sam has something to do with me, or you and Woolie would not have come down to the Patch at full speed. I've managed on my own many a day in the past." She lifted her head and looked straight into his eyes. "Please, Mark . . ." she pleaded. "I've loved you ever since I was about twelve . . . or something. Now I love you in a grown-up way. But it is right I should know what you know—*about me. Please!* Who is Sam? Why was he here? Why did I have a feeling of something familiar?"

Mark was silent, but it was a speaking silence. Nairee knew he was making a judgment of some kind in his mind.

"Come and sit down," he said. "On the old sofa. Guess we'll buy Gamma a new sofa as our wedding present." He was smiling now. He wasn't holding something of himself apart anymore.

He pulled her down beside him and put his arm around her. She put her head on his shoulder.

"Go on," was all she said. "I can take it, Mark . . . Especially now I have you—for keeps."

"There's nothing sinister or unholy to worry about, Nairee—*dear*," he said gently. "Notice how Woolie has taken off? A horse pounding back up to Great River? Woolie's off to consult her tribal chiefs about how soon she can carry the news to Gamma and . . . to Mrs. Lacey too."

Nairee lifted her head.

"What has it to do with Mrs. Lacey? I think Sam said he had once worked at Beelagur?"

"That's it exactly," Mark said. He had an arm round Nairee and the other hand held one of hers tightly.

"Go on," she said, not looking at him now, but looking straight ahead. Yet not seeing anything.

"Sam worked as head stockman on Beelagur. He was one of the best. Mrs. Lacey had a daughter who fell in love with . . . Sam."

Nairee closed her eyes.

"Caroline?" she said. "Caroline! *Caroline!*"

"Yes. That was Caroline when grown up. And something more—"

"Go on, tell me . . . I'm guessing."

"The daughters of rich well-born station owners don't usually run away with one of the stockmen. Not in those days anyway."

"Caroline? She ran away with Sam? Did they come home again?"

"No. There was too big a row. Neither party could forgive the other. Can you understand, Nairee?"

"Yes, and I know what comes next. At least I think I do. There was a baby? Did they marry, Mark?"

"Oh yes. They married, all right. But . . . and this part is sad, Nairee." His arm around her was tighter still. "Sam was a decent bloke in many ways. A man on his own can't manage with a newborn baby." He tightened his arms. "Caroline died . . . and Sam brought the baby back where it belonged and where it could have all the advantages of a full life. He gave the baby to Woolarooka down by the creek. There isn't anything the tribe doesn't know, Nairee. Even what's inside other people's hearts. They knew that Caroline's mother was not ready to forgive, and they told Woolie to take the baby to Gamma at The Patch. But to watch over it. And that baby—" he broke off.

"Is me!" Nairee said. She was staring past Mark, through the window. He nodded, then kissed her again very gently.

Nairee leaned back, and thought it out. Her heart was beating painfully. Mark said nothing, just watched her in a caring way.

"But why . . . ?" she asked at length, still troubled, but knowing she must *know*. "Why is there a head stone for Caroline? You know where those graves are by Beelagur's boundary fence? I mean . . . it's a *little* headstone. And the stones are there in a circle with one stone in the middle . . . like they are for me down by the creek. My spirit land, Woolie calls it."

"I'm sure that your circle was put there by the tribe, Nairee. Also the one for Caroline by Beelagur's boundary. It was their way of telling Mrs. Lacey that Caroline's spirit had come home. Mrs. Lacey left both there where they were put by the tribe. Her own tribute, I suppose. You know that our tribe hereabouts believe that when we are born each of us has a spirit that comes up from the ground. And when we die our spirit goes back to our own home—the same place, but somewhere in eternity."

Nairee's eyes had tears in them. Tears for Caroline. Perhaps tears for Mrs. Lacey too. She wasn't sure.

"That's why she was always so good to me," she said. "And the tribe watched over me too. And Woolarooka especially—"

"Yes, and Sergeant Jack and Mrs. Gray. Me too . . ."

"I've been lucky, haven't I?" Nairee said unexpectedly. And the tears dried away. "All the time I *did belong*. To so many people."

"All the time."

She looked up at him. "To you too, Mark?"

"Actually you are mine for keeps now." He kissed her forehead. "That's my mark," he said, and touched her forehead where he had kissed her. "Put your finger on it. Right. A circle of stones down by the creek, and now a spot on your forehead." His smile was wide, and endearing. Her own finger was on her forehead. "My mark made by Mark," she said, and though her eyes were still a little misty, she smiled up at him. "Mark, I do love you. I have for ages really . . ."

"Me too," he said. "Been in love with you—"

There was quite a silence, then Nairee spoke again: "And Sam? What do we do with Sam? My fa—" But she couldn't quite say it. She couldn't say "father" just yet. By and bye perhaps.

"We'll have a wedding," Mark said. "And we'll ask Sam to it. He ought to be the one to give you away—"

"No, Gamma will give me away. He's a stranger— well, all right, *almost*."

"I think you are right," Mark said. "But let us have time to think about it."

"You are thinking of Mrs. Lacey?" Nairee asked soberly.

"Agreed. But grandmothers don't usually give their granddaughters away." He watched her face. "Rather a lot for you to digest at one sitting." He spoke so gently that it almost brought the tears back to her eyes.

"And . . ." A new thought troubled her. Her eyes widened. Then suddenly she relaxed. She almost, but not quite, laughed. "*Dean* is my uncle. Oh Mark! What an *idea*! Yet it is true, isn't it? My *uncle*! What a *crazy* thought!"

Yes.

He held her against him for quite a time. His cheek against her cheek. The silence was long because she had so much to think about, and digest.

Then suddenly she lifted her head again.

"It's rather wonderful, isn't it?" she said, drawing herself back from him, yet looking into his eyes. "Now I don't ever again have to wonder, *Who am I*? A real grandmother, and a father, an *uncle*. I'll have to have a new name. Mark, what is Sam's surname?" Then her chin suddenly went up. Pride had come back to its place again. "Don't tell me just yet," she said quietly. "My name is 'Peech.' I'll only give that away for you, Mark."

"Well said, Nairee. You are Gamma's child, more even than Woolarooka's child. And Gamma is *ours*. Yours and mine. Right?"

"Right. Yes, yes. Maybe I'll soften up in time,

Mark. But now. Right now—would you mind holding me tight and kissing me long and lasting, all over again?"

She didn't finish her sentence. Mark had his arms around her and his lips on hers.

"Actually," he said at length, "I don't think you need worry about who is what, or what is who, at all. Remember, Nairee, I made my claim when I first arrived here at the shack. Today! I said, '*You belong to me.*' And that settles everything. *Mine*—"

"Thank you, Mark. Thank you so much. It is a wonderful way of putting it. I belong to you. I belong! I belong! I *belong to someone*—legally. Oh Mark, I am singing a song, aren't I?"

Epilogue

THE WINDS HAD DRIED THE WATERS LYING IN SHEETS on the land. Then came the bulldozers sent by the government to help restore the roadways and the arterial tracks.

It wasn't spring, but it was like spring in everyone's hearts.

Great were the comings and goings, the meetings, the radio conversations. Tears of happiness on some people's cheeks. Mrs. Lacey was pale, but dignified as ever as she made a public announcement in the *Coastal Press* concerning the forthcoming marriage of her granddaughter Nairee Peech to Mark Allen.

Somehow everyone in the district, including the tribe and especially Woolarooka, decided on the best place for the wedding. *Geko Station*. Hank Brown always gave the best—if sometimes the rowdiest—parties, anyway.

Mrs. Lacey bowed to the wishes of all with great dignity. She actually looked about ten years younger these days. It had been hard living a lie all those years, and now she was at peace. No more false pride about her own daughter's marriage to Sam Bellew.

Yes, Bellew was his name, and before the wedding Sergeant Jack Allen managed to track him down, made a fake arrest to bring him forcibly to meet face to face with Mrs. Lacey at Beelagur station. Nobody knew quite what happened next except that Beelagur's housekeeper was reported as saying Mrs. Lacey had ordered the best beef cuts to be cooked for dinner with her visitor. She, and Nairee with Gamma and Sam, sat down to it with all the paraphernalia of best linen, china, and silver that Beelagur usually reserved so it was said for Vice Regal visits, and those of heads of local government.

Mrs. Lacey did not talk much. But she did smile. So all were happy more than less.

Sam Bellew preferred his wanderlust days to settling down someplace. If he changed his mind someday, well . . . he would let Mrs. Lacey and Nairee know. Meantime he was coming to the wedding—if someone could advise him where to get a suit that would not displease Mrs. Lacey's idea of good taste.

Mrs. Gray from the welfare department in Alice Springs was to choose the material, do the cutting and sewing of Nairee's wedding dress. She bowed to Mrs. Lacey's decision to provide the wedding veil and the shoes.

Gamma, back at The Patch now that the floods were a thing of the past, was content to put up with people flying in and out, relaying messages on the radio while she endlessly played Patience. She was bent on achieving a certain extra finesse in deceiving herself, by having two queens extra in her pack and never divulging her secret to anybody else. She was not going to "give" Nairee away because she didn't believe in giving live people away at all. She was secretly enchanted with the idea of a new house—the rocks and mortar for foundations were already being brought in by anyone who happened to be out along the breakaway past the mesa country. She was also secretly on the side of

Woolarooka going walkabout with her tribe into their own secret land sites where they would make their own kind of wedding for Nairee and Mark with their own special corroboree. That would keep the *wurrawilberoo* (the devil) away from Nairee and Mark forever and ever. They'd come back and tell her as much about it as the elders allowed to be told to anybody outside the tribe. Secrets had to stay secrets forever—otherwise what would happen to the secrets that weren't secret anymore? "A good question," Sergeant Jack observed after thought.

So, on the given day all who could come assembled themselves, their families, stockmen, and other staff at Geko. The place was a tangle of people—big and little. There was even a special wedding cake made for the kids.

Hank Brown's hair was no longer a ruffled crown on his head (as was its wont). It was cut, plastered down, and neat. Mrs. Brown had ordered a new dress from the Camel store at the crossroads, a fashionable one but nothing to rival Mrs. Lacey's.

And Mrs. Lacey was elegant in a light-pink soft flowing lace gown. She wore beautiful new soft-leather shoes. And Nairee—?

Nairee was a dream in a long dress of white satin of which Gertie, the housekeeper from Geko, remarked, "It would be a plurry shame ever to wear it again for anything but a wedding."

Oh, what a day that was! Thy sky was so pale a blue it was nearly white. The trees and low growth in the bush were a sweet and lovely green—thanks to the earlier torrents of rain brought in the wake of the cyclone. The animals made a special occasion of the wedding. They were moving all over the place because Gamma insisted that all from The Patch should be loosed for at least half a day. The stockmen from Geko had undertaken to draft them in again when the sun went down.

Everybody was so happy, including Sam, who was forgiven by all for his long absence, and was only prevented from celebrating his return with too much home-brewed hop beer by being surrounded by Beelagur's stockmen, those from Geko, and a dozen or more drop-ins from outer properties. Gertie from Geko made the cake, Hank Brown's wife did the verandah decorations, and the music was provided by station hands who had such instruments as mouth organs, didjeridoo, ukuleles, and even one violin.

Nairee, wet-eyed with happiness in the manner of all brides, clung to Mark's arm as if she would never let it go.

And Dean! No longer guarded from too much attention to, and notice of Nairee by his mother, he gave the bride away.

A suitable role for him to play, it was agreed, behind hands, by all. Perfectly got up in a beautiful hand-tailored suit, he did his job with suitable dignity. He was the first, after the groom, to kiss the bride. It was a cool and appropriate kiss—on her cheek. And she returned it to his cheek.

The clergyman from the mission upriver performed the ceremony on Geko's front lawn.

When all was over, including the eating and drinking, the kissing, and a few sentimental tears, Mark took Nairee—now dressed in blue silk and, yes, a leghorn hat bought new by Mrs. Lacey, to his homestead, where they would live until their new place was ready.

The pink and gray galahs rose in riotous clouds, then formed as usual into chevrons of screaming delight as Mark's whirligig buzzer took off and headed for the breakaway country and the mesa range.

The kelpies, knowing full well they could not round up a helicopter in the air, took to barking wildly and rounding up anything from the visiting stockmen's horses to the cat, its kittens, and several of the very young children wandering around and wondering just what it was all about.

Uncle Jack had his arm around Gamma. In spite of his police duty he ignored the fact that Gamma had "borrowed" yet another pack of cards from the kitchen staff at Geko. She pointed out to Sergeant Jack the somber fact that she would have to return them next time she was invited to Geko. Meantime she wanted a loan of them, just to see if she could play them as well as she could play those at Beelagur.

There was a pause in time as all stood, those on the verandah, those in the stockyard, and those in the garden, and watched the "buzzer" rise and take off to the land of the big eagles, and of all birds that fly high. The setting sun painted the flat-topped mesas gold and crimson and shadowed blue. To the wedding guests, it really did look as if Mark and Nairee were flying into a heavenly dreamland. The curve of the mesa range was such that it looked as if it held out waiting arms.

The ladies dabbed their eyes. Dust must have been caught by their eyelashes for there was an untoward misting and dampness about those same lashes.

The men—including Dean Lacey and Sam—withdrew in the direction of the beer pots and wineglasses.

It was agreed that a good time was had by all.

Nairee, safe in the spare arm of Mark, knew that the whole of the future would only be a good time for her and that she *belonged*.

Alice Chetwynd Ley...
The First Lady of Romance

_____THE BEAU AND THE BLUESTOCKING   25613—1.50
Alethea's sheltered life could never have prepared her for the outrageous Beau Devenish or London in 1780!

_____THE GEORGIAN RAKE   25810 1.50
In England of 1750, one did not defy the social code...but Amanda would do _anything_ to prevent her sister's marriage to hellrake Charles Barsett.

_____THE MASTER AND THE MAIDEN   25560 1.25
Amid the violence of Yorkshire's Industrial Revolution, a young governess risks her future by clashing with the iron-willed master of Liversedge.

_____THE JEWELLED SNUFF BOX   25809 1.25
Set against the backdrop of Georgian England, lovely and innocent Jane Spencer falls in love with a nameless stranger who holds the key to her destiny.

_____THE TOAST OF THE TOWN   25308 1.25
Georgiana Eversley—admired and pursued by all the men around her, except one. Vowing to change this Buckinghamshire doctor's mind—she ignores propriety and eventually must pay the price.

_____THE CLANDESTINE BETROTHAL   25726 1.25
In Regency England an unspoken vow awakens young Susan to womanhood when she finds herself trapped in a lie and engaged in name only to Beau Eversley.

_____A SEASON AT BRIGHTON   24940 1.25
Reckless, impetuous Catherine Denham was too anxious to become a woman to remember to be a lady...something one never forgot in Regency England.

_____THE COURTING OF JOANNA   25149 1.50
While England is threatened by Napoleon's invasion, romance blooms between daring, spirited Joanna Feniton and a man who could destroy her future...and the future of England!

BB **Ballantine Mail Sales**
Dept. LE, 201 E. 50th Street
New York, New York 10022

Please send me the books I have checked above. I am enclosing
$........................ (please add 50¢ to cover postage and handling)
Send check or money order—no cash or C.O.D.'s please.

Name_____

Address_____

City_____State_____Zip_____
Please allow 4 weeks for delivery.   L-28

Available at your bookstore or use this coupon.